The Offering

Wolves of Wereduin, Book 1

Rosary Deville

As a beta in Wereduin society, Fern has no choice but to be mated when he comes of age. The ideal beta wereduin was subservient to their alpha, bears young, and knows their place in society.

Fern isn't like that.

Rather than become an extension of his alpha, Fern wants to play in his band, hang out with his friends, and stay himself. Now of age, Fern is to be placed in the Offering—an annual ceremony where alphas hunt and claim their beta mates. And whose attention does Fern attract? None other than Donovan Blackfang, a Highborne alpha who will stop at nothing but to claim Fern's heart, body, and soul.

DISCLAIMER

This is a work of fiction. Any resemblance to actual persons, living or dead, or actual races, cultures, or events is purely coincidental.

This is an m/m dark erotica recommended for mature audiences only. It contains graphic depictions of violence, rape, sexual assault, domestic abuse, emotional manipulation, forced marriage, slavery, torture, gore, death, and language. People who are triggered by the topics above should proceed with caution. Please store your files wisely, where they cannot be accessed by underage readers.

All characters in this book are of consensual age. Please do not participate in any new sexual practices, especially those found in BDSM/fetishes without guidance of an experienced practitioner. The author will not be responsible for any harm, loss, injury, or death resulting from use of any information contained in this book.

The entire story is fictitious and all spoken words and practices are notions of the author, and are not reflections of real-world religions. While references might be made to actual mythological or religious entities, they are the embellishments of the author's imagination and not the accurate religious beliefs of real-life parishioners.

For Lynn,

Without whom the world would never have met Fern and Don.

TABLE OF CONTENTS

ACKNOWLEDGMENTS

Special thanks to my cover artist Zoe Perdita, my editor, Sharon Stogner at Devil in the Details, my proofreader, Patricia Rowell, and my beta readers: Lynn Michaels, Jodee Arellano, Sam Bremmer, and Samie Forguson. Lastly to Derek and Brandon Fiechter for their Dark Fantasy Creatures playlist listed on their YouTube channel that provided me with a wonderful writing environment.

AUTHOR'S NOTE

Dear Reader,

Thank you for picking up a copy of the Offering. What began as a simple sexual fantasy, over the years, grew into a vastly complex world of different races, cultures, and customs. Due to its size, I've broken it up into two books, with this being book one. The second book will be right around the corner!

The Offering takes place in a fictional world of werewolves, called wereduin. Their culture is vastly different from ours, and what they perceive as acceptable would be absurd by our standards. I invite you to look at this book not as a condonement of physical and sexual violence, nor a promotion of rape culture, but as a commentary on a society that values appearances, brutality and strength, often at the expense of those most vulnerable, and how it shapes and affects the lives of the characters. I've included a glossary at the end of the book to help you keep track of the events, characters, and deities.

You will be following Fern, a young man who struggles against the societal roles thrust upon him, while trying to stay himself. You'll learn about the world of the wereduins through his eyes, and hopefully you'll be rooting for him to succeed.

I hope that you'll not only enjoy the action, feels, struggles, love, and steamy werewolf sex, but come away with the notion that sexual fantasies are healthy and normal. Everybody has them. After all, the Offering began its life as one. Even taboo fantasies that our society often views as depraved can be okay, and simply by having them doesn't mean that you support the behavior in real life. There's a proper time and place where these can safely be explored. One of those areas is through fiction.

Now take a few hours and step into Fern's world. Leave your inhibitions at the door and enjoy the ride!

~ Rosary Deville

Chapter One
The Hunt

The Offering rapidly approached, and this year everything changed for me. A few months ago, I came of age in Wereduin society, which meant I could participate.

I had no wish to go, absolutely none. I was too young to be claimed. I didn't want to bear some alpha's pups. I wanted to finish school. Play in my band. Maybe even go to college. Mom would hear none of it, though. The following night, I would be in some alpha's bed.

In Wereduin culture, betas were the ones who became pregnant. It didn't matter that I was a guy. I was a beta, so I could bear young like how my papa had my siblings and me. I wasn't aware of an alpha that didn't breed their beta. Mom had. She'd gotten three pups out of my papa.

Once I was mated, I would be bred too. *Yuck…*

As the beta parent, Papa made me a Mating Quilt, which was a tradition. It would be used when consummating the mating bonds.

Already he had been trying to teach me ways I could submit. How I could give the alphas a good chase. That was the thing—alphas didn't want betas to make it easy for them. If a beta didn't put up a good fight, it would set the couple back for months, maybe years in their relationship.

A beta was subservient to an alpha, but not their slave. Those who didn't put up a fight during the Offering would be little more than slaves. There was a name for weak betas, *slave betas.* Alphas who took slave betas could take more than one, and many alphas joined the Offering to pick off the weak ones.

No sir, not me. Not if I could help it.

Papa had also been teaching me the *Mating Song.* Once I was claimed, and the Offering was over, my alpha and I would recite vows to each other. That last night would officially bind us together.

Thinking about Mom and Papa saying those same lines to each other made it awkward and embarrassing. But Mom would have none of it. I learned the vows, and that was that. And the following day, I would be claimed. It would be the first of three claim marks that eventually would bind me to my alpha.

My stomach was in knots, and I could barely sleep. The Wolfsbane Papa had given me left a bitter taste in my throat. The medicine made it difficult to transform into a werewolf during the Hunt, so tomorrow I'd have to stay a wereduin—our humanoid form. Most werewolves lived as wereduin anyway because it required less energy than the werewolf form.

The wooden fan on the ceiling hummed as it spun. I stared out the open window, listening to the night—the echoing of the whippoorwill that lived in the oak tree outside the house, and the leaves rustling on the branch that grew through the wall. Werewolves liked to be surrounded by nature and often built houses around trees, not cutting them down like the other races.

I wondered how tomorrow night would feel. All I could hope for was a strong and beautiful alpha female like my papa had found.

The next evening Papa dropped me off at a large, open-aired stadium. It was located on the border of Nomans Forest, a vast woodland named by prehistoric humans that existed long before the Van Helsing line. Today, various races used it in their Rites of Passage ceremonies.

The auditorium buzzed with anxious chatter. Betas from all walks of life—some old, young, tall, short, fat, skinny, beautiful, or ugly—sat on the wooden benches or paced about the arena. Some betas bloomed late, hence the variety of ages. Others were kept from the Offering. Then, there were those who'd been sent away, or their alpha had abandoned them for some reason.

As for the youngest ones in the group, I'd heard stories of stricter Wereduin parents letting their child in early, either lying at registration or else making agreements with the future alpha to have them claimed on their birthday night.

Some betas looked happy to be there, excited even. I had never understood those people. Others looked scared. All I felt was determination and anger.

I was still in school. In fact, I should be doing my homework and getting ready for bed. But my parents had taken me out of it. Once claimed, it would be at the discretion of my new alpha whether I continued my schooling. The entire mating season took about a month, starting from this evening. The three Offering ceremonies were spread out evenly, with the days in-between for other ceremonies, banquets, and bonding time between couples. The last week was the week of the full moon and Mating Week. After being completely claimed underneath the full moon, I would be bedded for an entire week with my alpha.

Everything in my world was about to change, and once again, I didn't have any choice.

I kept tugging on my black curls, swirling them around my finger. My natural light brown showed at the roots, reminding me it needed to be re-dyed. Papa had taken my straight iron away, so I couldn't style it like normal. He worried I wouldn't be as attractive if my hair hid one of my eyes. He also refused to let me use hairspray or any cologne, so I carried only my natural scent.

I couldn't even wear my piercings and that ticked me off. The lip ring I understood, as some alpha might bite it off accidentally. But my industrial bar? It was a silver rod lodged into my outer ear. I doubted anyone could take that off.

Resigning to my fate, I entered the arena.

Then it hit me. Why did I have to find a partner at all? If I survived the night without being claimed, maybe I could put off mating for another year. Given the ages of some of these betas, it must be possible to pull that off. Plus, there had to be several hundred betas here. Maybe that could work to my advantage. More moving targets. I simply had to make myself undesirable and unruly. Most importantly, I had to not get caught by any alpha. Surely, with my attitude and the fact that I was on the track team, it would be like stealing kibble from a bowl.

I joined the line with the other betas waiting to check-in. "Fern Brightwood, of the Brightwood Den?" the wereduin at the check-in counter said when it came to my turn. He checked his roster. "You came of age two months ago?"

"That's right." Almost two months, not that I was counting. So what if I was now old enough to enter the Offering? I was still in school. I wasn't ready to become an adult.

"Here you are." He handed me a key to the locker the druids assigned to me.

"Remember no clothes shall be worn during the Hunt. Changing rooms are located near the lockers."

At my locker, I took out three trinkets.

The first of the Offerings honored Arduinna, Goddess of the Hunt, and our race's creator. This pendant would be a gift to her mate, Cerowain, the God of Fertility. If my gift pleased him, he would make me more fertile. My jade trinket depicted Cerowain's face. Although a werewolf like all the Gods, Cerowain also had stag horns. But the horns on my pendant were misshaped. Hopefully, that lost me some points with him. I definitely didn't want to become pregnant anytime soon, if ever at all.

The second pendant went to Arduinna's two worgs, her hunting companions she kept by her side. As they had her ear, it was best to be on their good side. This one was simple—a wolf made of wood.

Finally, the last pendant was to the Goddess herself. It represented the werewolf entering the Offering, so it needed to have personal value to the participant. Mine was a music note. Since it was to honor the Goddess, Papa let me make it out of obsidian. I loved the way it caught the light and glimmered like a diamond. Too bad it wasn't smaller. Otherwise, I could have worn it as a necklace. It would have gone perfectly with my emo-punk look. This pendant also served as a good luck charm and provided Arduinna's protection during the often-brutal events.

I stowed away the last of my belongings and stuffed the locker key into my backpack. It also contained an ointment Papa had given me and my Mating Quilt. Papa had finished the last of the stitching the night before. When we were claimed, our alpha had the right to the locker's contents, as well as the Mating Quilt.

Slowly, I removed my clothes, dreading the Hunt. My stomach tightened into knots. Some alphas were dangerous, and the weaker betas were always the first to go. But that would not be me! Absolutely not. No way. I was going to survive this Offering, and I was going to come out unmated. Even if it was the last thing I did…

We waited for the druids to arrive. These werewolves dedicated their lives to serving the Gods. Most were betas, but a few alphas occasionally took vows. Seldom did they leave werewolf form.

When they finally came into the arena, they herded us out the back and into the forest. Four at a time, we followed a worn dirt path. The deeper into the forest, the darker it got. Fog gathered around the thick oak trees. Their long, gnarled finger-like branches captured the remaining dim light.

Already I felt the presence in the woods, watching us. Maybe it was the sound of the wind or some other animal, but I swore I heard growling. Focusing on the soothing smell of moss and foliage, I tried to ignore the monsters in the woods, waiting to devour me.

The temperature had dropped by a good ten degrees and I shivered. Moisture in the air collected on my lips, and I rubbed my shoulders to chase away the goosebumps. So the alphas could fuck us easier, we weren't permitted to wear any clothing, even pseudo-clothes—special clothing made to handle shifting between forms.

We'd also been discouraged from transforming into werewolves. Alphas wanted us to appear weak, and in wereduin form, we looked basically like humans. But my werewolf fur, while not super heavy—more sheen and lush—

would keep me warm, so I morphed anyway, at least as much as the Wolfsbane in my system allowed. Its bitterness still lingered in the back of my throat.

Some betas stared at me with wide, scared eyes, others with chastising glares. So what. I didn't care if I broke the rules. That stupid one was *made* to be broken.

A bony, wolf paw rested on my shoulder, stealing my attention. The druid stared down at me, his eyes milky white. "You are to obey the Gods, young one. Now return to wereduin." He moved his paw on top of my head, and my body reverted. I had no control over it. My bare skin felt extra cold with only my almost non-existent wereduin fur.

The druid nodded to me. "May Arduinna and Cerowain forgive your disobedience and not take their punishment out on you during the Offering."

The druids were an eerie bunch, but he meant no ill will. However much it pissed me off, he was giving me a blessing of forgiveness. Inwardly, I grimaced. I felt bad going against the loving Goddess Arduinna. Still, I grumbled at how she allowed Cerowain to treat her beta children the way he did. Being a beta himself, you'd think Cerowain would be more sympathetic.

We trekked for an entire hour, so I had a very long time to think. Mostly, I pumped myself up for what was to come. Adrenaline coursed through my veins and gave me energy, resolution.

At some point they split us up. Given the size of the group, it was probably best we didn't all start at the same location. Otherwise, we might trample each other to death trying to get away when the Hunt began. My group went north, while the other two went east and west.

Finally, we reached an incline. Even though there was no handrail, the mismatched, wooden steps made it easier to climb. The top of the hill opened into a clearing. One or two trees dotted the field, but it was mostly clear of foliage. The last rays of sun had been squeezed out from the horizon, leaving a purplish-orange hue in its wake.

The druids gathered us around the archdruid in the center. The female werewolf addressed the crowd, praising the Gods before talking about the Hunt. With my heart trapped in my throat, there was no way I could pay attention to her speech. Besides, Papa had already told me what to expect this night. Standing in the clearing, hearing the growls in the forest and the whispering of the wind through the branches, I was glad he had prepared me.

I vaguely heard the archdruid reciting the ballad of Arduinna and Cerowain. I knew that one by heart from the bedtime stories read to me as a pup. The Goddess hunted for a mate, but none gave her chase like this stag she'd encountered. When she finally caught it, she transformed it into a God, which explained why Cerowain still had stag horns.

Hundreds of alphas hid in the surrounding forest, waiting for the hunt to begin. Waiting to claim their mate.

Some betas looked like they would become slave betas. Even though he was at least my age, a skinny boy who appeared younger than me switched his weight from foot to foot. He seemed both tired and restless, like he wanted it over quickly. Yeah, he would be one of the first to go down.

Finally, the druids backed away. They moved slowly like leaving a lion's cage without disturbing the beast. They were right to be careful. The time had arrived for alphas in their full glory to begin hunting their future mates. In the past, some alphas' aggression got so fierce they fought to the death. Sometimes betas didn't even make it out alive. It wasn't common, but it had happened. One year, a particularly beautiful beta stirred up too much of a crowd and was ripped in half by two fighting alphas. Well, that certainly would not happen to me. I wasn't about to wait around like a sitting duck.

I darted for the thicket. Not a second too soon. An alpha leaped from the trees and landed right where I'd been standing. The soon-to-be slave beta was immediately devoured as prey to the alpha's sexual appetites. As I ran, loud cries mixed with guttural grunts behind me. I was too curious. Even though I told myself not to, I looked back.

The beta dangled off the ground, held upside down. His knees whacked against the alpha's meaty thighs covered in thick fur. Pelvis thumping, the beast humped the beta's ass. The boy's face twisted in agony, his hands yanking tuffs of grass.

The alpha threw his head back in pleasure, and his fangs jutted from his gaping mouth, his tongue darting out. Right at that moment, his eyes cracked open, like he felt me watching him. His gaze rested on me, and he licked his lips.

I dashed off. To run faster, I transformed into a worg—our wolf form, as much as possible, given the medicine in my system. *Godsdamn the Wolfsbane!*

There was no way I would be on the receiving end of that large cock. I would not be raped by that asshole.

I can't be taken out now! It's much too early. I'll become a slave beta.

Shit, shit, shit!

He was gaining on me and obviously on the prowl for slaves. I was a goner if he caught me. Worse yet, if I found an alpha, I wanted a female. But gender didn't matter in our world. I'd belong to the alpha who claimed me.

Something massive and black leaped past me. With a heavy thunk, another alpha blocked the slaver's path. A huge, sightly beast, his majestic black fur shimmered in the moonlight. His eyes glowed neon blue. His white fangs glistened as they clashed against the slaver's, who looked like a shaggy dog in comparison.

Regardless of the black alpha's attractiveness, he was still male, and I was not interested. But I took a moment to study them. I needed to get the hell out of there, not stand around stupidly eyeing them. I had always been too curious. The black alpha looked familiar, but I couldn't place him. He was much younger than the slaver but held his own. In fact, he was winning.

Shit. Either of them winning meant bad news for me.

I raced in a different direction, hoping to lose them, looking for a place to hide. Papa told me to let the weaker betas—those destined for slavery—be caught first.

Low mist hovered near the ground and clumped around large nearby boulders. A wide oak competed with the rocks, its knees growing over some of the smaller ones.

I chose a nook between the oak and rocks and crawled inside.

I took out Papa's ointment from my backpack and applied it everywhere I could, including my genitals. It looked and smelled like the lichen that covered the boulders and would mask my scent. The ointment was short-lived, however. I couldn't hide forever.

Two alphas passed me from either direction. One was female. I wanted to jump out and get her attention, but then I kicked myself. I didn't want to be mated. Simply because I'd seen some large males didn't mean I was going to come running out with my tail between my legs. And besides, it was much too early in the game. If I was caught, female alpha or not, I would become a slave beta.

Cries and yells came from every direction. Roars. Growls. Sounds of fighting. More betas were being claimed, and by the sound of it, we had moved past the time when the weaker ones got picked off. As proof of this, I spotted a large beta running with three alphas in pursuit.

The beautiful beta sprang up like a frolicking deer—long legs, lean body, golden hair. There was nothing weak about this beta. Three alphas followed him, two females and one male. One slip up would be the beta's downfall. The two bitches fought to get ahead, giving leeway to the male. The beta darted into a narrow ravine.

Inside the valley, a small stream trickled. He still held the lead, but the muddier ground slowed him down. The alpha male reached him. Claws out, his fangs sank into the beta's shoulder. With a cry, he lost his footing. The two alpha females lost interest. Longing entered the beta's eyes as he watched the second female leave. He must've wanted her to claim him. Then he was topped by the large alpha male. The alpha grunted. The beta's panting barely audible. I no longer saw him since the alpha's larger body covered him completely. By the thrusting of the alpha's hips and the grunts of pleasure from the alpha, he was fucking the beta.

Fear spiked through me, and I darted out, running blindly.

I don't want that! Claimed by a large male, to be trapped forever beneath a savage monster. I didn't want to submit, period. But if I had to, then I wanted a female. In my panic, I ran out into a clearing, the treeless cliffside was rocky beneath my feet, and I almost tripped. Ahead, three alphas fought over a single beta. She cowered, and then her eyes found mine. Her startled gasp alerted them to my presence. Two gave her up and raced straight for me.

Shit.

While not very fast, they waited for me to slip-up. But after I'd watched that other beta get taken down, there was no way either of them would catch up to me, not with adrenaline pounding through my veins. As fast as I could, I sprinted toward the cover of the trees. That direction was toward that slaver alpha, but I had no choice.

I ended up losing them and ran along a winding stream, but *stream* was a generous word for the line of water that rolled through the rocks. The sound of moaning caught my attention. Up ahead, two alphas shared a beta—the female taking it from both sides. Her eyes were closed, and she moaned with them. She laid on top of one alpha. His strong hands held her down. The second alpha rocked into them as he rode her ass. There was something intimate about the scene that made me pause. I never thought the Offering, and especially not the Hunt, could be intimate. But these three looked that way. I passed quickly, having no time to contemplate them further.

Off to my left, another claiming was going on. A young boy resisted a large alpha female. She had tied his wrists to a branch. Knocking him over, she barred down on top of his dick, and he sank inside her. She looked in ecstasy. As she rode his cock, clusters of her alpha juices stuck to his shaft, like pollen on a bee. The harder she rode him, the more clumps collected on his cock. It was her alpha prowess. The beta's head fell back in a silent scream—his eyes cloudy, his mouth gaping. He jerked like something invaded his body. She was submitting him to her will, binding him to her. He was beyond hope at this point.

This was the first time I'd seen *Pollination* close up, even though I'd jacked off to it in porn lots of times.

Someone grabbed the nape of my neck. *Shit, no!* Why hadn't I paid more attention to my surroundings?

This alpha male was stout and gray. His jagged claws dug into my shoulder, and it ripped a cry from my throat. Out of the corner of my eye, I saw another beta. This alpha must have been cornering her before I showed up. She didn't look back at me as she made her escape. The alpha who had me could have come from my worst nightmares. He had a large scar across his eye. His thick, weather-worn hide told me he'd been at this game for a while. He could be my papa's age, not that age mattered for werewolves, but his face was truly menacing. The glee I found in his glowing red eyes terrified me. Veins riddled his muscular physique. One of his ears had been chewed off. He gripped my shoulder, tearing my skin. I clawed at his hands, face, biting wherever I could as he forced me onto the ground.

I felt sure I was a goner when he was knocked off of me. Growling surrounded us. It was the large, black alpha that had taken on the slaver. He snarled at the alpha who had been about to rape me. Slowly, I crawled away on my hands and knees. That was when he turned his fangs on me, growling. He didn't want me to leave, as if he already felt some ownership of me. Something in his eyes halted me and trapped my breath in my throat. I shook my head rapidly.

No!

There was no way I would be claimed tonight. And certainly not by a male. I took off running, leaving them to their fight.

It was over shockingly quick. The dark alpha won. *My* alpha. It confused me when I momentarily thought of him as mine. My body wanted to submit. Arousal grew heavy in my groin, heating me up.

Hell, no!

Instincts be damned, I was not born so I could have some male alpha's pups.

The black alpha picked up speed.

Just then, two alpha males sprang from either side of the woods. I ducked low, and they collided into each other. I dodged around them. The left one snatched me back before the alpha on the right knocked him to the ground.

Both alphas were beautiful—if I allowed myself to think something like that about the same sex. One was a scarlet red, while the other a golden bronze. Hopefully, the two would also stop the black alpha who still followed me, and I could make a getaway.

Both tried, not wanting to let a challenger slip by.

I dragged out a relieved sigh. Part of me was disappointed, and that part scared me. The rest of me was thankful. I didn't want any of them to win—especially the strong dark alpha.

It was apparent by their beauty that all three alphas fighting over me were from the upper-class. But my eye was drawn to the dark one—jet black with those piercing neon-blue eyes and riddled, muscular physique. Of the three, he was the most handsome. Shaking my head and trying to remove those unwanted thoughts about the beautiful alphas fighting for me, I left them to battle.

When I heard them following me, I stole a glance over my shoulder. My heart stopped. Both the scarlet and golden-bronze alphas chased behind me. The dark werewolf must have been beaten. My heart sank. I wanted to slap myself. Why did I feel so let down?

I ran blindly through the forest and over the rocks until I backed myself against a cliff. Both werewolves approached me, snarling. I retreated as far as I could go before I drew my fangs. There was no way I was going down without a fight.

Perhaps they formed an alliance because they no longer fought each other. Instead, they homed in on me. Was I about to be claimed by two males?

How would they take me? I only had one opening. Would they both try to fit? I trembled, but my beta brain started to submit. It craved having the alphas' cocks inside me.

Backing away, I shook my head and crouched low. They sprang at me, but before they could touch me, a black shadow leaped from the cliff over my head. He landed in front of me.

There he is again!

The black alpha.

Gratitude overwhelmed me, and I could do nothing but stare at him. I wanted this alpha. I ached inside. Precum dripped from my hard cock. I wanted him inside of me.

Violently, I shook my head. *No.* I did not want to be claimed by anyone tonight. I found a small opening created by their fighting and snuck out. The black alpha growled at me, and I couldn't stop my shiver. He wanted me to wait for him. He wanted me to let him claim me. Already, it felt like he had his claws around my heart.

No. I won't submit. I won't be bred or mated, not until after I graduated.

Barely aware of where I was going, I sprinted off in an unknown direction—my body sluggish.

Then I felt it. I didn't know how, but I knew their fight was over. Stupidly, I stopped running and turned around. Both alphas that had pursued me lay on the ground. Dead? Knocked out? I had no idea. It wasn't uncommon for alphas to kill each other in the Offering. One thing was for certain, the black alpha had won.

Panicking, I took off running again, but I wasn't moving fast enough. My body already wanted to obey him.

Two paths approached as I neared a fork. I prayed that I chose the right direction. I was mid-way in when I saw ahead of me...

I chose wrong. It was a dead end.

The dark alpha stood at the mouth of the fork. Boulders and mountains loomed above me on either side, the path barely a route through the peaks.

I had nowhere to go. The alpha knew he'd won. His smirk grew. The challenge blatant in his bright neon-blue eyes. He knew it. I knew it. My doom rapidly approached.

Despite my fear and my resistance, beta juices leaked from my asshole and down my thighs. My erection grew painfully stiff, more juices dripping from the tip.

He looked even larger as he neared me. His thick bulge grew beneath his ripped-up jeans. His eyes never leaving mine, he freed his massive cock—canine, hard, reddish-brown, and the largest one I had seen in my life. Its length and thickness grew by the moment while it gorged with blood. Cockhead swollen, prominent veins and grooves ran up the shaft. I swallowed. Something like *that* was about to go inside of me. Possibly forever.

I'll get bred by that?

No!

Spinning on my heel, I took off running until I came to the end of the path. He got behind me quicker than I imagined. I faced him with my back against the wall. Growling. Showing him my fangs to tell him to back off, I transformed into as much of a werewolf as I could. But there was no way he was leaving now. Not with the kill rapidly approaching.

For a moment, I froze. Time slowed to a crawl. This was it. If I let him do this, I would be claimed. I had no hope of winning, but it wouldn't be without a fight if I was going down.

I sprang at him. I thought I saw his brow raise and his mouth smirk. Before it was all over, he had me in his strong arms, my back against his chest. He tipped my head to the side, exposing the valley between my neck and shoulder. Sharp fangs broke my skin, and I cried out at the excruciating pain. His power tried to make me yield. I resisted as much as I could, but his fangs sank even deeper. I reached out, for what…I wasn't sure. For help, for freedom? He was claiming me hard, turning me from partial werewolf back into wereduin form.

His claws scratched my pack from my shoulders. He

caught the Mating Quilt while letting Papa's ointment and the locker key spill onto the wet grass with the rest of the bag. With the hand not holding me, he forced open the quilt. Throwing it, he spread it on the ground with his foot, then he stepped us closer until we stood on its edge. We sank down until my knees rested on my quilt. One of the corners got bunched together. So when he forced me to lie down, the side of my face and shoulder smashed into the grass. He was heavy on my back as he continued to bite me. My thoughts were so incredibly jumbled that I couldn't hold on to any of them. I felt vulnerable, like he had his hands inside my heart.

"Yield to me." His deep, gruff voice sealed my fate. I didn't want this. I didn't want to be claimed. Tears blurred my vision, muddying the dirt.

"You will yield to me."

Slowly I nodded, even though I continued to struggle.

"You're mine."

My skin felt clammy. My body slick with sweat—mine and his. A heavy pulse thudded from his cock; his thickness pressed against my crack...

Would it break my skin? Then, it found my hole.

"No!" I couldn't get him off me. He was far stronger and heavier. His teeth pierced through my skin straight down to the bone. It burned. Yet, I wanted it. I wanted him. He was my alpha and bounded me to him. Already, I lay in a pool of my beta juices. My hard cock dug into my stomach, and strings of precum added to the wetness beneath me.

His hands pinned mine against the ground. With one brutal thrust, he filled me, his balls slapping my ass hard. Pain burst behind my eyelids. My cries muffled into the mud. He grunted in pleasure and bit me harder, then he scooted me over, so I was completely on the quilt. He panted loudly against my ear as he moved inside me, turning the bitter pain into something almost pleasurable.

I had never had a cock inside me, spreading me wide open. I felt so full. He continued to grow until he cramped up my insides. I felt every inch of his massive cock, felt the blood pumping through the strong veins winding up the shaft when it moved in and out of my tunnel.

His grunts filled up the narrow space. I thought I heard footsteps running away past the fork. I wondered if they would hear him devouring my virginity. Wondered if they'd heard me...what sounds was I making? Small, almost helpless whimpers that turned to moans.

Every thrust shook my body. I'd had sex before when I dated a human girl, but not anal sex, and never with a werewolf. His weight and girth pushed me beyond my limits as he slowly broke me in. His enormous, solid build covered in soft fur pressed me into the quilt.

He got up onto his knees and pulled me against him. His larger frame completely covering mine. His arm held me like a belt strapping me to him. The contours of his well-built chest and rugged abs pressed against my back. The thick fur didn't stop me from feeling every inch of his muscles. Instead, they gave him a soft texture. He panted against my ear, and by the sounds of his pleasure, he was immensely enjoying his meal.

A clawed hand grabbed my erection. I yelped as the tips scratched my skin. I was so stiff, I ached. Stimulation overdrive. I could probably be hard all night with the way he fucked me.

He chuckled, his breath caressing my cheek. He held my cock steady, and I writhed against him, at the intrusion, at the force. I had never had another guy touching my cock, and the only girl I'd been with barely touched me there. It was nothing like this. He grabbed my cock like an instrument he knew how to play.

Slowly, he stroked. His leisurely pace was the exact opposite of his rapid humping. My body molded to his as he covered me like a shell. He trapped me between his sea of muscles, moving me as he desired.

A few times, I felt the dry burn when his fur and my skin were out of sync. His pubic hair scratched and cushioned my butt. Some of it had to get inside me as he fucked me bare, pumping more and more of his alpha essence inside me—as he tried to get me to submit.

His thrusting turned savage as he raped me like the beast he was. He had me kneeling, one hand grabbing my cock, the other supporting his weight on the ground. The more excited he got, the more weight he put on me. I sank onto my forearms, burying my face into the quilt. My mouth parted, and small trails of saliva rolled down my chin, pooling onto the quilt.

I didn't get out of being claimed. I had been naïve to think I could escape. I ended up with a large alpha drilling his rock-hard cock up my virgin ass, growing harder with each thrust. In one night, I had been changed from sheltered pup to yielding beta.

The large knot caught me by surprise. Near the base of his massive cock, it rapidly inflated inside me, and I cried out. My muscles clenched around it. There was no way he could leave me now. In the middle of his cock a second large knot grew. Both spread my insides wide, halting any semen from leaving my ass and forcing me to take all his cum.

The knotting had him fucking me harder, taking me down until I pressed into the quilt. He grabbed my hip and fucked me even harsher, not caring that his knots held me still. The friction was unbearably strong against my inner walls. My only relief was that he hadn't grown a womb inside me yet, so I couldn't become pregnant.

He came into me long and good, and it had me moaning on the quilt like a needy little slut, wanting it bad. When I finally spilled over into orgasm, I was so lost in the bliss that I forgot myself and where I was for a moment. It didn't stop. Like a series of waves, one orgasm faded only to be taken up by the next. With each new peak, he bent more of my mind to his will until I thought of nothing but him and the glide of his cock inside me.

The knots still connected us and held me firmly beneath him. He planned on fucking me all night, as was custom. My body was already exhausted even though I knew there were several more hours until morning.

My insides sang with pleasure and pain, and I barely noticed that his knots had subsided. Without the knots, his cock easily hammered into me, thrusting in and out.

Grabbing my hips, he flipped me over onto my back. He attacked my neck with his fangs, deepening the bite mark, making it more defined. All I could do was weakly grab his dark fur as he owned me. He kept thrusting into me, moving me up and down against the quilt, adding to the lewd sounds of my claiming. His pounding grew so intense that I almost fainted. Slipping out of me, he flipped me onto my side before he grabbed my hip and thrust back inside.

My arms lay limp against the quilt, my palms weak. My knee he wasn't holding up, moved haphazardly. I lay consumed as my alpha feasted on my body. My mouth fell open, cries, and saliva dripping out. I spurted cum like a fountain as another orgasm ripped through me, and it coated the quilt.

He pulled me into a position that allowed him to sink his fangs into my claim mark again. I cried out at the jarring pain. Reaching behind me, I dug my fingers into his mane as another round of orgasms washed me in bliss. His heavy knots grew inside me, binding me to him again.

Collapsing us face-first into the quilt, he bore down on top of me, utterly owning me. His hands covered mine and pinned me against the quilt, and he fucked me until the first rays of sunlight shown through the trees.

Chapter Two

Transitioning

Two days had passed since the Hunt, and I had been staying at my new alpha's house. My neck held the first of three claim marks. The red bite was stark against my pale skin.

Living with my parents was no longer possible. No, I was stuck with Donovan Blackfang. He went by Don.

I had been right. I did know my alpha. An aristocrat, his family was in the same social tier as mine, and while he was older than me, I had seen him at a few holiday parties. Whenever I had, he'd always looked so cool. He was fit, wore his silver-brown hair in a long ponytail, and had mocha-colored skin. He never paid much attention to the other little kids at the party or me, but I remembered he had a nice smile.

My parents were thrilled to have me claimed by such a strong alpha, but I hated him. My alpha? *Try rapist!* I didn't want to be anywhere near him. I tried to avoid him as much as possible. So far, I had been unsuccessful.

He was stronger and quicker than me, especially now. During the Offering—sometimes longer depending on the couple—something known as the *Dominating* began. This was when I would start becoming under my alpha's influence, mentally and bodily. So even though I ran track, my body grew weak around him, and I couldn't escape him. I didn't have a car. In fact, I wasn't even old enough to drive, despite coming of age in Wereduin society. But that didn't matter. I was getting the hell out of there. I would stay at Shamar's house. I hadn't had time to call my friend, but he wouldn't mind if I came over.

The moment Don was in the shower, I snuck out. The top lock on the door was a heavy padlock, but Don didn't use it, which worked perfectly. The solid wood door had a habit of sticking, and for a moment, I thought about leaving it open to avoid making too much noise. But that would alert Don that I'd left. He'd find out eventually, but better later than sooner.

Not even taking a set of clothes with me, I raced down the long driveway. Don's house, like nearly all wereduin homes, was walking distance to most things. Most werewolves didn't need cars. Only assholes like Don had one.

Don lived on a hill. His white, squared house was almost entirely made up of glass. Except for the supporting structure and, thankfully, the bathroom, most walls were windows. The large tree that grew straight through the center of the living room was impressive to see. Much as it made me bristle, Don had quite a classy place.

Fuck that!

Why was I thinking of Don's house as anything but my prison?

Shamar lived on the other side of the bridge that led into the bayous where most zombies lived. It was closer to my parents' house, but still only a bus ride away from Don's. Zombie and werewolf relations were decent enough that living side by side wasn't problematic.

I was in view of the bus station when a *Diamond-Lux* turned around the curb, its silver glistening in the sunlight— sporty and sophistication in one. Something about that car made my stomach tighten. The moment it neared, I knew why. Don sat behind the wheel. Slowing down, he pulled up alongside me.

"Fern. Get in." His tone lacked room for argument.

"Thanks, but I'm good."

"That wasn't a suggestion."

It was a long shot, but I had to try it. Not looking back, I sprinted down the sidewalk. Running from an alpha only incited them, but who cared? I never wanted to be paired with this asshole—a guy of all things.

Heavy footfalls gained on me from behind before I was caught and taken down to the ground. The grass wasn't thick, and the fall still hurt.

"Stupid, little pup, why are you running from me? What do you hope to accomplish? You're mine now. I own you."

I shook my head. "No, I didn't give my consent."

"Consent? Why would that matter, we're wolves? Now get in the car." Don had more than enough strength to carry me, but I fought him all the way. He yanked my hands behind my back and had me up in his arms. I kicked him again and again. "I said, stop it, or I will hurt you."

Like I cared at this point. But his punch to the stomach had me barreling over. "Damn…you."

"Uh-huh." Don picked me back up and slung me over his shoulder.

"Put me down!"

"Yeah, yeah, yeah. You're coming home with me, and I'm going to teach you a lesson. You will yield to me as I will not tolerate disobedience." I knew this period would be a power struggle. Papa had mentioned that to me, as did Mom. But the experience was far more horrible than I imagined.

He dropped me forcefully into the car, and my head slammed into the seat. I rubbed the back of my skull to soothe it. That distracted me enough for Don to close the door, clicking the lock the moment it shut. He unlocked *his* door and got in.

"Bastard! I won't accept you."

"You already have. Your body accepted me, and I won you. End of story."

I shook my head. "Not for me. I won't stay with you."

"You will. When we get home, I am fucking you senseless."

My stomach knotted with dread. Don was so excessively big. My smaller body still had to get used to the intrusion. Papa had given me a cream to help stretch me, but it was infused with Don's alpha prowess, so I had no intention of using it. The more of Don's essence that got inside of me, the easier it became for him to submit me. Besides, at best, the lotion didn't seem to be made for my comfort, but rather to stretch me open so Don could better plow into me. Papa didn't see it that way, of course.

We arrived at the house way too quickly. I clutched the door handle.

Don rolled his eyes. "If you don't behave, I will hit you again. You got that?" He got out of the car.

I clung to the door handle with a death grip, but Don was still stronger. Yanking open the door, he tugged me out from the car seat. I kicked at his legs, but this time Don tripped my feet out from under me, and I fell onto my butt.

He glared down at me. "I will be fucking you. It is inevitable. Stop fighting me and submit. Or I will make this very hard on you."

He yanked me up and slung me over his shoulder. I grabbed the car door, but the slippery metal popped out from under my fingers. Soon we were in front of the door. I kept kicking him to make it harder for him to get his keys. Don growled. The next second, he slammed me against the door. His hand constricted my throat.

Leaning closer, Don whispered, "Unless you want me to knock you out right here, I suggest you stop struggling. You are mine now. End of story."

The threat in his tone made me hesitate, and it was all that was needed for Don to unlock the door and drag me inside. He locked the large iron bolt at the top of the door that he hadn't used before.

He took me all the way to the walk-in shoe closet before releasing me. The moment my feet touched the ground, I raced for the door. I pulled at the lock with all my might, but it was super heavy and didn't budge.

Don snorted. "Yeah, good luck with that." He went about removing his shoes, not at all in a rush.

"I don't like you. I don't want to be mated to you."

"Oh, yeah? And why is that?"

"You're a guy for one. And you're a bully."

"Only because you fight me." Don was behind me in a flash. "As for being male, I will stretch you out soon enough and have you craving my cock so much that no female will be able to satisfy you again."

I could not stop my whimper. His breath tickled my neck. I had always felt the most sensitive there, and even more so after receiving the first claim mark.

Don smirked against my skin. His teeth sank into the red, shiny bite mark, and my knees buckled. My whimper became a moan as I sank into the pleasure-pain of getting bitten by him. My new alpha was biting me.

New alpha? That thought upset me. Since when did I plan on calling anyone alpha? There were two more Offerings left, and Betas Night, I could still shake him. I had to be free of him.

He hoisted me off my feet, wrapping my legs around his waist.

"Ahh, stop…no, I don't…I don't want it!"

"And what part of the mating process requires your *wants*?" Don groaned as he sank his teeth back into my neck, deepening the claim mark. I clawed at his back, but his alpha influence weakened my resolve, and my instincts called me to submit. Compared to my werewolf claws, my wereduin ones seemed like blunt fingernails, especially against Don's impenetrable hide—alpha skin was thick even as wereduin. Unfortunately, his essence prevented me from shifting forms.

He took me into his bedroom and threw me onto the bed. He removed my clothes with haste, popping off a button snagged by his claw.

"No…" I tried to get away, but I was too slow. Already his prowess invaded my senses. "Stop…get off me…"

Don flipped me onto my stomach. Stretching my arms out above my head, he pinned my wrists. When he breached my body, I screamed into the mattress. His thickness tore my inner walls. It hurt so badly that I could barely think.

"You're making this difficult. I would take time to prepare you if you weren't always fighting me. But no, you want to do this the hard way," Don's words hissed into my ear. "Do you think I'll ever let you leave me?" Again and again, he pounded into me. "No matter where you run, I'll chase you down. I'll never let you get away from me. You belong to me, Fern. I'll be fucking you for the rest of your life, got that? You are mine, and I will breed you and own you. And you will be obedient to me."

I lost the battle to contain my moans when pleasure overtook pain. Each of his movements brought me to life, awoke sensations inside my body that I hadn't known existed. To try and stifle my moans, I bit the mattress. But it was no good. Trapping me beneath his firm body, he fucked me into submission.

Shamar spotted me in the hall. "Fern! Praise the loa, you're safe! I wasn't sure I'd ever see you again." Like all zombies, Shamar practiced the Voodoo religion. While he wasn't particularly religious, he was always saying *Praise the loa, this,* or *Praise the loa, that.* On his most emotional days, he upped his game and said, *Praise Ayida-Weddo!*—who according to him, was the loa who created the zombie race.

The moment he was in front of me, he threw his arms around my neck. Palpable anxiety poured off him. Receiving hugs from zombies was never a warm experience, given their naturally cool skin. Shamar's green color was common for a zombie, most ranging from green to brown. Of all my friends, Shamar was the one who didn't need to dye his hair black. His mangy hair always looked uncombed, like he'd just gotten out of bed and sprinkled a bit of dirt on it—a trendy style among zombies our age.

I smiled awkwardly since Shamar still hugged me, but he'd always been a touchy-feely friend. Oddly, he never seemed to do this to anyone else but me. He and I clicked instantly, liking all the same metal bands, like the one printed on the worn-out *Zombie Blood* t-shirt I wore to school. Despite fading from too much love, the front still looked awesome, depicting the face of a human girl looking like a zombie voodoo doll. Stitches wove down the middle of her face. More sowed her lips together, then crossed her face to her ears. It had been their original album cover. That was the gig where I'd met Shamar. We had collided in the mosh pit and had been friends ever since.

He hugged me tighter. "You won't believe how worried I

was. I barely slept last night. I wasn't sure I'd ever see you again." When did he plan to let me go? He always overreacted to anything that remotely caused me discomfort. Arduinna help it if I got sick.

"Yeah, well, it's not that common for betas to die at this stage." I winced when his arm squeezed down over the claim mark, pulling away. The black scarf I'd hidden it under didn't make it any less tender.

"You got bitten?" he asked, genuinely shocked as if the entire purpose of that madhouse was for anything else. "But I thought you didn't want to be mated?"

I started to get defensive. "It's not like I didn't try to get away…geez, you make it sound like I wanted this."

"I knew you'd get claimed."

"What great faith you have in me…"

Shamar shook his head. "I don't mean it like that. I knew you'd put up a good fight, but you're a Highborne. And compared to a lot of others, you're…" He shut his mouth. Shuffling his feet, he looked down at his worn-out shoes.

"What? I'm what?"

"Never mind."

Alphonse and Lucian caught up with us. Lucian had an arm around Alphonse's waist, the two of them laughing. It was common knowledge that even though all four of us were friends, Lucian and Alphonse were besties, like Shamar and me.

"So, you made it in one piece, then?" Lucian always sounded on the arrogant side. Must have been his vampire blood. Of all the races, they were the most pompous—Highborne werewolves included. The antiquated design of his ruffled tie and billowed sleeves made him look like a prince leading a princess. All he needed was a cloak and his image would be complete. Given his attire, he made me think of the vampire actor Dracula.

Alphonse would make one awkward princess, though. His black tees normally contained either band logos like mine or funny slogans. While both wore black, it was apparent where the vampire began, and the human ended. This close together, their height difference was more pronounced, with Lucian being the shorter of the two. That was ironic since vampires normally were taller than humans, and beta wereduins and zombies too.

"Wow, you-you must've been so sca-scared!" Alphonse had the courage of a mouse, despite being a descendant of the legendary Van Helsing like all humans in our society. "I he-heard you guys can-can-can actually die in that cer-ceremony." He also had a terrible stutter—something he'd had as long as I'd known him.

I looked away. "Yeah, well…"

"Who-who'd you get pa-paired with?" Alphonse sounded like a giddy schoolgirl with a crush. "Is she a-a hottie?"

Lucian snorted, but he didn't comment. He released Alphonse's waist, sulking in the background. He was always moody. It went with his look. While the rest of us were emo with a hint of metalhead, Lucian was the goth in our group. He liked to make his already pale skin whiter with make-up, and he put black blush on. He applied thick extravagant eye make-up and lipstick—all black, of course. Vampires had crazy long ears that stuck out at an angle, far past their heads. Lucian riddled his length with piercings.

I sighed. "I wish—" A distraction interrupted me before I could start talking about Don. Figuring it was something to do with people I didn't care about, I ignored it. "He's bossy and full of himself, not to mention a real jerk. He wants me to do everything his way."

"I know, bu-bu-but." Alphonse looked over his shoulder at the commotion. The tallest in our group, seeing wasn't a problem for him. "Isn't that wha-what *all* your-your alphas are-are-are like?"

"Well, I guess. But he could've at least been a strong female—"

"Who-who's that?" Alphonse interrupted. "Shit, he's hot!"

"I don't see it," Lucian grumbled. He sneered at who

Alphonse had pointed at. Shamar and I looked in that direction too. My heart clenched.

Damn it…what is he doing here?

"Him?" Shamar asked, and I realized I'd spoken aloud. "You know this guy—wait, don't tell me he's your alpha?" His eyes narrowed, and he furrowed his brow— distinct anger in his tone.

I nodded. "Yeah, why does that jerk have to show up at my school?"

A flock of betas surrounded Don, but his height made him stand out. Pompous, full of himself, jerk. Of course, all this attention was the worst thing for him. For me rather…his big head was probably being blown to even larger proportions.

"And he's an asshole?" Shamar's voice turned bitter. Alphonse seemed to be the only one impressed and showing active interest. Both Lucian and Shamar scowled at Don.

"Big time. I fucking hate him."

"Does he?" Shamar looked away, sadness in his tone. His feelings confused me. "Force himself on you?"

"What the hell, Shamar?" Lucian glared at him. "Don't say disgusting stuff. As if I want to think of gross werewolves like that. No offense, Fern…"

I shrugged. I wasn't offended. I didn't like to think about vampires having sex, either.

Don spotted me and maneuvered the betas out of his way, heading in my direction. I was even more pissed at him. Took him long enough to stop flirting with all those betas. What did he think this was anyway? Did he think he could have me and other slices of ass on the side? *Hell, no.*

"Fern." Heads turned in my direction when Don directed his voice at me.

Alphonse sucked in a breath. "He e-even sounds hands-handsome."

"Whatever, I'm outta here." Lucian walked off without looking back. But *walking* for Lucian looked more like gliding with his back straight as if he had something stuck up his ass.

"Wait! Lucian!" Alphonse turned to us. "S-sorry, guys,

gotta go. I'll talk ta you later, o-okay?"

"Yeah, all right." I wanted to take off with them, but that jerk would chase me down.

"What are you doing here?" I glared all the hatred I could muster at him when he stopped in front of me. "Thought you had tryouts today?"

"I'd almost think you'd listened to my schedule." He gave a wry smile. "But nah, they're not for another few hours."

"So shouldn't you be practicing? And literally anywhere else besides here?"

"You left without a word this morning, so I thought I would swing by since I have some free time. After all," he leaned in close, and his voice tickled the soft fur on my ear, "you're my beta now."

I knew what he was implying. *Yeah, right!* We were at my high school, not some sleazy club where he could take me into the back and do what he liked with me.

His hand hovered near my face before I slapped it away. "Not yet; we still got two more Offerings."

"Right!" Shamar said. "So you can't just come into his life and try and change it." An ever-faithful friend, I could always count on Shamar to help me out.

"Zombie, huh?" Don cleaned his ear with his pinky finger. "I don't feel like dealing with yet another brat, so try to be good."

"I'll hex you if you don't leave him alone!" While Shamar wasn't particularly good at hexes and spells, he was learning from his grandmother, a highly-skilled Voodoo witchdoctor. Voodoo shamans and witchdoctors dominated the hexes and spells industry because they worked and could be quite effective. At some point, even Don would have to quiver.

Ignoring Shamar completely, Don grabbed my hand.

I tried to fight him. "You're such a jerk!"

He tugged me against his chest, whispering into my ear. "Do you want me to submit you right here? I don't have to wait until we're alone. So, unless you want your entire school to see you taking it, like my needy,"—he nibbled the tip of my pointy ear, accenting each word—"little," —"beta," even in wereduin form, his canines still pricked, "then I suggest you follow."

I bit the inside of my cheek to stuff down my frustration. He'd make good on his threat. *Asshole.* It looked like I had no choice but to give in to his perverted demands, and at my school of all places.

"Sorry, Shamar, I'll have to catch up with you at lunch."

Shamar looked ready to fight on my behalf. But I waved him off since Don was already snarling. He could easily hurt my friend, and I couldn't allow that.

Leading me into the bathroom, Don glared at two students. "Get out."

The boys, both zombies, took off at a brisk pace. When they were gone, Don bolted the door.

"You can't just lock it." I already felt my body responding as if Don were touching me. "What if others need to come in here?"

He stalked toward me like the predator he was. I slowly stepped back. When I bumped the sink, his lips twisted into a smirk.

"Nowhere to go, my little pup?"

I swallowed. "Le-Leave me alone."

Don shook his head. "You are never to leave the house without coming to me first." He caught me in his strong arms, lifting me up to sit on the sink counter. "I need to stick my cock inside you first."

A whimper escaped my lips. He nuzzled my neck, tilting it to the side and up toward the ceiling. He nosed my black scarf until he found my skin and ran his fangs along my neck, nipping me, sucking, and kissing. I knew what he planned on doing. Digging my claws into his shoulders, I weakly tried to struggle, but I needed my werewolf claws to break his skin, so I had no way to fight him off. His fangs bore into my exposed claim mark, reopening it, making it more defined.

"I'm going to enjoy this." Don sank his fangs even deeper

as he spoke through clenched jaws. "Breaking you in. Making you mine. Owning you. Right here at your school."

He tugged my shorts down to my ankles until they dangled off one of my legs. He must have been using some influence on me today since it was extremely hard to fight him. But maybe that wasn't it. Maybe I didn't want to put up much of a struggle. Not because I enjoyed it or accepted him by any means, but I didn't want to make too much noise. I didn't want people at my school to see me humiliated in this way.

"Let this be a lesson to you the next time you leave the house without my permission." He yanked off my underwear and angled me to his cock and plunged into my ass. I thought it would hurt, but to my embarrassment, I was so wet inside, juices dripped down my thighs. He growled. "Look at how wet you are. At how much your body was craving this. It belongs to me now." He leered at my hard cock that pressed into his stomach. "Even here," he grabbed my shaft, pumping it. "You are so hard for me. Admit it, my little Fern, I own your body, if not your heart."

He moved inside me with deep thrusts, forceful, pushing me up against the counter. "This isn't enough." His voice sounded distracted or preoccupied before he lifted me. Still buried inside my ass, he took me up against the wall. He pinned my wrists above my head with a strong hand while his other one held me up. The new position allowed him to pump feverishly into me. I gasped, crying out in wanton desire. It felt too amazing. But it also trapped me. I should have known better, but this moment made me realize how fucked I truly was in this situation. How most likely I would end up having him for a mate and have his cock inside me whenever he chose. As he ravished me in the school bathroom, the realization finally set in.

He worked my body like putty in his hand. I couldn't believe how deep he could get inside me or how hard he was. Knots grew inside his cock and rubbed against my inner walls until they had completely plugged up my ass. Despite the knots, he came so much inside me that it streamed down his cock.

"I plan on doing this to you every morning. Where you choose to take it is up to you. But know this, I will have my cock inside you, nailing you to the bed, every morning, or I will come and find you." Tears from the overwhelming sensations spilled down my cheeks. "And then I will fuck you against anything I like. Next time, I will bend you over your own desk and let the entire class see you take it up the ass."

I nodded weakly, saliva spilling from my parted lips. As it ran down my chin, he licked it off. Pleasure from his thrusts drew me to a state of euphoria like he invaded my body and soul until I was utterly consumed by him. At that moment, I would let him do anything to me, and there was nothing I wouldn't do for him. My body worshiped him. Deep inside me, my mind rebelled, still not wanting to surrender. But right then, he had all the power, and he lorded it over me, making me feel claimed, owned, devoured by his appetite.

"I didn't hear you, *beta*," his voice, rough and needy, whispered into my ear. "Who will be fucking you every morning?" I didn't want to answer him. He found a different angle and fucked me harder, and the pleasure ripped even louder cries from me. I didn't want my entire school hearing me taking it like his good little *pup-maker*, even though he had made me into one—one he planned on breeding soon as the law gave him ownership of me.

"Y-You."

"Where will my cock be every morning?"

"In m-me." I could barely think over the intense sensations. I threw my head back against the wall, exposing my throat. He attacked my neck with forceful strokes of his tongue, staking his claim on me, making me yield. "I'll ne-never…"

"Never what?"

"Ne-Never do this again…"

"Good." He licked from my open mouth to my chin, trailing down my neck until he found the claim mark. This time when he sank down, I had to bite my lip to stifle my cries. This would certainly teach me not to evade him in the mornings. I had no doubt he would make good on his threat and fuck me inside my classroom. Whether they disapproved or not, the teachers would not be able to stop him. As his beta, he could fuck me anywhere he chose, especially when the Offering was going on.

Fangs never leaving my claim mark, he continued to fuck me until I spilled my cum all over his stomach.

Shamar was the first of my friends to arrive at our lunch table. His expression warred between worried and angry. His pale lips stretched across abnormally straight, white teeth. He'd look scary if I hadn't known him for years.

"He raped you, didn't he?"

That felt like a slap to the face. It wasn't like I wanted that broadcasted, nor did I want to talk about this with friends.

"Well, fuck you, too," I said in what could have been a greeting.

Shamar sighed. "You know what I mean. I'm not trying to take out my anger on you. It's just, this is so frustrating. I don't know what to do with these feelings!" Shamar wasn't one to hold back what he thought or felt. His animated voice held a faint scratchy sound. Whenever he worked himself up and talked too much, he sounded like there was something grainy scratching the back of his throat.

"Calm down, will yah. Geez, I'm the one actually having to deal with this jerk, and you're the one freaking out?" Taking a seat across from him, I opened my lunch box. I was planning to buy lunch or go on a hunger strike since I didn't have any *ules* to pay for it, but Don had brought it to me. At least *that* hadn't been his only reason for coming to my school. Normally, Papa would make my lunch. I missed that. It made me feel homesick. Being a beta sucked.

Don's lunch actually looked pretty tasty. I would've rather thrown it in his face, but my stomach didn't agree, already grumbling loudly. Wereduin needed to eat more calories to maintain forms. Without the extra energy, we'd regress back into worgs. I guess I took the amount of effort it required to stay in wereduin form for granted, as I'd been able to shift since puphood. For us, it was the equivalent of humans learning to walk. I worried about tiring in werewolf form, though. Hopefully, that would change with time, like it did after learning to shift as a pup.

"Thought you weren't able to stay with your Papa anymore?" Shamar probably referred to the homemade lunch I'd brought in.

"Yeah…looks like assaulting me wasn't the only reason that jerk came by."

"I wouldn't eat it."

"Easy for you to say, I'm starving."

"You don't know what he put in it. Maybe it's more of that mind-controlling thing you guys do?"

I sniffed it. "Doesn't smell like it."

"Here?" He offered me what looked like a crispy chicken finger, only I knew better. "This is amazing, once you look past what it is."

I shook my head when Alphonse's voice came from over my shoulder. "Like he wants ta-ta-to eat human fingers? He's a werewolf, and they-they used to be hu-human once." That was a theory, but it had never been proven—and certainly not what we believed—although humans liked to link every race's origin back to them.

Shamar took his *chicken fingers* away. "You wouldn't be the one eating it, so what do you care?"

Alphonse and Shamar had a rocky relationship. This was made stronger by the fact that Shamar, as a zombie, ate human parts. It wasn't always human flesh, but it still made Alphonse queasy. Thankfully, Shamar hadn't yet come of age. In the zombie world, in the final rite of passage into adulthood, zombies went as a horde to attack humans for their brains. Shamar had said he would never participate in that, especially since he knew Alphonse.

Of course, the humans were little better. Maybe they just needed something to hunt since they still officially called themselves *Hunters*, even after making nice with vampires. They'd have to be out of their fucking minds to try and hunt alpha werewolves, so zombies seemed to be their new targets. The only way civilization didn't crumble was because both races could only act on their animosity during rituals and stuff, which was why you didn't see human and zombie students fighting in the halls. Thankfully, though, it seemed like among us younger people, we didn't share the same beef against each other as our parents did, so maybe both sides were on the mend toward reconciliation once the old farts kicked off. But knowing human arrogance and zombie appetites that might be a tall order, even for the next generation.

"You don't have to rub it in his face, though." Lucian resembled a bulldog ready to defend its master with how he crouched beside Alphonse.

"Okay, okay, guys." I threw my hands up to draw their attention and prevent what could turn into a fight. The distraction worked, and Shamar was back to being the concerned best friend. A look of compassion crossed his face.

"S-so-so, what did hap-pen?" Alphonse also took the bait and no longer looked like he wanted to throw up or run away crying. Lucian took longer to return to normal. He got super protective when it came to Alphonse, but then again, they were best friends.

I sighed, wishing I hadn't stolen the spotlight. What was I thinking? I didn't want to divulge any of this embarrassing information. It was humiliating enough. "I really fucking hate him. Wish his stupid *spawn* tryouts didn't start so fucking late, then he wouldn't have been able to——"

"Wa-Wait! He's a *spawn* player?" Alphonse's eyes almost bulged out of his head. Of all of my friends, only he followed the sport. Basically, he fell off the grid when it was playoff season—much to everyone's frustration, particularly Lucian.

"Yeah, he's trying to go pro." I scoffed. "Like he needs a bigger head than he's already got."

I didn't know anything about *spawn* until I got with Don, as sports had never been my scene. It was basically a giant capture the flag game that involved two teams and a lot of fighting. I actively tried to avoid anything *spawn* related.

"I know bu-but-but *spawn?*" Alphonse rubbed his hands together, his eyes looking even brighter. "What team?"

Not like I paid much attention. I shrugged. "I don't know, something *fury…*"

"Iron Furies? Like *the Iron Furies?*"

I rolled my eyes. "What does that even matter? It's a stupid sport anyway."

Alphonse looked so happy, like he had died and was now dining with the Gods in the Moon Vale. "I can't be-believe-believe it. Wow!"

"So?" Lucian grumbled. "Big deal. He plays *spawn*. Not like you need brains for that—"

"Ah, man!" Alphonse grinned widely, talking over Lucian. "Now I wish I'd stayed to get an autograph."

"Well, he hasn't made it yet, so cool your balls, Alphonse." I scowled and started to play with the food he'd made me. It was a tuna salad sandwich, truffled potatoes, carrots, and dessert—a mini chocolate cake that made me hope it contained a creamy center by the swirl of frosting on the top.

"Still, it's the fu-fuck-fucking Furies we're talking about!" As he scanned the items in my lunchbox, Alphonse's eyes lit up even more. "He-He-He made all of this? Looks tasty! Hot lunch su-sucks today."

"Sure, have some, I guess." I gave one of my sandwich slices to him and traded it for some spicy boar-wings.

"Holy shit, this is-this is good!" Alphonse eagerly talked with his mouthful.

Next to him, Lucian sipped his drink, a sour expression still on his face. He usually brought in a shake—this one a fancy mixed drink called *Bloody Mary*—even though they served O-positive blood drinks in the lunch line. He thought school lunch was beneath him—typical vampire.

"Al?" A noticeable pout entered Lucian's voice until he got Alphonse to look over. He rubbed his face in Alphonse's shoulder. "Since you're having that, think you'll be strong enough today?"

Alphonse smiled. He brushed his auburn ponytail off to the side. Some of his long, dyed-black bangs had slipped free and framed his face. He tugged down his oversized collar, revealing his neck—his family's dress code demanded that every shirt have collars that, when straightened, covered up to their ears. I had learned this information when I spent the day with them. When they all wore similar clothing, I had to ask him what the heck was going on. He said it had served as a line of defense against vampires back when the two races hated each other, and the custom never went away.

"Sure, I don't mind." Now visible, Alphonse's Adam's apple bobbed when he swallowed. It stuck out more when he slouched his neck.

Lucian licked his forked tongue over the spot he intended to drink from on Alphonse's neck. Then his fangs broke the skin. Normally, their typical behavior went by unnoticed, but my own bite mark ached beneath the scarf that hid it. Tiny thrills danced up and down my spine as I recalled the pleasure of Don's fangs entering me. Shaking my head, I was filled with self-loathing. Why did I even have to like it anyway? Why couldn't I only get those thoughts that hated everything Don-related? It really did suck to be a beta.

Turning away, I tried to focus on something else. That was when I noticed Shamar was avoiding looking at Alphonse and Lucian, too. Our friends' display of intimacy never used to bother Shamar, either. Perhaps, like me, he also was pissed at that asshole, Don.

My stomach growled loudly, and I eyed the food. Alphonse's excitement made me curious, so I tried it. And, yes, it appeared Don could add cooking to the list of things he was good at—like he needed another thing to blow up his already fat head. *Arrogant bastard.* Still, the food tasted amazing, and despite cursing the cook, I ate it all.

That evening we walked home from school together, laughing. My neck still hurt, but I had no intention of telling my friends that…especially not Shamar. It was the four of us. Until Don pulled up in his silver *Diamond-Lux*.

Asshole. Was he going to follow me everywhere from now on? *Probably.* Alphas were very possessive during this period. Last night, Don held me beneath him for what could have been ten minutes. During which he had deepened my claim mark, biting it again and again. It had hurt, but that was nothing to how pissed I was at him for stirring up my emotions. With every bite, Don ejected his alpha influence into me, trying to submit me. No fucking way. I was going to hold out as long as possible. The Offering was far from over. There was still a chance to rid myself of his arrogant ass.

"Fern." He pulled up right beside us, lowering his window.

My knees weakened at the sound of his voice, and that pissed me off. So, I took it out on him. "The hell do you want? Aren't you supposed to be at tryouts?"

"Long over with. Besides, I told you I would pick you up from school." He smirked. "Why do I get the feeling that you haven't forgotten but are purposefully trying my patience."

I snorted. "Bingo! I told you I walk home with my friends, so piss off."

Alphonse looked from me over to Don. "Fern," he whispered, twirling a strand of his long hair around his finger, his hand trembling. He'd freed his ponytail on the way home, and now his shaggy auburn hair hung passed his shoulders. "Go. You-You're gonna ma-make him mad. G-Go-Go with him already." Alphonse tried to hide behind Lucian, looking like he wanted to be anywhere but here. Despite slouching to not be that noticeable, he was still plainly visible to Don.

I sighed. Alphonse was quite the courageous guy. Wasn't it him who wanted to get Don's autograph?

I glared at Don. "Let him get mad for all I care. Come on." I directed my friends away from the car.

Don growled. "Fern, do you really want to test me right now?"

"Now's as good a time as any."

"Why you—wait a second, who told you that you could be around Fern, brat?"

It took me a moment to realize he wasn't talking to me this time, but instead, his gaze fell on Lucian. *Right.* The old vampire-werewolf grudge.

"I did." I glared at Don again. "He's been in my life a hell of a lot longer than you. As I see it, you have no right to dictate who I can hang out with."

"As your alpha, I forbid it, now get in the car. Unless you want me to drag you in here."

"You might be his alpha, but you're not his slave owner. Fern is allowed to have friends without you trying to take that away from him." At least Shamar was a good friend—Lucian was too busy scowling at Don, and Alphonse was too busy cowering.

Don's eyes narrowed. "Do you presume to tell me what rights I have over my own beta?"

"Yeah, I do." Shamar met his gaze with confident, cold eyes. "Fern is his own person and can make decisions for himself. What does it matter who he hangs out with? No one's getting in the way of him and his alpha, so you have nothing to complain about."

"Are you about finished, brat?" Don spoke like he talked to a five-year-old throwing a tantrum. He stopped the car.

My first impulse was to run, but instincts would have Don chasing me down and fucking me right on the street. And I had way too much pride to let my friends see me so helpless.

"Seriously, what the fuck? Why can't I hang out with my normal friends?"

"Because you are no longer a normal high schooler, but my mate. Now fall in line unless you want me to submit you right here."

I glared at him, wishing all my hatred onto him. Too bad Shamar hadn't brought one of his hex bags to school. Don caught my hand.

"Let go!"

He slung me over his shoulder like I weighed nothing.

Glaring at Lucian, he advanced on him. "If I ever find you around Fern again, I will kill you."

"What the fuck? Lucian's my friend. You have no right—"

"That's where you're an idiot. I have every right to you. Every right. Got that." I kicked at his chest and pounded my fists into his back. Don began to transform. His dark skin sprouting fur, his blue eyes becoming more neon in the evening sunlight. "Get. The hell. Out of my sight. All of you!"

Unfortunately for me, none of my friends were bold enough to directly take on a terror like Don, a full-blooded alpha. It wasn't uncommon for them to kill potential threats, especially during the mating season. Shamar looked like he was debating charging at Don.

"I fucking hate you!" I said. Opening the passenger side, he threw me into the car. Immediately I went to open it, but he blocked it.

"Stop it! Leave him alone!" Shamar went to help me out. Only to be met with the back of Don's arm, raising his hand to strike Shamar if he advanced.

"Okay, new rule. All annoying brats better head home now before I break some bones."

There was no way I could win against him, and I didn't want that asshole to hurt my friends.

"Forget it, guys. I'll see you tomorrow at school." I had to yell this out Don's window as he'd locked my side of the car the moment he slammed my door shut.

Getting in the car, Don sped off. I glanced back to my friends, all bearing expressions of anger or fear—as was the case with Alphonse. Last I saw, he trailed behind Lucian toward Lucian's Coven and the Helsing community where he lived. His slouched gait barely kept up with Lucian's that seemed to glide over the sidewalk.

Shamar stood with clenched fists watching us drive away.

"You will not be around that vampire anymore, Fern."

"Fuck you. We're in a band together, and he's my friend—"

"And you are my beta."

"So?"

"So you belong to me. And there's no way I want my mate anywhere near those untrustworthy bloodsuckers."

"They're not bloodsuckers!" I unleashed all my anger—at him, at the world, at my stupid parents for pushing me into his arms. "If anyone is the asshole here, it's you."

Don gave me a cold glare. Without a second thought, he pulled the car over. I shivered despite my anger. I felt the livid frustration rolling from him. My body begged me to seek out forgiveness—to give in to my alpha. Instead, I narrowed my eyes. In no time at all, Don crossed over to my seat, lowered it, and stayed on top of me. He was well-built and heavy, and that made it difficult for me to breathe. I shoved him hard, trying to knock him off. I went to strike him, but he pinned my wrists down. A predatory smirk lit his face.

"You're quite lively, aren't you, Fern?" His husky, sensual tone took me by surprise, and I forgot all of my angry comebacks. "But..." He nibbled my cheek, breaking the skin. His tongue licked up the small droplet of blood that appeared. "You will soon learn who your owner is." He grabbed both of my wrists with one hand. His other popped open the button on my shorts and went inside. Against my will, my body responded to his touch.

"I am going to break you in, bend you to my will. And you. Will. Obey me." He growled—blue eyes hinting neon as the evening faded. Slowly, he transformed on top of me. He hadn't taken me while in werewolf form since the Hunt. His already strong body grew even larger, and his added weight crushed me into the seat. His muscular chest expanded, making his firm pecks huge. Fur spouted on his chest and tickled my skin. The car's metal roof screeched as the frame adjusted to his enormous size—all cars were made to accommodate alpha werewolf transformation, courtesy of witch engineering that specialized in doing the impossible. Witches also had a hand in the making of pseudo-clothing—a reason that wereduin and witch relations were fairly good, despite our cultural differences.

Don reached under my shirt—claws scraping my abdomen—and yanked it over my head.

"S-Stop it," I growled. "You're gonna rip it."

He nibbled my ear, again making me bleed. "Like I care."

I let out a high-pitch sound somewhere between a whimper and a moan, and it pissed me off.

Pinning me down, his hand invaded my briefs as he nibbled my chin.

I forced my head back to get away from him—bad move. The scarf had loosened in all his manhandling and exposed the claim mark between my shoulder and neck. He sank his fangs into my skin, deepening the wound.

"Fuck," I moaned, lost to the intense sensations as Don continued to dominate me. He tugged down my shorts before freeing me from them completely. His cock throbbed with blood, making the head swell. His enormous girth breached my tiny hole, and my body trembled. He was a full-blown werewolf, while I was a wereduin. I was going to definitely feel the size difference.

He's gonna split me in half!

But a tiny voice whispered from the back of my mind.

Break me. Open me. Put me in my place beneath you.

I shuddered. A moan escaped my lips, sounding like surrender.

His massive cock drove the wind out of me. As a werewolf, it was more bestial, turning reddish-brown. Two knots grew until they lined his shaft. The harder he got, the more pronounced they became. Thick muscular veins overlapped them and glided over my inner walls.

He didn't stop to let me adjust to his size, but shamefully, my beta juices had already slicked me up. The dammed fluids served a role in making me submit to my alpha. The more I produced, the more semen he could put inside of me. And the more that happened, the more I craved him and desired to belong to him.

Don bottomed out—his balls slapping my ass. I could

barely breathe against the intrusion. A trail of saliva spilled down my chin and met with tears leaking from my eyes I'd screwed shut.

He licked my chin, cleaning them both away.

"Are you full of me, my little Fern?"

I could only nod.

"Good. Feel this. This is my power over you. I will fuck you as many times as it takes for you to learn your place. Soon, you'll memorize every inch of my cock. You'll feel me inside you even when you sleep." He had succeeded in taking away my ability to think. All I wanted was for him to move inside of me and to make me feel good.

I bit my lip, my need so strong it pierced my stomach, and I ached down to my groin.

He rolled his hips, tantalizing me. "What is it, my little Fern?" Leaning down, he nibbled my cheek. He trailed his canine snout through my hair, breathing in the scent of my dark locks. "Tell me." Don nipped my left ear, tugging on the floppy tip until it straightened into a peak, and I let out an embarrassing whimper.

Unlike my right ear, which was pointy like normal, this one drooped—a leftover from puphood, before I could fully leave worg form. His smirk puffed air against my skin, and I shivered. His tongue delved inside, invading even more of my body.

My face burned. My body ached, craving the friction. Desperately, I bucked my hips, but his weight barely allowed the movement. "M-Move…" I struggled to get the word out.

"You want my cock to move inside of you?"

"F-Fuck…" My head lolled back, only to be caught firmly in the palm of his hand not pinning my wrists. His large hand could have been a bear's if not for his humanoid fingers. My curls snagged on his razor-sharp claws massaging my scalp. "I want…"

He forced me to look at him. "What do you want?"

Fucker!

Tears of pent-up frustration spilled down my cheeks.

Don's fingers holding my face rubbed the wetness into my skin.

"Ass-hole," I growled.

"I want you to say it. Otherwise, I will keep you here all night, wet and needy for me."

"Fin-ne. You. I want…*you*."

"You want me to what?"

"Bas-tard!" I bit my lip until it bled, but I couldn't hold in my whimper. "Mo-ve, fuck me!"

Don tsked at me. "You forgot to say please?"

I was about to explode.

Gods dammit! Fucker!

A strangled cry ripped from my throat. "*Please!*" Inside I was so pissed off at him, at myself, but I had already lost the battle with my lust, and there was nothing else left to do but beg. But knowing that asshole, he'd probably make me beg forever before he met my demands.

Don's smile crinkled his eyes, and he kissed my brow softly. "That wasn't too hard, now was it?"

He thrust his hips into me, and my brain dissolved. Pleasure danced like tendrils over my skin, making me tingle all the way to my fingertips.

To my surprise, he picked up speed. "This is how good it feels to submit to me." His stiff cock moved up and down my entire length, stirring up delicious friction that felt too amazing for words. "I will protect you, Fern. I will keep you safe. You will never know hunger or loneliness. I will make you into the perfect beta. And you will love it. You will beg to have my pups one day."

I fisted the back of the car seat, digging my blunt nails into the fabric. I could still hear his whispered words like a poison in my heart despite my constant moaning. The worst thing of all was that I wanted everything he was saying. I wanted him to make me his beta and fill me to the brim with his pups. I wanted to serve him and please him. There was no stopping these stupid thoughts. And worst yet, I started to think they were no longer stupid. He knew he was getting to me as if he had peeled back the layers of my skin and was openly watching my heart.

He didn't allow me to transform as he fucked into my smaller body. I knew what he was doing. He was stripping away my power and binding me to him. I wouldn't have felt so full in werewolf form, nor would his body feel as big and heavy. As a Wereduin, I was closer to a human in strength, not only appearance, and he dominated me completely. It was addicting and desirable, and I lost myself to the pleasure.

When I came to, he grunted on top of me before he spilled his load. It kept gushing until it pooled from my hole and stained the car seat underneath. He didn't stop coming.

Two knots swelled with his semen and plugged up my ass, forcing me to take in all of his cum. Then a third one grew closer to the tip.

Three? That's new!

The knots expanded until there was no way for his cock to leave my body. I tried to adjust to him, but he was so big, and the knots stretched my insides to the point of pain. Immediately, I was afraid and began shivering. It hurt, and yet it felt good, confining and liberating at the same time.

He collected me into his arms and held me tight, continuing to fill me up. By now, long streams of his cum spilled down the base of his cock—not even his knots could contain his heavy load.

"Breathe, breathe with me, Fern." He whispered gentle words into my ear. "Come on, you can take it. You can take me. Surrender to your alpha. Surrender to me, Fern. I will take care of you and protect you. I won't let any harm come to you. Now give me your heart as well as your body."

I couldn't say anything. Instead, I focused on his cock. The knots expanded fully, but the other places on his shaft that weren't engorged quivered and sent pleasure spiking up my spine.

I am yours already. Again, that inner voice. *Stop all of this trivialness and claim me. Make me know my place at your side.*

He dug his claws into my back the moment I spilled over

the edge. It was a good thing wereduin skin was tougher than a human's. Otherwise, he'd have gored my back and got my blood all over his car. Colors danced behind my closed eyelids. The pain added an edge to the orgasm as it traversed my body. He thrust his hips into me like a madman until I gasped and moaned like a horny, little *pup-maker*. Finally, he released the last of his seed, still holding me close.

The tension broke around us, and for a moment, we were naked in front of each other. Not literally—he still wore his clothes—but it was the intimacy of the moment. The way he held me like I was precious. He rocked into me gently, relishing in the afterglow of our sex. His claiming. My submitting. Our lovemaking.

That last thought stopped all others.

Lovemaking?

Was that what had happened?

He was no longer tense or angry. Tired and spent, he panted against my ear, still intent on holding me. Instinctively, I nuzzled into his neck. Slowly, he returned to Wereduin form. His cock was still inside me during his transformation. The rough grooves smoothed out, and the knots lessened before they were replaced by the soft feel of his skin.

Pulling back to study me, he kissed down my forehead. Before closing my eyes, I glanced at his face. It held intimacy, caring, and…love? That was weird, but I was too tired to fight against the flow. At that moment, Don completely dominated my heart.

Chapter Three

Life and Death

Werewolves, in full or mixed forms, passed Don and me as we walked through the bazaar. Red and orange merchant stands lined either side. An old zombie witchdoctor sat behind a table. She ground up something in a mortar with a pestle, and she didn't spare me a glance. In front of her sat large tubs filled with seeds, herbs, salts, and other voodoo ingredients. I recognized the black salt and a type of Wolfsbane because Shamar had used them. Burlap voodoo dolls and spell and hex bags dangled from the table and out into the street, close enough to touch, but I thought better of it. I doubted the seller wanted my paws all over her wares.

On the next stand, Vampirean china glowed from the eerie orange cast from the crisscrossing street lamps. A tall vampire male stood behind the counter. He wore a black cloak over his head, but his long ears stuck out from the sides. He narrowed his hawk eyes, watching me, perhaps fearing I would nick something—*arrogant asshole*. Like I wanted that fancy crap anyway.

The scent of raw meat overwhelmed my nostrils. Flanks of flesh hung from the next stand over. Since the seller was a zombie, I knew a good portion of them were human. The tables displayed small cuts of meat as well. My mouth watered at the sight of fried frogs and sparrows. I licked my lips. I could almost taste the sparrow wings crunching under my canines—it was the best part! I wouldn't stoop so low as to ask Don for ules to purchase anything, though. I trailed behind him, silently.

As a Warrior, Don had to obtain special weapons for the next part of the Offering. The Warriors were a sect of fighters and trainers who served the Twins of War—the War Goddess, Babd Catha, and her twin, the God Camalus. They sold the weaponry Don would need.

In addition to weapons, Don sought his trainers' counsel

and to get some last-minute practice. He visited the trainers a lot. I had quickly learned that Don was a brilliant fighter, so his career choice of professional *spawn* player made a heck of a lot of sense, especially given how violent that sport could be.

Don also belonged to not one but three sects—Arduinna and the Twins, but I didn't know the third. At near-genius level, he served as a trainer sometimes. It would have been awe-inspiring if it didn't give him yet another reason to be a pompous jerk. In no way would I ever compliment that asshole.

We had passed a stand selling pickled fingers when one partially transformed werewolf sneered at me. "Hey, tasty." He had a gray, mangy coat. "How about I make a feast out of you?" His yellow eyes narrowed, and two protruding fangs glistened as he leered at me. I quickened my pace. And banged right into Don. He'd stopped to converse with some Hands of the Moon, beta wereduins devoted to the Moon Goddess Luna, the Mother of the Gods. Being impotent made them unappealing to alphas, and they did not mate. Instead, they dedicated themselves to serving the community.

Don turned his head. Immediately, I straightened up. I didn't want him to think I needed him when I most certainly did not. "Don't tell me you're letting them scare you, huh?"

"Yeah, right." I puffed up my chest, trying to appear bigger than I was. "I was getting away from a mosquito."

"Uh-huh." Don's smile started low. "Let's just keep going." He dragged a hand through my hair, messing up my curls.

We entered the town square, where large trees grew around the cobbled stones. Don headed to a monstrous sequoia-oak at the center. Carved out from its trunk, a path spiraled up the tree. Inside, several sections of the trunk had been hollowed out into large rooms. Surprisingly enough, the tree still lived. Along with the Twins, the sects of Arduinna and Dagda, the All Father resided there.

Don smirked. "'Course, you're not scared, right? So, how about waiting here for me until I get back?"

I didn't like that idea of being left with the lone wolves, like that one taunting me earlier. Also, a few crones walked the square. Those witches scared the hell out of me, not that I would let on. I had to save face. "Fine, I will." I leveled Don with a challenging look. He was so possessive and protective of me; surely, he wouldn't leave me out to be prey for street wolves?

Don rolled his eyes. "You wouldn't make it a minute after I left. Stop being foolish and follow along." I hated that Don was always right. The stupid jerk.

I stuck up my nose.

"Fine, suit yourself." Don spun on his heel and headed off to the giant tree. As I watched him go, my fear grew. I really needed to swallow my pride, especially given where he had left me.

A skeletal hand rested on the back of my shoulder, and I jumped. Spinning around, I faced the crone. According to some, these witches sold their souls to Cursed Sprites. Now they lived off the flesh of others. They didn't attack outright. Instead, they tried to lure their prey to their homes. Even though everyone knew a crone's game, they still provided spells. People often tried to go with them to trick them into giving out a spell—some survived, many did not.

I backed away from the crone.

"Come n' see, Oy've a spell to rid yah of yur master. Fer jus' a finger, Oy'll give it to yah. A finger n' tis' all yurs." That was another thing crones would do, beg for body parts that they would either eat or use in their spells. For one moment, I dreamed of being rid of him, not having to live with him anymore, and finally having my own life back, but crones were tricksters. Whenever they could get away with free meat, they didn't hesitate.

"Sorry, but I'm good."

The old crone cackled. "If ya change yur mind n' don't wantta be a fuck toy, ya come ta see me."

"Sure, I'll keep that in mind." I had moved toward the sequoia-oak where Don was before I even realized what I was doing.

The crone retreated into the square and found her next target—a female wereduin by herself. She looked anywhere between mine and Don's age. She must have been an alpha since she was alone, but it was hard to tell. The old crone started talking to her. I wondered how this would end. In our world, it was dog eat dog. If the crone succeeded, then she was more than allowed to feast on her prey. No one would punish her. It didn't look like the female was buying it, though, and soon the crone was off again on the hunt.

"What's a tasty treat doing all by yerself, pretty?" A large alpha put a hand on my shoulder. Even in wereduin form, he still looked intimidating. His heavy claws dug into my shirt, tearing it. *Fucker.* Though not my favorite, I still liked my *Meat Skuwls* tee.

"I'm not alone. Obviously. My alpha is inside."

"Oh?" He dragged out the word, twirling one of my curls around his claw. "If I were yer alpha, I wouldn't be leavin' such a tasty morsel on its own." He circled me, closing in on the kill. "Otherwise, you might get lost or…stolen."

"Stay back." I was through being intimidated. I wasn't weak, and I didn't need an alpha to protect me. Not when that alpha was who I needed protection from. I grabbed the hand on my shoulder and threw it off.

The alpha smiled, his front fang cracked down the middle. "Feisty, arent'cha?"

"I said, stay back. I'm warning you!"

"Or what?" His chipped teeth elongated into sharp fangs, his werewolf rising. Slowly, I backed away. "How abutja put on a show for me? Go on, show me yer power? If ya think yah can fight me, go right ahead."

I growled low, hating his mocking, belittling tone. I wanted to slash his face off. My werewolf rose—claws extending, sharpening at the tips, canines lengthening into full fangs. Now werewolf, my body was stronger and five inches taller—average size for a beta werewolf as some could reach heights of six feet. My skin became thicker, straight down to the canine padding on my palms and fingers. That made walking, trotting, and even climbing easier. The latter because, however bestial, my hands were still humanoid enough to climb. I had gotten used to the pain from shifting as my bones and muscles elongated, to the point where now it was simply a dull ache. When I first shifted, it had hurt so badly—my tail the most painful, since it went away in Wereduin form—I had to take time off from school to rest.

"Fine." I charged at him, my claws out, ready to kill. He smacked me off to the side and laughed. My lip hurt, and I tasted the coppery flavor of blood.

"That all you got? Ooo, this is gonna be fun."

Baring my fangs, I flew at him. He grabbed me and bent my hand back. Pain spiked down my fingers and wrist, and I lost focus, my werewolf waning. The thick canine padding on my palms softened until my skin became smooth. I was wereduin again—my humanoid body smaller, weaker. He threw me into the dirt. Laughing.

I winced when my leg hit the cobblestone surrounded by dirt. It hurt to move it, but that didn't deter me. Legs trembling, I got to my feet and shifted back into a werewolf. The moment I charged him, he caught me again—his sharp claws digging into my forearms. He shoved me backward, and I smacked the ground. Roots and rocks dug into my sore back, but I wasn't about to give this asshole the satisfaction of seeing me cry. Forcing my body to shift one more time, I tried to ignore the pain in my leg. Slowly, I got to my feet. I was losing too much energy to stay a werewolf for long. This would most likely be my last shift.

My claws and fangs out, I slashed at his midsection, but he side-stepped me. "Feisty, little pup, aren't cha?"

This time I tried to catch myself, but my foot snagged a root. My ankle screamed out in pain, and I thudded against the ground. I returned to wereduin form, panting heavily, exhausted.

A shadow fell over me, and someone bent beside me. Don checked my bruised lip. "You did well." He sounded sincere. Then he turned to the alpha, growling, his humanoid features rapidly transforming until he was full werewolf. He was infinitely more beautiful than the mangy wolf I'd been fighting. For a moment, pride welled up in my chest. Don came from a breed of wolves that this lowlife would never dream of being. My mate was strong. And handsome. And…I wanted to smack myself. I didn't feel any of those things for stupid, mean Don.

Facing the alpha, Don's tone hardened. "My turn."

They clashed with each other, but I wasn't afraid of who would win. Don could handle himself in a fight. Instead, I sat back and nursed my bruised backside, trying not to move my ankle too much.

The fight ended quickly. Don stood at an impressive height of over seven feet. His shimmering black fur covered his massive shoulders, well-built chest, and python-sized arms. His dagger-length claws dripped with blood, and he roared as he threw his head back—human and beast in one. The other alpha backed down, cowering with his tail between his legs.

With the alpha gone, Don turned to me. His werewolf features faded, and he was handsome again. His eyes no longer glowed neon. Instead, they went back to startling blue. Upon becoming wereduin, his pseudo-clothes appeared, like they materialized from his fur. His height reduced to his normal six feet, four inches. He still towered over me. At five foot three, I barely came up to his shoulder.

Seeing Don's pseudo-clothes made me curse. Had I known I'd be in a fight and need to shift into a werewolf, I'd have worn pseudo-clothes too. Not that I had many, but I had enough. Then my transformation wouldn't have torn my *Meat Skuwls* shirt and ripped my shorts. *Fucking alphas…*

That's when I realized we had an audience. Several betas in the crowd swooned, each trying to be noticed by Don in all his prowess. Those who had alphas got growled or snipped at until they submitted. That didn't stop them from staring at Don. A thrill shot up and down my spine. I was the one who got Don. Not any of them. Only me. I hated those feelings the moment they showed up and dashed them down quickly. But not quick enough.

Don let out a sigh. "I told you to follow along. Look what you did to yourself." Gingerly, he touched my leg then trailed his fingers to my ankle. I winced. It was probably bruised, maybe strained? While fighting, I hadn't paid much attention to the pain and focused only on attacking.

I swatted his hand away. "I'm fine."

"Right," Don drawled out the word, then had me up in his arms. "Stop being stubborn. You've done enough to yourself for one night."

He carried me all the way to the car. I hated it, but even though I fussed, he ignored me. Afterward, we drove out into the countryside, where the Second Offering would take place.

He carried me upstairs to our rented room and sat me on the bed. "Let me find a first aid kit."

I pouted. "I don't need one."

Don rolled his eyes. "You're persistent. But you can't hold out on me forever. Why not save yourself the trouble and yield already?"

"If it's all the same with you, I'd rather take my chances with Ugly on the street."

Don laughed and messed up my hair. I quickly tried to correct it, but with my curls all over the place, there wasn't much I could salvage. Since Don didn't own a straight iron, I had to wait until Papa brought mine from home. Until then, I was stuck looking like I did as a pup. Even *correcting it* didn't make it look cool—I missed my emo style.

Don rubbed aloe over my wounds, and I sighed in contentment. It felt soothing, peaceful, and something more. His alpha influence was healing my bruised leg and sprained ankle. Then he ran a bath for me. It was all great until he got in too.

I sat in his lap with my head resting on his chest. My body felt drained and fatigued, and I wanted to lie in the warmth of the tub forever. Don's cologne smelled like balsamic vanilla. I found the spicy, floral undertones calming when mixed with his natural masculine scent. Not that I would admit any of that to him. He seemed content to hold me and pet my hair. I nestled back against him before I realized what I was doing. When I felt his thickening bulge, I tried to back off. He captured me in his arms, preventing me from pulling away.

"Still so cold to me?" Don whispered into my ear. His rock-hard abs pressed firmly against my body. His giant cock poked my back as it rested in my ass crack. He dragged his cock between my cheeks, making me feel every inch of his growing erection. "I have ways of getting you to submit."

A thrill tingled down my spine and I shivered. I shook my head, my body flushing. My inner walls dampened, preparing for my alpha. Arousal escaped my lips in a whimper, and I moaned. Embarrassed, I covered my mouth with both palms. Don smiled. It was a real smile. Not a smirk or a teasing one, and it caught me off guard. How could he look so handsome? He used my moment of hesitation, gathered me into his arms, and carried me to bed.

That night, Don spooned me before he entered me. Then he had me on my hands and knees in puppy position. At the overwhelming sensations, I sank to my forearms. Grabbing my thigh, he flipped me onto my back. He had to pull out a little to allow the movement. My face burned with embarrassment. I felt like a dirty, little *pup-maker* spreading my legs for him like that. He hoisted my legs onto his shoulders, making me bend, raising my lower body into the air. He drove his cock inside me, and I couldn't stop the groan. I wanted to punch the smug smile on his face, but he devoured me with rapid thrusts, turning me into a mush of sensations. It felt amazing and left me crying out for more.

The Second Offering began the next day at sundown. Often called the Silver Offering, it honored the War Gods— the Twins of War—whose symbol was a pair of silver, crisscrossing blades.

We traveled far into Hummock Prairie, which, as the

name suggested, was a vast prairie littered by dunes or hummocks. The hummocks were tall enough to climb but not overly wide. Wild grass covered the earth as far as the eye could see, and when the wind rippled through the grass, it looked like a green sea with the hummocks standing out like islands. It would have been peaceful if not for the molebats.

Werewolves had very few natural predators, the deadliest known as molebats. As their name suggested, these creatures looked like a mixture of bat and rodent. Their faces resembled bats with their beady eyes, pig-like snout, and large bat ears. Inside their mouths were rows of tiny, jagged teeth with two fangs on either side. Their skinny arms stretched out like a bat's but were not wings. They had knife-like, retractable talons on their three fingers. They could walk upright on two legs or crawl on all fours. Their legs, toes, and tail looked like rats, and they scurried when they moved, much like rodents. While their arms were naked like bats, their faces, bodies, and legs were covered in fur. They lived underground in burrows, which were a complex network of tunnels. Molebat drones gathered prey and brought the carcasses back to the colony.

Although much smaller than wereduin, they were vast in numbers. Often entire colonies attacked at once and could overcome a lone wolf or a small group. Molebats could not climb like wereduin could, but the hummocks weren't steep. It would slow them down but not prevent them from coming.

Civilization kept molebats at bay by forming cities as a means of survival. But out in Hummock Prairie, it was molebat territory. Anything, or anyone that the molebats could turn into food, they did. After sundown, the entire area would be teaming with molebats hoping to feast on weak alphas or unprotected betas.

Alphas had to keep their betas safe, and most importantly, alive. There was no room for the weak in wereduin society, especially among alphas who planned on breeding. This Offering tested alphas and weeded out the weak ones.

I'd avoided thinking about the Silver Offering because it scared the shit out of me. For the last two days, I almost didn't want to go to school because Shamar's anxiety over the event only made it worse. Alphonse's palpable fear also wasn't helpful. His stutter worsened tenfold whenever the subject came up. The only one who acted normal was Lucian, who seemed just as bored as always, but every so often a worry line appeared on his forehead.

I understood they cared about me, and it wasn't uncommon for betas to die at this stage—a lot of them did—so perhaps I couldn't expect them not to worry. Knowing Shamar, he wouldn't sleep tonight, and I'd probably find my cell swamped with texts and missed messages from him. I'd definitely have to let them all know, especially Shamar, that I was okay when I got home.

If I got home.

I shook my head. No. I couldn't think that way. Besides, I had Don. He was Mom's best student from the way she talked about him. He could protect me, right?

Fuck. As if I wanted to rely on Don for anything. *Godsdamned jerk!* It was his fault I was in this hell to begin with.

We arrived early enough to claim a good spot. Don found a particularly tall hummock. It wasn't overly steep but had a defined incline to limit the molebats coming.

I'd taken one step up the hill when another alpha passed us. His eyes lingered on me. From over my shoulder, Don growled. The alpha kept walking. Three slave betas followed him. He had two boys and a girl, and none of them looked at me. I wondered what made them become slave betas. Maybe it was fear? One boy looked around with wide eyes. The other boy kept on walking with his head down. His shuffling gait and slouched shoulders indicated to me that he'd given up on life.

"Get moving. It'll be dark soon." Don's command reclaimed my attention, and I followed him up the hummock. When we reached the top, it confirmed my first observation. Our quilt, and the three feet of grass surrounding it, made up its entire square feet.

Rolling my eyes, I spread the quilt. It still contained the

stains of my first claiming—my blood, cum, and beta juices never to be washed out. An offering to the God Cerowain, the quilt would be a constant reminder of my submission to my alpha. I bristled at the thought.

The slaver and his slaves camped on a nearby hill, smaller and wider than ours. All three betas shared a quilt and went about spreading it while their alpha surveyed the area. I watched them work. The girl was the most puzzling, though. She must have felt me staring since she looked right at me. There wasn't dullness in her eyes, but life. *Fight.* How the heck was this girl a slave beta? Maybe she might prove herself if she survived this night…

My mind returned to one of my family's holiday parties. A friend of mine had lost a cousin who fell into the role of slave beta and never got out. His alpha hadn't even defended him against the molebats. I shivered at the thought—being eaten alive inside their burrows.

"Sit closer to me if you're afraid." Don's voice caught me off-guard.

I scoffed under my breath. *Yeah, right. Like I'll ever do that.* I didn't want to be closer to that asshole. My wrists were still sore. He had ended up tying my hands together. Pinning them above my head, he fucked the life out of me. He kept trying to get me to submit. And the worst part was, this time he'd come close. More than physically, he'd gotten into my heart, stripping me down to the core—demanding my soul, not just my obedience. I hated him so much.

"I'm good, thanks." I scrunched up my nose. "I'd rather not even talk to you if that's all right, *master.*"

He growled low in his throat. In two seconds, he had me on my back—the white peaks of his fangs showing. Trapping me beneath his firm muscular frame, he stared down at me with those mesmerizing eyes. His mocha-colored skin made the startling blue stand out. The more his werewolf rose, the more neon his eyes became until they glowed in the dark. His long silver-brown hair spilled over his shoulder, feeling heavy against my chest. "Are you trying to get me to take you again?"

"Get off." I bared my teeth, wishing my pointy canines were more intimidating. Our eyes locked in a staring match. His gaze never leaving mine, he leaned close and nipped my nose. Then he licked along the freckles that culminated at the tip in slight discoloration—another leftover from worg form. I'd hoped the dark patch would fade the more I stayed as a wereduin. So far, no such luck.

"Your will is crumbling, my little Fern. You're mine." He nibbled my chin. "It's only a matter of time." My body shuddered. He must've felt it; his mouth twisted in a triumphant smile. Then he rolled off me. Tying his hair back into a long ponytail, he went back to marking our territory.

I wanted to fight him, but that was when I heard it. *Scurrying.*

Our hummock was tall enough to provide a terrifying view. Molebats advanced from every direction until the entire valley was teeming with them.

High-pitch cries came from their open mouths—sounding like a million little voices speaking all at once at a crazy speed.

Fear stoked in the pit of my stomach. My mouth went dry. As a pup, all the horror stories told to scare us into good behavior involved molebats attacking, carrying us off into the burrows to be eaten alive. I was so scared I could barely breathe, and my stomach ached.

"Stay down." Don stood in front of me, his legs like sturdy poles. Maybe it was instinct from all the times he'd schooled my body for his ownership, but I scooted closer to him. Inside, beneath many layers of fear, I still wanted to fight him. Wanted to shove him away and run off down the hill. Runaway and never let him catch me. He was just a rapist who had captured me against my will.

Waves of molebats clashed into the werewolf pairs that were still on flat ground. People screamed all around me. The molebats had started to attack their victims.

Would we survive the night? These were molebats. Could Don fight them all by himself? But then again, he trained under my mom, and he hoped to play *spawn* professionally. I heard that sometimes they released beasts into the playing field to add more of a challenge. So maybe he was used to this, right? At the least, more prepared? I could only hope.

Don lit the four torches he received from his trainers yesterday and placed them at each quilt corner. These special torches burned if the alpha lived. They served as an offering to the Twins. They also symbolized life, not only the alpha's but their unborn pups.

If the alpha failed to protect himself and his beta, then this was where it ended for them. The torchlight would die out, and they would be shamed for their weakness—only the torches served as their funeral. They weren't permitted to enter the Moon Vale, nor did they even go before Arawn—the Twins' beta and the God of Death. Instead, Arawn's servants would escort their souls into the Shadows, where they would be forgotten.

I wasn't certain what happened to betas who died at this stage. It wasn't considered important enough to be mentioned. I assumed that, like everything else involving alphas and betas, they went together.

While Hummock Prairie had a lot of hummocks, the Second Offering needed to take place at the center so as to have the most exposure to the molebats. Because of the hundreds of alpha-beta pairs participating in the Offering, not everyone was lucky enough to find a hill. Those that hadn't, weren't doing so well.

One alpha looked at her limit, five molebats attacking around her. She moved so fast that she blurred together. Not far away, her beta fought with all he had. A molebat came from behind and drove its knife-like talons through his back. The alpha threw a dagger at the molebat attacking her beta, but it missed.

The molebats took the boy to the ground. They didn't even wait before they sliced off his arm, followed by his leg. Then tail. He screamed in pain, crying out for his alpha, but it was all she could do to not die herself. She yelled his name, fear in her voice. That was when I recognized them as the small boy who I'd seen during the Hunt being injected by his alpha female's essence after she had tied up his wrists.

I swallowed the lump in my throat, sadness ripped at my heart—also, appreciation. That made me feel terrible since others were dying all around me. But right then, I appreciated the overly punctual bastard who always showed up early. Otherwise, we wouldn't have gotten our hummock, and I may have been that unfortunate beta getting ripped apart by molebats. The alpha still stood, surprisingly, but she hadn't the strength to save them both. I wondered if Don would have left me to die, but compared to her, he was the better fighter.

A blood curling, high-pitched shriek rang out from down the hill.

It was the slave girl beta. How had she gotten so far down her hummock and away from her owner? Two molebats had her, one attacking her leg, the other her shoulder. She screamed, trying to shake them off. Her cries echoed around me as they tore her skin off—glee in their squinty eyes.

Color drained from my face.

She kicked the snout of the molebat attacking her leg. Claws out, she shredded the face of the one eating her shoulder. I couldn't express how badly I was rooting for her. She had to getaway. She just had to. Otherwise, I was about to watch another person get murdered.

Don could help her. He could. Why didn't he?

Freed, she started climbing up the hill on her hands and knees. Her alpha sat at the plateau. That was when I noticed the other two slave betas. The one who had shuffled his feet and looked at the ground earlier had already been overcome with molebats. They sliced up pieces of his body, passing it to their comrades. It reminded me of ants cleaning their kill.

The other beta tried to fight them off with a stick. Unlike the girl, he hadn't been bitten yet. He looked so scared. I wanted to help them, and at the same time, wanted to hide my eyes. The girl spotted me.

"Help!" She skirted off the ground. Instead of going to

her master, she raced towards our hummock.

No, don't come here! Don't! Don wouldn't save her. He wouldn't protect her. If she wanted to live, she had to make it back to her alpha.

The closest molebat snared her hair with its claws, and she tripped. She let out an ear-jarring scream as they collected on her back. I had to stop this, but my body froze up.

A memory surfaced of a previous holiday party I went to with my family. I saw the face of the same girl, laughing with three other betas.

"Stop!" I leaped to my feet. "Myrtle!" I didn't know why I lost all fear. Maybe it was because I didn't want to see a person I knew killed. Maybe I assumed that Don would protect me. No rule said he had to, though, not if I left my quilt.

I raced down the hill toward Myrtle, her hands reaching for me. The molebat's razor-sharp talons severed her foot from her ankle. Blood seeped into the reddening grass. Her screams were broken by tearful sobs.

"Myrtle!" I ran to my doom, running to save a person beyond my help. They were already carving her up. The last look of pain and fear shown from her eyes before they closed for good. Two molebats scavenging her remains.

They looked up, and their black beady eyes homed in on me. I was a considerable way down the hill. Don hadn't followed me.

I couldn't move. My body paralyzed with fear.

Molebats scurried toward me—their skinny arms reaching out for me.

My body jolted to life. Shifting forms, I sprinted up the hill. It was quicker to run as a wolf since I hadn't mastered this as a werewolf. I didn't change completely. There wasn't time, but I had more speed running on all fours. In my mind, was her foot being severed clean off.

With the wind roaring in my ears, I raced up the hill—their high-pitched voices right behind me. I could almost feel their ragged breaths on my neck.

Almost at the top!

My quilt was empty.

Don?

Where had he gone? Had he abandoned me?

A black shadow leaped over me. The heavy mass landed somewhere behind me and shook the ground, knocking me over. Instinctively, I blocked my face, returning to wereduin form to protect myself with hands and not paws, from the fangs and talons I expected to come. But they never did. Opening my eyes, I noticed someone fighting off the molebats some feet from me.

A full-fledged werewolf, Don tore into molebat flesh, slicing up multiple targets at once—tearing off their ears and their naked, bat-like arms.

One sank its teeth into his shoulder. For a moment, my mind doubted. Could Don really get eaten by molebats? And if so…

It would be my fault for leaving my quilt. Any beta who left their quilt, either thrown out like Myrtle's asshole alpha or else left in fear—or in my case, stupidity—was fair game to the molebats. Nothing was forcing an alpha to go after them. Yet Don went for me.

Had I doomed us both? *Please, Mother Goddess Arduinna, protect us!*

Don severed the head of the molebat who bit him—blood splattering all over the ground and trickling out of its pig-like snout. Growling, he leaped forward and pinned three molebats beneath his body. On their backs with their stubby rat legs and tails up in the air, they would look funny if they hadn't been covered in Myrtle's blood. Don bit open their throats with no regard for their lives.

The molebats that were still slicing up poor, dead Myrtle paused to watch the unlucky three bleeding out. Don turned his fangs on them, bloodlust in his neon-blue eyes. For a moment, he scared me more than the molebats. They didn't approach him but continued to dissect Myrtle's body. He wanted them to come at him. I saw it in his eyes, felt it in his stance. His fangs dripped of blood. When they didn't attack, he didn't pursue. Not turning his back on them, he walked up the hill, still crouched low in a killing position.

I was still on my knees when he stopped in front of me. He yanked me off the ground and backhanded me hard, throwing me onto the quilt. Salty tears stung my bloody lip.

"You little fool! Do you want to die?" Don grabbed me up by my hair and slapped me in the face again and again. I blocked as best I could before he threw me back onto the quilt. I couldn't stop the tears. I saw Myrtle's face—the terror-stricken look of one who didn't want to die. Clinging to the quilt, I sobbed into the fabric. Don didn't hit me anymore. He was quiet, standing over me. "Stop it. You're embarrassing."

"Fuck you." Sobbing hard, I barely got the words out before I screamed up at Don. "Why didn't you help her?" I yelled like we were equals, like he hadn't been smacking me around.

"Help her?" Fangs out, he pinned me to the ground. Droplets of his drool dripped from his open jaw and collected onto my cheeks. "*You* are my beta! You, not her. You stupid little fucker. Do you know I have the power to let you die?" Menace shown from his startlingly neon-blue eyes. "Stupid little idiot. You almost died. And next time you do something so foolish, I won't be risking both of our lives. You got that?"

Rolling over onto my stomach, I clutched the quilt and wept. Don didn't comfort me, but he didn't yell or hit me. Our scuffle drew more molebats' attention, but his menace stilled them. Their bat ears twitched, looking as if unsure whether to attack. I could almost hear the question in their scuffle of jumbled voices.

Don's lip bled, but he licked it off. There was something feral about him. It sent shivers down my spine and gave me the first air in my lungs that I had since Myrtle got ripped to pieces. His terror meant my protection. He was angry. Livid. More furious than I had ever seen him. But his ruthlessness was keeping them at bay. He looked like he wanted to sink his claws into every single one of them.

"You," low snarls came from his throat, his voice deep

and guttural. "Sit in the center, and don't you dare move." I nodded. "If you do," his werewolf features showed none of his handsomeness. "I'll kill you myself."

I crawled to the center of my quilt and closed my eyes, trying to block out the loud cries all around me. My curiosity got the better of me, and I glanced up. It was the remaining slave beta, he finally tired and lost his footing. The molebats swarmed him. My stomach churned.

"No, you don't." Don's voice had me swallowing the bile that crawled up my throat. "Not on this quilt, you fucking don't. And if you get up from this spot, I'll crush your skull in."

Burying my face into the quilt, I cried out my nausea and fear. I kept expecting the molebats to come for me, too.

Don growled, real and threatening, and it made me look up. They surrounded us, swarming the hummock like ants up a hill. Their terrible, high-pitched voices were the only sounds I heard. I clutched the quilt with white-knuckled fists and screwed my eyes shut. Sickness filled the pit of my stomach—fear, sadness, and terror spilled down my cheeks in large, salty tears.

Don fought them. I couldn't look, too afraid, but I heard the commotion. The wailing death screeches. The scurrying of hundreds of trotting feet. The swipe of his claws sent wind across my back. The ground trembled as he leaped from corner to corner.

None of them touched me.

Not even one.

I still couldn't look up, but I heard them dying. Don was killing every single one of them. Tears dried on my cheeks, and new and different emotions filled me. Admiration. Gratitude. Relief.

I braved a glance up from my arms, clinging to my quilt like that alone protected me. Two molebats raced toward me from the front corner, puffs of air coming from their flaring nostrils. Their jaws opened, revealing tiny, dagger-like teeth—two protruding fangs flashing in the moonlight. Throwing my head down, I hid against the quilt. But they never attacked me. I felt Don's presence in front of me. Felt the wind in-between his claws, the ground rumbling underneath his feet. Heard the loud tearing of flesh and bone his fangs made.

I cracked an eye open. Don was amazing. He fought a never-ending mob. It must've been an entire hive attacking us, climbing up the hill from all sides. But thanks to his choice of location, only so many could come up at the same time. Don moved super-fast, looking like he fought them all at once. His training from his teachers had come into play and something else.

Whatever side he was not on, a mirage of himself materialized so that four Don's fought simultaneously. The mirages changed places with him if he moved in their direction, perfectly mirroring his last location, so Don never actually stopped moving.

I looked at a trident made entirely of onyx, driven through the quilt into the ground. From it, golden lights flowed like veins. Where they ended, the mirages formed. The light connected all four directions—north, south, east, and west. When Don replaced a mirage, the light connected to him like he was the image.

I recognized this weapon. Don had received it from his trainer when he'd left me alone in the bazaar. He had placed the trident at the center of the quilt, close to where I sat. I could have touched it if I didn't fear for my life.

I glanced at the other alpha on the nearby hill, the asshole who let Myrtle die. He, like Don, fought like Hell's demons. He didn't have the trident that Don had, but he held his own. He'd set up a barrier around him, also made of the same golden light. It held back the molebats perfectly, blocking his back and sides, so he only had to worry about one direction.

The quilt his betas had setup earlier lay forgotten in the dirt—molebat corpses and blood all over it. My anger grew. If he could kill the molebats, why hadn't he saved his betas? He had claimed them. Why not protect them? All three would've easily fit inside the barrier behind him. But I knew the reason.

Slaves were disposable.

The asshole had probably used his betas to buy time to set up his barrier, too. Don and he indirectly helped each other. Every molebat killed by Don was one the slaver didn't have to and vice versa.

Finally, they stopped coming.

Don crouched defensively in front of me. His claws dripped blood. His growls loud and menacing. I was still terrified but no longer of him. When no molebats came up our hill, Don started breathing hard. It was for a couple of seconds, but even Don needed to catch his breath. He rounded on me.

Immediately I covered my face, but he didn't hit me. "You're all right." He sounded like he said this more to verify his own internal questions. "No marks. No nothing." He huffed. "And Mites's wrong. Of course, he's fucking wrong."

He wasn't making any sense to me, but then, the guy had faced death and lived. Moreover, no harm came to me whatsoever…well, I had almost gotten killed, but that wasn't on him. Obviously, that had angered Don. Maybe I shouldn't be upset at him? After all, my foolishness could've killed us both.

"I'm sorry." I bowed my head. "I almost killed us. I'm sorry."

Don snorted. "Fucking do that again, and I won't be saving you."

"I know. I'm sorry."

Don kept pacing the four corners, his mirror images doing the same. "There'll be more of them. Don't look if it will terrify you. And don't leave the quilt."

"I won't, I won't. I'll stay here."

"Good." Don stopped pacing and took a knee, momentarily reverting back into wereduin form, most likely to conserve energy. He dug out a water bottle and drank deeply before he splashed water on his face and neck. Then he looked down at me, his voice sharp. "Get some sleep."

"Not likely." My body felt exhausted. If not for my years

as a wereduin, I would've reverted into a worg. I definitely hadn't the energy to shift into a werewolf.

Don hadn't yelled at me, even though adrenaline made him sound cruel. He sat beside me, dripping with sweat. Molebat blood dotted the quilt. While his sweat also soaked through in multiple places, the molebat blood only covered the corners and nowhere else. Plenty of carnage served as offerings to both War Gods. Corpses piled up in the grass near the hummock's edges and around the quilt, but nothing dead touched the quilt. That would have been disrespectful to Cerowain, the God of the Offering.

Depending on the sect, an alpha needed to fulfill certain rules and rituals to the Gods. The more sects an alpha joined, the more their status elevated, but it also meant more rituals to observe. Messing up or skipping some subjected them to penalties from the Council.

One alpha survived the night but still lost his beta because the Council thought he'd made too much mess on the Mating Quilt, and it displeased Cerowain. Don belonged to three sects, so my slip-up could've been costlier than I'd realized. I suppose I took for granted how unbelievably strong Don was, even by wereduin standards. Yet, he had managed to do it all, keep me safe, and observe the rituals required. No wonder he was exhausted.

For a moment, I appreciated him. Really appreciated him. He put his life on the line to save me, and it wasn't necessary. A beta who didn't obey his alpha could be costly, and some alphas for that reason alone would've let the beta fend for himself. But not Don.

"Thank you," I whispered.

My soft words got his attention. He nodded at me. "Get some sleep. We're not over this, not by a long shot."

Glancing down the hill to the flat plains, I saw a mixture of horror, including an alpha, brought down by the molebats. His beta still fought while the alpha's ears and tail were cut off as he was disassembled piece by piece.

Looking over at the alpha-beta pairs lucky enough to be

on hummocks, I found the two alphas and their beta from the first trial. Their hummock was taller and pointier than ours, limiting the number of molebats attacking even more.

They had their beta between them. Her eyes screwed shut. Both alphas wore the same weapon. They didn't have tridents like Don, but I had seen him wield that weapon before. It consisted of five long razor blades that went in-between the fingers, the equivalent of having double claws per hand. This iconic weapon was another symbol of the Twins of War. They were one being but contained two torsos, each having a single arm. On either hand, both Twins' fitted the weapon between their fingers.

Golden lights from a barrier joined the alphas together, with their beta in the middle. This allowed the males to use weapons in both hands and protect the female even when distracted by killing molebats. They tore through the creatures, moving as one.

They looked close in age and fought so in sync that I wondered if they were twins. That would explain why both shared a beta, as was custom. I didn't know which sects they belonged to, nor the rules they had to play by, but they had torches around the edges of their Mating Quilt. The molebats swarmed around them, but the torches stayed lit—a result of the Twins' will. One thing was for sure, that trio would survive the night.

I thought about Myrtle, and my stomach hurt.

Don's large hand covered my shoulder. It made me look up at him. He pulled me close, and I fell against his legs. The musky smell of his sweat comforted me, and I pressed my face into his calf. He rested a firm hand on my head and kept me by his side. Maybe he was reassuring me I was safe, or maybe it was for him. To reassure himself that I hadn't run down the hill to a painful death. He'd gotten blood—molebats and his own—in my hair, but at this point, I didn't care two shits about something so petty. With my body extremely fatigued, I ended up passing out against his legs.

I awoke lying on the quilt to dead silence. He must have

moved me off his legs, most likely so he could continue fighting while I slept.

My nerves piqued for danger, expecting molebats to march up the hill, jaws opened, their beady eyes fixated on me.

Don knelt beside me and watched the moonlight. I knew he would not be sleeping tonight. "You awake?" I nodded. He placed a hand on my head. "It's almost over now." His encouraging words helped me breathe a little easier.

"What happened? Is everyone dead?"

Don nodded. "Those that were too weak are being taken home as dinner for the molebats." Thinking of Myrtle, I looked away bitterly. "But there's no way that will happen to us. You are safe with me, Fern. Just know that." I tried to nod, but instead, I stared at him dumbly. He sat on the quilt. "Come." With a flick of his wrist, he called me over. "Stay close to me. From now on, you must always be touching me."

I remembered the molebats had a cleanup crew. Bloodwhispers. These silent blood suckers craved live blood. Those too tired from fighting—or more likely, betas unprotected by careless or tired alphas—made good prey. Bloodwhispers evolved to be deathly silent, being too weak to attack in the open. They were two feet long and inched on the ground. Their centipede-like bodies were covered in soft hairs. They could draw blood without inflicting pain. This last wave of stragglers had killed betas in the past. Don wanted me close so he could feel every part of my body. That way, they couldn't drain me in the shadows.

As the morning drew closer, a layer of mist covered the ground, making it difficult to see more than a foot away. Bloodwhispers liked to hide in the haze and drink from their victims when close enough. When they prepared to feed, they arched their long, skinny bodies upward like a worm. Their feelers—resembling antenna on both sides of their head— could prick a victim, and he'd never be the wiser.

I didn't protest but instead climbed into Don's lap. He held another weapon. This one looked like a thin, long blade, jagged like a saw. He thrust his elbow back, taking the sword underneath his arm. I heard it stab a bloodwhisper.

It appeared Don had entered into a pact with a Talon Blade. This weapon housed the spirit of a lesser deity that served the Twins. It replenished his strength and energy when it fed upon bloodwhispers. To detect its prey, it sent out pulses that only full-fledged werewolves could hear. Don had reverted into a wereduin—perhaps he too lacked the energy to maintain werewolf form anymore—but if he let the blade guide him, he wouldn't be caught off guard in this heavy mist. If I stayed where he could feel my body completely, I was safe. He kept running his hand over me—up my arms, down my legs, along my back. He sat in the center on the quilt, cross-legged, but spread enough so I could fit inside, and pulled me against his chest.

"You're safe, you're safe." It was weird hearing him say that, especially since earlier, I would've given anything to hear those words. Of course, he was no longer doing his dance of death. "I promise I'll protect you. I promise, Fern." He was like another person. Dare I say, nice? His strong arms made me feel secure. Nodding, I closed my eyes.

A chilly wind blew against my leg. I couldn't see anything around me other than fog. Don thrust his blade in that direction, and it struck something solid. The sword glowed a faint yellow, and the world was revealed to me again. The creature looked more like a large, fuzzy caterpillar wiggling on the blade, its body twitching. The blade's jagged edges, resembling teeth, came alive and devoured it, eating it whole. I cringed, but I was too tired to care much about the bloodwhisper's fate. Upon finishing its prey, the sword's light went out.

The mists had a calming, sleepy effect. Bloodwhisper secretions floating in the mist left their victims comatose. Don's blade had a resistance to the mist. It was forged with the bloodwhispers' natural predator whose soul still lived in the sword, its resistant properties carried over. If Don held it, he would stay awake despite the tranquilizing effect of the bloodwhispers' mist.

I pressed my legs against him, trying to touch as much as I could. My smooth skin brushed over his rough hide; my sparser hairs mixed with his coarser ones. The mist grew thicker. Something fuzzy tickled the back of my neck.

"Don!" I clutched his leg and buried my face into his neck. He speared the bloodwhisper. The blade chomped loudly near my ear as it gorged on the dead creature.

"You're okay. I've got you. There's no way I'll let anything in this mist hurt you. You're mine, and I'll protect every bit of you, from the curls of your hair to the pores of your soft skin." Why Don recited a poem to me, I had no idea. It seemed a weird time, given the circumstances, but the time had come for alphas and betas who had survived to bond.

My mind filled with the call of my alpha, asking for my loyalty, making me want to yield of my own free will. Making me feel safe for the first time that night. Nodding into his neck, I clung to his chest. His arm, not holding the sword, held me tightly.

"Don't ever scare me like that." I had known this time would be an emotionally driven one, but hearing Don expose his vulnerability was humbling. "When you were running down the hill, I feared I wouldn't make it in time to save you." He hugged me tighter. "All I thought was that I didn't want to lose you." He pressed his lips against my head. "But I got to you, just in time. I protected you."

When he wasn't being all jerky and full of himself, Don could actually be a caring and gentle guy. "If something had happened—if I hadn't been strong enough…" He held me so tight breathing became difficult.

Already I'd heard his blade move twice, once to the side, and the other close enough to feel a rush of air on my shoulder. This time the bloodwhisper didn't even get a chance to breathe on my neck. "I'll kill them all for you, Fern." He growled through the words. "Every last one."

I swallowed. Hearing my name spoken like that made me feel vulnerable. "Don?"

"I protected you that one time in the gym lockers. I could

never forget you. The way your eyes looked scared yet sad. I wanted to give you everything, to protect you, to make you happy. I remember thinking how perfect you were. How if I had to pick a mate, it would be you. How you were the only one I wanted. Now and forever." Don's grip loosened until it wasn't so painfully tight, even though he still held me securely.

I was at a loss for words. Don had protected me in school that time?

I'd been in middle school, and a group of seniors—all alphas—started bullying me. The leader was an alpha named Brigacos, although everyone called him Brig. He was the most vicious to me.

He'd begun taking off my clothes to humiliate me, but before he could finish, a voice had stopped him. I never saw the speaker. Commanding but caring, he had told me to run away, and I had listened, never turning back. Not even when I heard them fighting. After that, Brig and his posse never messed with me again. Never in my life had I imagined Don was the owner of that voice.

"It—that was you?" I nuzzled into his neck, my eyelashes collecting the sweat on his skin. I had been to many holiday parties after that incident. All that time, Don had noticed me? I never would have guessed that given we never spoke, and he always looked so cool, like he didn't have time for pups like me.

His sword hadn't been idle, still feasting off slain bloodwhispers, him moving it as we spoke.

Don's soft smile was in his voice. "You were adorable and sweet. You needed someone strong to protect you. To help you grow. When I became an adult, I waited for you to join the Offering. From the first moment I saw you, I wanted you. Needed you. Fern, I love you."

Hearing those words froze my mind. Don loved me?

Don tipped my head up, and his lips covered mine.

He kissed like he fought, demanding and with intent, making me take it. Of all the times we fucked, he had never tried to kiss me. Now he claimed my lips like he had every right to them. The coppery taste of blood lingered in my mouth—mine, his—and something else. His taste. Masculine. Addicting. Calling for my submission. Sounds trapped in my throat, encouraged by the way he molded my lips to his, yet silenced by his mouth on mine.

When our lips parted, he cupped my face. "Give me everything, Fern." Gently, he licked my split lip caused by his strike, cleaning it up for me. Tender. Caring. His gesture comforting, and in a night of nightmares, I craved this safety.

I ended up falling asleep and awoke beneath his weight. He'd trapped my hands on either side of me. Pulling back, he took some pressure off me. He was a full-fledged werewolf. His claws dug into my aching wrists, drawing blood. His tongue soothed my bruised cheek from earlier before his fangs reopened the wound, making it bleed again. Slowly, he put more of his weight on me. I tried to break free. Realizing I was helplessly trapped, I whimpered uncontrollably. Gently, his tongue caressed the wound again before it dipped beneath the skin. At the prick of pain, I sucked in a breath.

He nudged my head to the side. My bare skin tingled between my neck and shoulder, where he planned on putting his second claim mark.

He was one mark closer to having the legal right and ownership of my body. He sank his large canines into my skin, and nothing could stop me from crying out. His fangs dug deeper, and blood pooled from the bite. Tears crowded my eyes as he claimed me hard. Pulling back, he licked my cheeks, leaving a hot, sticky trail of what smelled like blood where my tears used to be.

He got off me enough to free me completely of my clothes—ripping my shirt, tearing open my pants. Then he threw my knees apart and got between them.

In the moonlight, his reddish-brown cock looked more like a spear waiting to puncture my ass. Its bulbous head gorged with blood. The base swelled with seed, the knot already growing.

Shivers raced down my spine. I prayed he'd stop and desperately wanted him to continue. I needed him to put me in my place. I belonged beneath my alpha. He needed to make that clear, once and for all. I hated those thoughts, but my instincts blinded me, making me yield.

He grabbed my thighs and aligned me to his cock. My body ached with arousal, and my inner walls slickened with beta juices. His shaft plummeted into my hole, its large, mushroom head spreading my ass wide. Pain, pleasure, and everything in-between had me twitching and gasping. A heavy pulse thudded along the vein in his cock and sent tremors down my hole. Throwing my head back, I screamed at the sky. He growled down at me, my blood dripping from his fangs. His knot plugged up my ass.

"Fuck…" I dug my fingernails into the Mating Quilt, helpless but wanting to grab onto something. His fangs sank into my first claim mark. Tearing open the wound, he feasted on my blood. My body trembled beneath him. Inside me, his knot held me in place while his sperm filled me. His cock poked and pressed against my inner walls, looking for a place to hollow into a womb. That would allow me to carry his pups. Each movement wreaked havoc on my nerves. The pleasure was so intense it danced over my closed eyelids. Shameless cries escaped my parted lips as I moved with his thrusts.

"Submit. To. Me." The thickness of his cock glided along my tunnel. He planned to cum inside me, deeper this time like he was breeding me. "Say it."

"I submit," I whispered. At some point, the knot swelled so large that it restricted his movement. He continued to pump inside me anyway.

"Again, my little Fern." He branded me with his cock, rubbing me raw, marking his territory. We weren't official, and he shouldn't be giving me a breeding mark. He did anyway. Pain blurred into pleasure until no distinction could be made. "Who owns you?"

"You!" I screamed in agony before I moaned loudly, falling over the edge. I chased my orgasm, drowning in hot waves of pleasurable bliss. The more I sought release, the farther his seed traveled in my body. Don growled a purr of contentment. He kept coming until he finally finished and rolled off me.

I panted, fully spent. He collected me in his arms and nuzzled my cheek. His breaths were harsh against my ear. I couldn't believe he'd given me a breeding mark. Those were supposed to happen after the mating process was complete. Like a signature, each alpha had a unique breeding mark, but he didn't need one for him to create a uterus in me—his cock and alpha essence were enough. That wasn't why he'd marked me. By giving me his mark, Don had signed his name inside me. Gave me something final. He must've been extremely confident he'd win me in the Third Offering. Whenever he set his mind on something, he always got his way. I was a lost cause. And worst yet, I wanted it.

I awoke in Don's king-sized bed. I must have passed out hard because he'd had time to not only carry me to the car but take us all the way to his place.

Don's scent was on the pillows. And the sheets. And me. Rolling over onto my back, I hid my face behind my arm. I could still feel him inside me.

Last night had been the most horrific of my life, and Don protected me through it. I didn't get a single scratch from the molebats. My lip was busted, and my cheek was scabbed from Don's strike, though. I remembered his fangs reopening the wound during sex. While I was high on arousal, I had said some awfully embarrassing things to him. I replayed our conversation in my head. How he had commanded me to submit. He had even got me to say the words on my own volition.

My cheeks burned, and I didn't want to face him. Most disturbingly, though, were my thoughts when he dominated me. That pissed me off. There was no way I was going to accept that mean, abusive jerk. In my mind, his neon-blue eyes and wolf features faded. I heard his heartbeat as I leaned against his chest. His whispered words of *I love you.*

I didn't know what to make of any of it. Don loved me? No, I couldn't have heard that right. He was the abusive asshole trying to change my life as I knew it. He didn't love me—couldn't love me. He just wanted to own me. That was his lingering adrenaline speaking. After all, we both could have died. Surely that was all it was, and I decided to think no more about it.

My phone glowed on the nightstand next to my side of the bed.

Shamar! I had to let him know that I made it.

I had over twenty missed calls, and he spammed me all night with texts like *are you alright? Don't worry, I've got a protection spell on you. Fern, please be okay.* And on and on it went…

After the terror of last night, I couldn't berate him. I almost died. He'd been right to worry.

Texting seemed a bit insensitive, so I called him up.

The phone had barely rung when he picked up. "Fern!"

"Yeah, it's me."

"You're okay." Shamar sighed heavily. "Praise, Ayida-Weddo!"

I sprawled back onto the bed, closed my eyes, and listened to the sound of his breathing. I was safe. My life hadn't ended. Things would go on for me—school, my band. I hadn't been murdered by monsters last night.

He did most of the talking, which was good because my mind was still jumbled. But it was comforting hearing his voice. By the time we ended the call, I was feeling much better emotionally.

Getting out of bed, I went over to the walk-in closet. I was starving, my energy levels were depleted to the point I was surprised to still be in wereduin form. I didn't feel like devoting time searching for an outfit, especially since most of my clothes were either in the hamper or packed away in boxes. I wasn't fully moved into Don's house.

I settled on one of his tees. It was big on me, but whatever. I opened the door to the rich smell of coffee and something wonderful frying.

My feet padded on the cold, wooden floor. The living room walls, made up entirely of windows, provided a magnificent view of the woods outside. Fog lingered between oak trees, mostly driven away by the mid-morning sun.

Not many separators divided his spacious house. From the living room couches, I saw him in the kitchen. Wearing only his boxers, he had his back to me. I took a moment to study him. His long ponytail fell in the valley between his broad shoulders. His silver-brown hair complimented his dark mocha skin.

A large tattoo spanned the entire length of his well-defined back. I recognized the design. The Twin Gods of War. Their two torsos shared a single lower body and connected such that their heads faced away from each other. The War Goddess, Bahd Cava was taller than her twin, Camalus, the War God. They shared two legs—one side male and the other female, although given their bulging physique, they looked similar. Their pose made Bahd Cava more prominent. With her arms and claws out, she slashed through some unseen foe. She held the same weapon those two alphas from that trio had used last night. The blades fitted between her fingers, successfully doubling her claws. Red blood glistened from the tips and dripped down her knives and fingers alike. Camalus held the same weapons. He too struck at some offstage enemy. Large, glowing red eyes completed their terrifying faces. Their jaws were wide open. Drool and blood dripped from their fangs. Fire and smoke surrounded them as if the Twins waged war against the old gods of Hell invading the Moon Vale.

The reds and true blues of their armor, black fur, and piercing silver blades were strikingly vivid. Like a work of art, every minute detail looked painstakingly defined.

Some parts of the tattoo, like the fire and smoke, were softer, and the contrast made them appear like pastels on canvas. Up until now, I'd never seen Don's tattoo this blatantly. I knew he had one from the many times he'd fucked me, but this was the first time I could take it all in. How long had something that size taken to complete? Had it been painful to undergo?

I wished I could move Don's ponytail out of the way. The hair drawing a line through the Twins almost seemed fitting.

My eyes followed the curve of his spine to where the tattoo ended. Then traveled lower to his ass. Even though I was not into guys, I had to say it was nice. Firm and muscular. Mid-thought, I grew angry. I absolutely was not attracted to that jerk. Nor would I feed his bloated ego by complimenting his good looks. *Good looks? As if!*

"Morning." Don looked over his shoulder, and his smile reached his eyes. He smirked as he took in my appearance. "Looks good on you."

Shrugging, I ran a hand through my messy curls to get them out of my eyes. "Well, not like I got a choice. You took my clothes, and I'm too drained to go through my boxes."

"For washing. They were disgusting."

"Oh, yeah?" I felt the need to fight him. "Well, who got me that way, huh? You're the one who has to constantly touch me!"

Don raised his brow before he went back to frying. "How do you take your eggs?"

I scoffed at him. "You just gonna ignore me now?"

"I'm not ignoring you. Your eggs? How do you want them?"

My sigh came out as a tired growl. "Sunnyside up."

"There." His smile returned. Was he mocking me? "That wasn't so hard."

Brooding, I sank into a chair at the breakfast nook. The black marble was cool beneath my fingers. I tapped my foot against the chair's tall legs.

"You should give your parents a call."

"What?" Those words sounded weird to me. For a moment, it felt like I'd just had a sleepover with my buddies, not woken up from demanding sex with my alpha, forcing me into submission.

"Your parents. Call them." He tilted his head over to the

landline. Who still had one of those nowadays? Feh…old-timer. "The Silver trials are deadly. I'm sure they must be worried."

Knowing them, they probably weren't.

"I doubt it. You can't do any wrong in their eyes," I said before I realized this was going to bloat his already huge ego.

He set down my plate. It looked super delicious, with sunny-side eggs on two pieces of toast. I took a whiff of its heavenly smell before I realized what I was doing. Feeling pouty, I wanted to rebel and not eat his food, but my stomach growled painfully.

"I'm flattered and all." He was more than flattered by the pompous way he puffed up like a balloon. "But all the same, call them." He served himself next and took a seat beside me. Right beside me, not a seat in-between us. It made me feel vulnerable. This person could rape me, hurt me again. I was no match against him. Don knew that as well as I did.

For a moment, I was terrified. That was strange given how mouthy I was to him and not likely to stop anytime soon. But my cheek stung in a reminder of his strikes.

"You don't have to fear me." He ate his food as if a teenage boy wasn't trembling beside him. "I don't intend on hurting you."

I took some calming breaths. I hated this person. Why did I have to be afraid of him, anyway? *Stupid body.*

"I'm not afraid of you." I was glad my voice came out snappy, defiant.

"Uh-huh." He opened the newspaper, confirming once again how old he was, the old pervert.

"I'm not."

"Call your folks. I mean it."

"Or what?"

He put down the paper, and I flinched. "I said I won't hurt you, so stop it already."

"Well, who made me like that, huh? You hit me."

"Only when there's reason."

"Sounds like what an abuser would say."

Getting up with a sigh, he grabbed the landline and put it into my hand. "Not all betas survive Silver. Remember your friend."

Myrtle. Her scared face would torment me for the rest of my life.

He sighed again. "Don't go getting all emotional again. Gods, are you sensitive."

"Sensitive?" I glared at him. I wanted to throw my plate at him, but I was too hungry. "I saw them cut her up! While she was alive! And her face. Her eyes…she was so scared."

"Of course, they were killing her. How else was she supposed to feel?"

I pushed back my chair, making a scraping sound on the floor. "Unbelievable. You don't feel anything for her? To die like that. And for what? Some stupid archaic mating trials?"

"Archaic, huh?"

"Yes, that *is* what it is. I'm not your property simply because you kidnapped me."

"Man, are you annoying. Maybe teenagers are too young. Maybe I should've given you a few more years."

"What?"

"I would have, but there was no way your mother would not be putting you in the Offering as soon as you came of age."

"You…" His words took me back to the night before. "You said something like that last night."

He smiled softly. "Yeah. I did."

"I don't understand."

"I pursued you. Wanted you for a while, actually." I studied him, looking for understanding in his blue eyes, which were still startlingly blue, although no longer the neon when he transformed.

"And now I've got you." His smile brightened.

Grumbling, I sat back down and picked at my food. That was until I tasted it, then I was shoveling it down. "Wow, this is really good!" I hadn't intended to compliment the arrogant asshole, but my mouth was singing praises all on its own. I was starving.

He messed up my hair. "Good." He poured himself another coffee. "Your parents. Start calling. Now."

I breathed and slowed my chewing. I decided to call them to help pace myself so I didn't upset my stomach, pigging it all down. I punched in the number for my parents' house, thankfully remembering it, even though after cellphones, I'd forgotten most phone numbers, Shamar's included.

Papa picked up on the first ring. "Fern!"

"It's me, Papa."

His deep breath of relief made me feel guilty. He must have been worried sick. "Thank the Goddess."

"Always for Her kindness," I answered with the chorus of the psalm out of habit. "Didn't mean to worry you. Is Mom okay?"

"Your mother? She has been my rock. Believes in your alpha."

Grumbling, I rolled my eyes. "Of course she does."

"And she was right to trust." He sounded like he both reassured and chastised himself at the same time. "I won't doubt anymore."

"Why? He's still a jerk to me."

"Jerk to you?"

"Yeah, he hit me."

Oddly, Don didn't interject and instead kept reading his paper.

"For what? Does this happen often?" Leave it to Papa to worry.

"Yes. That jerk hit me last night! And it still stings."

"Are you okay?" For a moment, I wanted to play on his anxiety in hopes that he would let me come home, but I heard the strain of exhaustion in his voice. "Wait... Last night? During Silver?" Mentioning last night had been a mistake.

I swallowed. I swear I saw the ghost of a smile on that jerk's face. "Well, yeah..."

"Did you leave your quilt?"

"I had to." Myrtle's scared face resurfaced, distracting me.

I was much more upset about what had happened to Myrtle than about Don hitting me. "I saw…" The words stuck to my throat. "Myrtle…she was…"

"I know, Fern. I'm so sorry. Her family was informed early this morning." Papa sighed into the phone. "They'd hoped that she'd last long enough to be freed from slavery. Her father had been trying to get other alphas to challenge that beastly slaver. He wasn't having much luck, though, because that alpha who claimed her happened to also be a Highborne. Still, I'd heard at least one was interested." Papa released a breath. "Thank Arduinna that Donovan claimed you during the Hunt! I don't even know what I'd do if you had become a slave. Not that your mother was worried, given all of your many suitors." Pride entered his voice.

I'd long stopped listening. All I could think about was Myrtle. Had she survived the night, she might've been saved from slavery. I balled my fists. "Fuck the stupid Offering! I shouldn't have waited so long to try and save her!"

"You did *what?* Fern, you could have been killed."

I looked down at my food, and I diverted my eyes like Papa was here disciplining me. "I know."

"Donovan was right to strike you. The Silver Offering is never to be taken lightly."

I shoved out of my chair and started pacing. Thankfully, the landline was cordless. "You don't have to tell me that. I've never been so terrified. I thought I was going to die…"

"And you could very well have. I'm sorry that had to happen to Myrtle, but just the thought of losing you…I can't bear it. You will put Donovan on after this, so I can thank him properly."

I blew out a breath. "He's my alpha, Papa. You don't have to thank him."

Papa hummed into the phone. "I guess you're right. But no matter how old you get, despite now that you're mated, you'll still be my little pup."

Mated…shit. That was right. Don and I were one Offering away from him officially being my alpha, my dominant. Forever.

My body trembled. I remembered the way he sucked on my skin until it bruised. How he didn't let up on my nipples even though I begged him. It hurt. But it was intoxicating too, addicting. For a moment, I wanted him to knock everything off the table and take me right on top of it. I wanted him inside of me.

"Your mother wants to speak with Donovan. And I do, too. Put him on the phone, please, Fern."

"Wait, wait, Papa! I don't want to live with Don."

"Fern, he's your mate. Law has it—"

"I'm too young to be mated. Can I at least live with you guys until school is over?"

"Of course not, Fern. You are Donovan's beta now, and if he wants you to live with him, then you have to follow his wishes."

I headed into the living room, away from the back of the newspaper, where Don was either pretending not to listen or else not caring in the least. Maybe because he knew I was trapped with him. He had won me, claimed me twice now. My neck still stung in both places where he bit me.

"But Papa, I can't stand him." I knew I was whining, but I didn't care. The wooden tiles beneath my feet had warmed up since this morning. I paced the spacious, wide-open living room and went over to the oak tree. It grew straight through Don's living room and out of the roof. I pressed my hand against the bark, feeling the bumpy edges against my fingers.

"I know this is a trying time," Papa said, voice softening. "You've got a strong spirit. Much like me when I was your age. It took your mother and I longer than the month of Offering to complete my *Dominating* period. Let yourself submit to him, Fern. He is a good wolf. He will protect you and treat you kindly. And when you birth his pups, you'll be the happiest you've ever been."

I shook my head. "No, thank you."

"Fern, this is why Donovan punishes you. You need to let go of your stubbornness. You are mated now. You belong to

Donovan. Treat him as your alpha and do as he says. I promise you that after the *Dominating* period, things will get much better, as they did for your mom and me." I didn't believe him, but I didn't get to tell him that because he wanted to speak with Don. And Mom was probably waiting for her turn, too.

I would not be permitted to talk to my mother until after the *Dominating*. She was another alpha, and until Don broke me in completely, her presence could be seen as a threat, regardless that she was my mother. Papa could talk to me because he was a beta.

I heard Mom talking to Don. It was clear when he changed from talking with my dad, who was no doubt thanking him, to talking with my mom.

"By Babd Catha's hand, I protected him. And let not a single blow befallen him."

He was quoting literature, referring to how the Twin Gods of War protected their beta, Arawn the God of Death, from the old gods who wanted to rid *Death* from the world.

It sounded more like a skit, and it made me think of the mating vows. These official vows, spoken on the Final Offering, were also a skit of sorts. Thinking about saying those lines to Don made my chest hot, and my lower body ached faintly. I turned my thoughts off that topic, or I would be standing in a pool of my own precum and beta juices.

My mom's muffled words responded to him. I couldn't make anything out, but it made Don smile. A real smile. "Thank you, Teacher Brightwood." Then his tone returned to being serious. "I swear to take care of your pup at the cost of my own life."

I kind of wished I knew what they were saying, but at the same time, I didn't care. Most likely, it was more pompous alpha crap. Instead, I decided to watch some TV, but not before grabbing my plate of Don's tasty food. That last part upset me, but I was too hungry to pass up breakfast.

Chapter Four

Punishment

From the little I saw of Shamar over the next few days, he looked like death. He'd excused himself to throw up in the bathroom on *Belsday,* and now on *Twinsday,* his normal green skin had taken on a sickly yellowish hue. The bags under his eyes kept getting saggier. Despite being zombie, he was still living flesh—not living the way Alphonse and I were, though—as he hadn't undergone his Change.

He was untalkative and secretive too. Something was up with him, and I had to go find out.

Don and I had finished dinner, him picking up the plates to start washing.

"Um, hey, Don?" I went into the living room, knowing my voice would carry, despite the light rush of water from the sink.

"Hm?" Don's strong back muscles looked more defined in the sky-blue shirt he wore. When had he gotten that shirt?

"Gonna ask me that question, Fern?"

Snap out of it! Dammit, stop thinking about stupid Don. Like hell, he's sexy!

"Who said it was a question?"

"I did."

"All right. I was thinking about going to check on Shamar. He's been super strange this week. And he keeps getting sicker and sicker."

"Oh, yeah? The whole week, huh?"

I nodded. "Yeah, since *Belsday,* and he didn't even call over the weekend, either."

"That's too bad."

"I know, that's why I want to go over and check on him."

"No, I mean, that's too bad, but you're not going anywhere tonight. You've got school in the morning anyway. Just see him then."

"But something's up with him. Honestly, the way he

looked, I doubt I'll see him tomorrow."

Don didn't seem to think my problems were really problems. "Then talk to him when you talk to him."

"No."

The water stopped. Don stood in the separator between the kitchen and the living room. "What was that?"

I shivered, then bit my lip to cover it up. "I said no." I looked up and met his eyes. "He's my friend, who's possibly in trouble, and I'm gonna see him tonight."

Don's eyes darkened. "You will go where I allow you." I stood my ground. Don still held the towel he used to dry dishes. "Fern, do you dare to test me?"

I looked away before I felt the fire burn within me. "Yes. Shamar's my fr—"

When I looked up, Don was right in front of me. He grabbed me by the arm and slung me over his shoulder.

"You really like pushing it, don't you, Fern?"

"But he could be hurt?"

"Think about it. He's been sick all week. He's around that age." Opening the door of the bedroom, he threw me on the bed. "He's most likely undergoing the Change."

The *Change*. I knew about this zombie phenomenon that happened when they reached adulthood. I was no expert by any means, but Shamar needed me. He came over when I was sick, and it always made me feel better.

"Well, more reason for me to be there for him."

"Stupid boy." Don shook his head, letting out a sigh. "You have zombie friends. Aren't you aware of what their Change entails?"

"T-They die."

"Exactly. So why the hell would you want to be around that?"

"'Cause Shamar's my friend. And it's gotta be terrifying to be dying. I'm not gonna let him do it alone."

Don looked ready to get onto the bed with me. I crawled back on my hands and knees. I didn't want to fuck. I needed to be with Shamar.

He crossed his arms, revealing his prominent muscles and making his sky-blue shirt show off even more of his solid physique. *Fucking shirt!*

He headed for the door. "You go there, and you'll get yourself killed. Wait until you can see him in school."

Relief fell over me. He didn't plan to fuck me. My relief was short-lived though. He pulled the door shut behind him, and I heard the click of the lock.

"What the fuck? Don!" I sprang from the bed and onto my feet.

"Appears like this is the only answer you'll take."

I pounded my fists against the door, but the wood held firm. Even if I transformed into a werewolf, I didn't have the strength to break it. If I was an alpha, that'd be another story. It wasn't like I didn't get stronger in werewolf form. I did, but betas evolved to be more beautiful than powerful.

"Stop that. You're not coming out. So get ready for bed. I'll be in in a little while."

"What the fuck, Don? I'm not a little pup!"

Don scoffed, his voice teasing. "Oh, really?"

"Fuck you."

"Now, now, stay in there and reflect on your actions." His condescending tone pissed me off even more.

"Dammit, Don!" There was no answer. He had clearly tired of me. "What the fuck?" Pounding on the door was getting me nowhere. And I needed to be there for Shamar. I remembered his look of fear when the skin on his face peeled off while we washed our hands in the bathroom sink. He had been terrified. Sick and alone.

Of course, he had his family. Maybe I shouldn't be worried. I wasn't a zombie. How in the hell did I think I could help? His parents and older siblings were much better equipped. But not being a wereduin had never stopped Shamar whenever I got sick or needed his help. He was even willing to take on Don for me.

Fuck.

Going over to the bed, I flopped down hard. I wanted to

kick and scream on the floor, but that would really confirm my pup's status. And I didn't want to give Don the satisfaction.

A light drizzle fell around the mini dogwood tree that sprouted through the bedroom. As the tree grew below the house, and the opening that surrounded the tree concaved, the water did not bounce off any surface. So instead of getting all over the floor, it simply fell and soaked into the dirt. The netting at the top of the house, which wasn't visible from this angle, kept the bugs out.

Wait a sec…if water could get in, then I could get out.

Like all werewolf pups, I grew up climbing trees, so climbing up the dogwood was a piece of kibble. Now to do something about the netting.

I hadn't taken Wolfsbane since the night of the Hunt. So far, Don's alpha prowess wasn't suppressing my ability to shift. Technically, it made me instinctually not want to shift and disobey him, but the end effect was the same.

As a werewolf, I might not have had the strength alphas had, but my claws were still sharp. And the netting above the tree was meant to keep the bugs out, not werewolves.

I put on one of the few pseudo-shirts I owned—a plain tee—and shorts. Normally those kinds of clothes weren't made for betas, only alphas. Thankfully, I hadn't put my pseudo-shoes in the coat closet but left them in the room.

The dogwood bark held my claws nicely. I had always been quick when it came to tree climbing and won whenever my little sister and I raced.

When I reached the netting, a simple slice of the claws ripped it open. Don's house was practically one large window, so I had to be careful not to be seen. It would be less conspicuous to crawl.

I stayed in werewolf form to run on all fours and still maintain a humanoid shape. But I quickly tired because it required too much energy. So I shifted somewhere in-between werewolf and wolf and stayed close to the ground.

The living room lights illuminated the surrounding foliage. That asshole was probably watching TV. What the hell gave him the right to lock me in our room? *Our* room? *As if I'd ever call it that! Fuck him.*

I made it to the street and trotted to the bus station. The extra padding on my palms and fingers prevented the gravel from digging into my skin. Despite the physical exertion, I always felt safer and more in control the closer I was to werewolf form, probably why alphas prevented us from transforming, especially early in our relationship.

I knew the bus route by heart. There were a few more stops before I reached his house than when I'd lived with my folks.

When I got on the bus, I realized I hadn't taken any ules. "Fare?"

"Put it under Blackfang Pack." Thankfully, I now had Don's family name behind me. As a pup, I couldn't take ules from my family's vault. But as Don's mate—even unofficially—I could withdrawal from his Pack's treasury under his name. All I needed was one bitemark to identify as a Blackfang. Every family member of age had unlimited access. But it was common courtesy for individuals to put more in than they took out in a given month. Theoretically, I could withdraw any amount I wanted—assuming Don didn't prevent me.

The bus driver, an old, flea-bitten werewolf, gave me the once over like he didn't believe I was old enough. Tugging down my collared pseudo-shirt, I revealed Don's bitemark.

He squinted but finally nodded. Then he took out a digital scroll containing a roster of family vaults. It didn't take long to find the correct one. As vaults were expensive, only Highbornes and other aristocracy had them. Normal banks were run by goblins, but underground vaults were maintained by gollums. Although small, these rock beings could turn to stone anyone foolish enough to look them in the eye. The price they charged was insurance for any accidental damages.

The driver marked three tallies next to the name before he handed me the digital quill to get my signature. The tallies were a placeholder. Don would have to pay the fare later.

Every transaction in the vault would be under his name. I'd already seen him take out his unofficial monthly quota when I caught a glance at his laptop. Another transaction would make him look bad. Unfortunately, his family wouldn't notice a measly three ules—their vault probably overflowed with ules, remedies, and other treasures. Too bad. That jerk deserved it for treating me like a pup.

I took a spot in the back.

Five more stops and the bus veered down the main street and crossed over the bridge leading into the bog. All around us, tall oaks grew, their thick knees waded in the swampy water. Moss dangled from the branches with a full moon peeking out between them. It wasn't only werewolves that honored the full moon. Other races did too, so maybe it played a role in the zombies' Change.

Finally, I came to Shamar's stop. It was at the fork of a dirt road, yellow lights on two lampposts lit the path. The moment I stepped off the bus, I was enveloped in the sounds of bullfrogs and crickets. I swatted the gnats away from my eyes.

Shamar's family lived down this street. It was kind of creepy at night. It made me think of my horror movies, which always got me excited. I loved being scared.

I passed several circular bog homes with wooden porches and steps leading up to the door. Poles on either side of the bog home stuck into the mud and prevented the home from sinking into it. That allowed zombies to live close to the swamp. Warm glows came from inside the homes. Shamar's was the third to last one on the block.

At his bog home, I thought about knocking at the door. But all the lights were off. If they were asleep, I probably shouldn't be inconsiderate and ring the bell.

I changed back to a wereduin. Going around the home, my feet sank into the muddy ground, the tall cat willows got my shorts a little wet.

I forgot why I hated to skip the door and go straight to his room. *Fucking swamp.*

No way I would be changing back into either worg or werewolf form. My pseudo-shoes would be gone, and I didn't want mud on my feet. It always got in between my claws.

A faint light came from Shamar's window. Not warm yellows like most of the bog homes I'd passed, but a soft, reddish-orange glow shown behind the whicker.

Zombies didn't share our love for trees. But bog homes were made entirely of wood, so I might be able to climb to his window. My wereduin claws were plenty sharp. Maybe I could make it if I went up lightly?

First, I better get his attention. "Shamar?" I tried to make my whisper loud and quick. After searching for a stone, I threw it at the pane.

The lights flickered as if someone was there.

"Shamar?"

No answer.

He had to be in there. Maybe he was too sick to come to the window. It pissed me off that as a zombie, Shamar was subjected to a curse that killed him before reanimating his body. When they awoke, they were a full-fledged zombie.

And I thought the Offering was bad.

I climbed the side of his house, cringing at the scratch marks my claws made. It wasn't nearly as easy as I thought, and it made me appreciate trees even more. Finally, I reached the ledge of his window and gave it two knocks.

"Shamar?" I kept my voice low to not wake up his family.

Silence. The light flickered. Someone was there.

"Shamar? Don't get up if you don't have to." I started opening the window. "I know you've been feeling sick and all—"

All thoughts left me.

Shamar stood in the center of his room. Naked. His green skin glowed. His eyes closed. Lightening danced on his skin— long tendrils of energy, in various reds and oranges, coming from ritual mats around him. Voodoo trinkets and incense produced a haze.

I watched him, shocked. Had it already happened? Was

Shamar officially a zombie? "Shamar?" My voice was barely a whisper.

Slowly his eyes opened. He had been facing the window, and the moonlight reflected a yellowish-white glow on his skin.

His glossy white gaze was unfocused. His head dangled to the side, neck up before it rolled to the other side. His green skin had ripped, and some of it was shedding off. His body seemed more like a voodoo doll in how it contorted than the boy I knew.

His mouth opened, dirt and grime rolled down his chin—some of it poured out from his shredded skin. He looked terrifying, but I could never be afraid of my best friend.

He made a low moaning. His eyes grew wide, blackness filling up the milky-white orbs. Still glossy and unfocused, they were directed at me.

"Shamar?"

He took one step toward me and stumbled, falling straight onto his face.

"Shamar!" I jumped from the window ledge to help him up. The moment I reached for him, his hands shot out and grabbed my ankle, and he sank his teeth into my skin. I screamed in pain and instinctively kicked him off. I accidentally kicked his head, and his neck snapped to the side with an ugly popping sound. "Shit, Shamar! Snap out of it! What the hell is wrong with you?"

Grabbing his head, he cracked his neck into place, then lunged at me again. Raspy growls slipped past his stretched lips. His eyes watched me with a vacant stare like he didn't know me at all. Like I was nothing but a meal of flesh he'd brought for lunch. Only he wasn't smiling, or laughing, or being his super overly emotional self.

I raced to get out of the way, but he took me down to the floor, and we rolled around until he pinned me. I held up both hands against his chest to stop him from biting me.

"Fuck! Stop, Shamar!" I transformed into a werewolf and used that newfound strength to roll him off me. He was ungodly strong. Normally zombies were the weakest race, but not this Shamar. He was like a never-ending source of power. I had barely gotten to my feet when he charged, slamming me into the wall. "Shamar! Stop! It's me, Fern. Stop!"

"F-errrrrn." I thought I heard what sounded like my name in his guttural groans.

"Yeah. Fern, your best friend. Who's been really fucking worried about you. So stop trying to fucking eat me!"

"Brrraiiinss!"

"No. *Fern*. Not *brains*. *Fern,* dammit!" Okay, maybe Don had been right. What the fuck was I doing here? I was about to get my brains eaten by my undead friend.

Being best friends with a zombie, I assumed I knew what to expect. Sure, I wasn't an expert, but we did talk about our races sometimes. Didn't we? Actually…perhaps not as much as I thought. We normally discussed bands and music whenever we hung out.

Right now, Shamar was *Raging*—when zombies became mindless killing machines. But I didn't think that happened until *after* their Change, not *during* it. I thought he would be bedridden or something, not chasing after me like the walking dead!

I wished he didn't get so tight-lipped during conversations about his culture. Maybe then I would have seen this coming? But when it came to anything zombie-related, Shamar liked to shoulder his burdens alone. Take his Change for starters. He hadn't even told me it was happening! Shamar cared so much about my problems but shut me out when it came to his. If I didn't know better, I'd say he was embarrassed. But why? I thought zombies were pretty cool. That didn't mean I wanted to be eaten by one.

I dashed for the window, making it to the sill when he grabbed my back and bit down on my shoulder.

"Ah! Stop!" I cried out at the spike of pain. As a werewolf, I was used to being bitten, and zombies didn't have nearly enough fangs to really hurt me…at least not right away. Thrusting my head back, I banged his forehead, and he let go. At the sound of popping bones over my shoulder, I looked back. Shamar's head dangled to the side from my force. "Shamar, stop! You're gonna hurt yourself!"

Shamar rearranged his head and neck once more, correcting what I had dislodged. Without another thought, I jumped out of the window and landed on all fours. My claws dug into the muddy ground.

"Brraaainssss!" Shamar reached out of his window, then leapt out after me. I thought he would break something, but lightening—the reddish-orange stuff that had surrounded him before—struck his body, and he landed on his feet. Upright. He looked taller. His menacing, black eyes bulged out. Grime and dirt seeped out from his open mouth; my blood stained his teeth. Still naked, the moonlight revealed the damages his body had undertaken probably from the curse—rips and tears all over, some spots open, revealing milky-white muscles or jutting bones. "Bbrrraaainsss!"

"Shit, shit, shit! Shamar! Wake the fuck up!" I backed away from him straight toward the marsh behind his house. He was walking me out to a place where it would be hard to escape. Already the mud stuck to my paws and made my steps sluggish. "Shamar, stop!"

He charged and knocked me on the ground. I bared my fangs. Rolling over onto all fours, I tried to run away. He collapsed onto my back, his fingernails tearing off my fur. He bit down on my shoulder, shaking his head as if to gnaw the flesh off of my bones. If I hadn't been wearing pseudo-clothes, he would have torn my shirt apart.

I reached behind and clawed his shoulder, but that spurred him on, and he attacked the back of my head, savagely biting me. "Bbbrrrrainnss."

I cried out as his teeth broke my skin.

Suddenly he was yanked off me and sent flying into the bog. Don stood there, a full werewolf. He growled at me. "You. I fucking told you to stay put."

"Don!" I was too relieved to be afraid of him and his wrath.

Shamar rose to his feet. "Brrraiins." The throaty words

rumbled from his dislocated, hanging jaw.

As he approached us, he picked up speed.

Don sighed. "Fucking little brats." He drew his claws.

"No, wait! Shamar's not himself. Please don't kill him!" I threw myself onto his legs like that would hold Don back from attacking Shamar. It was laughable, though. Don easily dragged me along. "Please wait!" Don growled, approaching Shamar. "Wait! Please! This was my fault! I should have listened to you. Please, Don, please!"

Shamar lunged at us—hands reaching. Wails and furious snarls escaping his lips.

Don caught him up by the scruff of his neck. Holding Shamar dangling off the ground. Shamar swung his arms, trying to grab Don, but he couldn't reach. As a werewolf, Don dwarfed my friends, making them like the gnats outside were to me.

"Don, please! Please don't kill him! Please!" I had begun to cry. My sobs choked me up. "Please, I fucked up! Me. Not him—he's my best friend!"

"Be quiet already." Don sounded annoyed. Grabbing me with his other hand, he yanked me off his legs and held me out to his other side. When he noticed my presence, Shamar stopped trying to grab Don and instead reached for me.

"Bbbraaaains!"

"Fuck, this is annoying." Don's anger grew. "And not how I fucking wanted to spend my night." He walked us around to the front of Shamar's house, then dropped me, and I fell, muddying my knees. He knocked on the door, still holding a thrashing Shamar. Losing his patience, he banged on the door louder.

The door cracked open. Shamar's grandmother, an old witch doctor, stood in the doorway, dressed in her nightgown. Also a zombie, she resembled her grandson a little with the same green skin and wide black eyes. Her face held indignation before she saw Shamar thrashing in Don's grip.

"Sorry to bother you," Don spoke nicely to her despite his gruffness. "My idiot mate interrupted Shamar, and this happened." He brought Shamar before his grandma.

"Oh, dear…" Shaking her head, she rushed into the house. Her voice carried from behind the door. "Hold him for a second longer." She came out with a voodoo doll that looked exactly like Shamar. She closed the doll's arms together. Shamar stopped reaching out blindly, his arms resting by his side. Then she did the same with his legs before she made him sit. I stood there flabbergasted that she could move Shamar in that fashion.

"Now, be silent, you." Her tone was on the chastising side, and it reminded me of a witch I'd seen once disciplining her cat. She closed her hand around the doll's head, then used her finger to swipe down over its eyes, nose, and finally mouth. At the touch of the doll's eyes, Shamar closed his. When she got to his mouth, he stopped biting the air in a wild frenzy. "Now that's better." She smiled like a witch who'd finished stirring her cauldron.

"Very sorry about this." Don grabbed me by the shoulder and tugged me over. "Apologize, Fern, for the trouble you caused." I felt like an unruly pup, but it was my fault, not Shamar's, so it wouldn't be fair to get him in trouble.

"I'm sorry. It's my fault. I thought Shamar was sick, so I decided to check on him and make sure he was okay."

She nodded. "Praise the loa, you've got this one here," she pointed at Don. "Else, I'd be cleaning your brains off my yard tomorrow."

"Really, really sorry, Ganmi." It meant *grandma* in Zandien—the language most zombies used—and was one of the few words Shamar had taught me.

"I know, Fern. You're forgiven." She looked to Don, then nodded at Shamar. "Thank you for not killing him."

Don gave her a smile. "Good night, again, sorry to have troubled you."

The moment she shut the door, Don growled at me. My stomach fluttered—anxiety setting in. He was livid. He was going to beat me for sure.

"Come on." Giving me one last growl, he headed toward

his parked car. I dragged my feet. Palpable tension filled the space between us.

We drove in silence. Every so often, he growled low, and it stole my attention.

Finally, we arrived at his place—it didn't feel like our place, just his. Not since I had first come to stay with him did I dread entering it as much as I did right then. His silence was killing me.

"Um, Don?"

"Did I ask you to talk?"

I flinched at his sharp tone and shook my head. It pissed me off, my rebellious side fought for control, but my self-preservation had full reign.

He got out of the car, and even though he didn't slam the door behind him, it still sounded loud. I felt the tremors from the force. I couldn't stay in the car forever, but I didn't want to go inside. There lay my doom. I wanted to stay in the car. But this was ridiculous. If I didn't get out, he would most likely drag me out like he had before.

Slowly, I exited the car. He wasn't waiting for me at the door.

That shocked me. I wanted to run because I knew he would hurt me the moment I entered the house. But at the same time, I didn't. Inside, somewhere, I longed to have him submit me. To be beneath him. Apologizing. Servicing him. Being punished by him.

My body tingled as I walked to the door. I wanted him to hurt me. To make me sorry I ever defied him. I was his beta. I didn't have that right. He needed to put me in my place. My instincts craved it, almost like I would lose respect for him if he wasn't on me the moment I stepped through the door.

I paused; my rational brain screamed, trying to take control. *No. I don't want to be punished. I haven't done anything to deserve punishment. Shamar needed me. Right?*

My hand rested on the doorknob, but I couldn't open it.

He would hurt me.

I wanted him to hurt me.

But I didn't. I didn't want that. I dreaded it.

How long would he be patient with me? Maybe he'd think I'd tried to run away again. That made me tremble. I wanted to run, to run away and never come back. But my instincts were strong, calling me to walk into my doom.

Opening the door, I stepped inside.

Don stood in the hallway. His handsome features were a mixture of werewolf and wereduin. "Get over here, beta." I flinched like he had struck me. "You deliberately disobeyed me." His eyes narrowed. "Come here!"

I shuffled my feet until I stood before him. He towered over me, and our massive height difference had never been more apparent.

Immediately, I felt weak. I wanted to bow before him. All my resolve abandoned me as my beta instincts kicked in.

"What do you say, beta?" Don grabbed my head and forced me to look at the floor. I yelped as it was the spot where Shamar had bitten me earlier. "Yes, it hurts. And it could've been a lot worse."

I swallowed.

"I told you from the beginning that I wouldn't tolerate disobedience. Didn't I?"

My beta instincts craved this, and I had no choice but to surrender to them. Already he was using his alpha prowess against me.

I nodded.

"Answer me, beta."

"Yes, you said that."

"And still you chose to defy me."

Punish me. Punish me. Make me beg. Make me regret ever leaving—for even thinking that I had the choice.

Shit. What the hell? Stupid thoughts. Shut the fuck up. But there was no stopping them.

"You said it, and I disobeyed."

Don snorted. The next thing I knew, he had me over his shoulder. I thought he'd take me into the bedroom and submit me like normal. Instead, he went into the living room.

My heart was trapped in my throat as my stomach knotted. Somewhere underneath my instincts, I hated showing him submission. But I didn't have the right to voice that. At this moment, he was king.

He dropped me onto the couch. Even against the soft cushion, his force still knocked the wind out of me. "Stand up."

I stood. He sat on the couch. His posture was erect, focused.

His mouth curved into a smile, but there was nothing friendly about it. "You disobeyed me, like a little pup. So now, you will be punished like one. Take off your pants." He leered at me. "Roll them down to your ankles, don't step out of them. Do it!"

My fingers trembled for a moment as I undid my fly then brought my pants—still damp from the mud—all the way down.

His hand cupped my groin, and I hardened beneath his touch. "That's right. Your body already accepts my ownership. It wants to be punished." He was right, and the goosebumps that sprinkled my arms and legs confirmed it. "Now your *panties*." He gave me a squeeze before he let go.

I wore the equivalent of tighty-whities and burned with embarrassment. Did he have to call them *that?* "Fuck…"

With an open palm, he smacked me across the cheek, and it turned my head. It startled me more than hurt.

"Did I ask you to talk?" Shivering and stunned, I shook my head. "Then, don't talk." He leaned back and massaged my balls with his socked foot. Heat collected in my groin, and I failed to stifle my moan. "What are you waiting for? Remove your panties." I hated him calling them that, even more humiliation…I hated it. But I had no choice. He could seriously hurt me if he wanted to. Slowly, I tugged down my underwear until they joined my pants around my ankles. "Get over here." He grabbed my arm and had me over his knee.

"W-Wait. I'm not." I wanted to struggle, but instead, I stayed perfectly still, regardless of my protests. "Not a pup…"

He squeezed my ass cheek and teased, "You are to me." He dug his claws into the meaty part of my ass, and it hurt, but it felt grounding too, like his claws anchored me to my proper place. I still tried not to show it. Yes, he had the upper hand at that moment, but I had my pride. Maybe I couldn't speak, but that didn't mean I would give him the satisfaction by crying out.

His hand smacked hard against my bare ass, and I jumped. It stung. I wouldn't be surprised if he left a large, red handprint on me.

His hand rose, then came down hard on my ass again. I bunched my lips together, trying to contain any sounds. He struck me again and again. And again. His open-palmed hand smacked against my skin. The pain was getting unbearable, and I wanted to get away.

He leaned closer. "What's this? Not gonna cry, my little pup?" I bit my lip at another hard smack. "Holding out on me, huh?" A devious edge entered his tone. "We'll see who can hold out the longest. I will not stop spanking you until I have you crying in my lap." I screwed my lips together. No way in hell, I was giving him that satisfaction.

Air whooshed against my back as his hand drew back. *Whack. Smack.* Down and down it came. My ass stung, some of my skin prickled with blood. This time when his hand came down, he extended his claws, and I lost the battle and yelped in pain.

"Ah," he said, voice smooth as butter. "You liked that one, huh?" With every spanking, his claws dug into my ass until he had me crying out. "This is the one that does it?" He didn't always use his claws, but now that he had broken skin, every whack hurt. He spanked me so hard, I became delirious, my ass heating up.

"S-Stop."

"What was that?" I doubted he could hear my whimper over his angry tone. "Did you say something?" Again and again, he spanked me. I shook my head. He covered my mouth with his other hand. "Do you wish to say something to me?"

He squeezed my mouth tighter, and I couldn't speak even if I wanted to. "Well, do you?"

I shook my head, digging my fingernails into my fists to have some control. He was hurting me so badly. But I was growing hard. The tip of my cock dripped with my beta juices.

He leaned down and purred into my ear. "Are you hard, my pet?"

I whimpered. His hand raised again, but this time, he rubbed my ass, smearing the blood. It felt soothing. There was something else too. Don used his alpha prowess to soothe the burning. He rubbed my ass gently, and I moaned against his palm. It felt amazing.

His hand went away. When he returned, I expected to get more fondling, so his sharp smack had me crying out—my muffled cries hidden behind his hand. The pain, the pleasure, continued. He would rub my ass to soothe my bruised skin before he returned to spanking me.

Finally, I was at my limit. Pain and pleasure mixing into something unnamable—my mind escaping to a place where they became interchangeable.

He grabbed my hips and lifted me off his lap, then I was face down on the couch. I ground into the leather to relieve my aching erection. His heavy weight on my back stopped all movement, and I whined helplessly, but he wouldn't allow me to move. This was yet another punishment.

"Not tonight, Fern. Tonight, only I will be coming. You," he nipped my ear, pressing more weight onto me until breathing grew difficult, "will take it up the ass until I've had my fill of you. Until you learn your place is beneath me, obeying me." He didn't prepare me, but my beta juices already streamed down my cheeks. His cock felt harder, thicker, and it spread my hole wide like he was nailing me to the couch.

He pumped my ass, fucking me rough and brutal, and it shook my body. With his weight on me, there was no way I could come. Whenever I came close, he reached between my legs and squeezed my balls. I cried out in pain. Streams of tears trailed down my face.

"No, Fern. Not tonight. Tonight, you will serve me completely. And until I say otherwise, you won't be coming at all."

I whimpered in pain, pleasure, frustration, and want. He fucked me until he filled my ass with his cum, but he didn't knot me. Instead, he ground against me until he grew hard again and then returned to thrusting.

All night he fucked me. My hole ached, and my back was sore.

It was early in the morning when he finally got off me. I tried to stand, but I staggered. I would have fallen but Don caught me.

"You're not going to bed, Fern."

"What? Why?" I was sexually frustrated and exhausted.

"Because you're not. I don't need to give you any reason." He got behind me and pulled me flat against his chest. "You won't be going to school today either. I've got other plans for you." He took me into the bedroom. "Starting with this." We stopped at the dogwood. "You broke it, you fix it."

"But, I'm tired."

"How's that my problem?"

"And sore."

He laughed, and it sent a shiver down my spine. "And you're going to get even sorer." Going over to the dresser, he pulled out a black butt plug. "This is going up your ass until I say otherwise."

I swallowed. I wasn't underplaying my soreness. He had fucked me so hard through the night, and I didn't even have the blissfulness of orgasm to numb my mind periodically.

I shook my head and darted for the door. "No! No, it'll hurt!"

He trapped me in his strong arms. "Then you should've thought about that before disobeying me, destroying my house, and nearly getting yourself killed. Nearly killing your zombie friend too. If I had been in the mood for blood, I would've ended him."

As he spoke, I struggled with him, but he got the plug

near my ass and stuffed it inside, clogging up my channel. I quivered, all strength leaving me.

"This. Right here. I want you to feel this. Every time you disobey me, I will punish you like this, for as long as I want, doing what I want. You belong to me, Fern. You are my little beta, and you will obey me, or I will break you open from the inside out." I sagged against his chest. The plug reawakened my soreness and fatigue, and I had no way to fight him. "Now shift into a werewolf."

Holding me captive in his arms, his alpha prowess invaded my senses and called to me. My body began to transform as if beyond my control. His influence must have provided me with some strength; that was the only way I could shift, given my depleted energy levels.

In werewolf form, I knew he found me beautiful. Unlike alphas, beta bodies were graceful and humanoid, not rippled with muscles. Our fur wasn't as thick and much softer. He licked my neck and nibbled my skin, teasing my nipples from underneath my shirt. "I am going to have you replace the netting." The moment he left me, I slumped to the floor. My body too weak to hold me up.

"I-I can't."

He returned with some sealant netting and—

A cock cage?

He was serious about not letting me come. At this point, I would even need his permission to pee. I didn't have the energy to fight him when he caged me. He dragged me over to the dogwood. "Now climb and fix it."

I stared at him, helpless, falling asleep. "I-I can't. I'll fall."

He smirked. "Then, you fall."

Asshole. Fucker. I was too exhausted to voice anything. It was all my tired brain could do to not sink to my knees.

He helped me mount the tree. "If you fall, I won't catch you. Remember this the next time you even think of defying me."

My arms shaking, I pulled myself up, digging my claws in. That was the only thing holding me to the tree.

"Aren't you forgetting the netting?"

Godsdamn asshole. Fucker. Fucking ass jerk.

I paused and crawled down a little until I could take the netting from his hand.

"Well, get moving. I don't have all day."

I fucking hate you. I hate you. Asshole. Fucking asshole.

"I know you do."

I must've spoken at least some of that out loud.

"Let this be a lesson to you. Now move."

The butt plug made my knees weak, and the cage kept getting caught on the tree's bark. Thanking every deity I could think of that this wasn't the oak tree I was climbing, I dragged my ass up the entire trunk to the slashed-up netting at the top. I carried the new netting between my teeth.

"If you make a mess up there, what you've experienced so far will be trivial by comparison."

My body trembled. The plug made my legs wobbly as pleasure danced along my back, but the cock cage secured my dick and tightened painfully around my balls. There was no way I'd come.

Reaching up, I slashed the old netting until it came free, and the entire sheet fell to the ground. Taking the new netting from my mouth, I went about fixing it into place with one hand. All the while, I barely hung on to the tree with the other. If I wasn't a werewolf and using my full-length claws as anchors, I'd have fallen for sure. It was a wonder I could even maintain werewolf form at this point, and that had me thanking the Gods even more, for someone up in the Moon Vale loved me. That, or somehow Don's influence was still fueling me a bit.

The last lock snapped into place, and my body gave out entirely, and I let go. Too fatigued to save myself, I fell asleep midair.

I didn't hit the ground.

Strong arms caught me. In a dream state, I felt a muscular chest against my head and then a soft mattress beneath me before I entered Caromeith's World of Dreams.

"Can't I at least put something on?" The butt plug stuffed in my ass and the cage on my dick were the only things keeping me from being completely naked.

Don scoffed. "You'll wear what I tell you. You're being punished for your disobedience last night."

"Punished, some more? You fucked the life out of me all night. I barely slept. And I still haven't gotten off." I grumbled under my breath, "Jerk."

"Think of this next time you decide to defy me. Now get on your knees."

My knees wobbled as I lowered to the floor. The butt plug wiggled inside me, sending jolts of pleasure dancing along my spine. The wooden floor bruised my bare skin. "But the wood hurts my knees."

"And that's my problem, how?"

"Jerk."

"You've no one but yourself to blame." He headed into the kitchen. "Come, I'm hungry."

I was starved, but I got the feeling only his hunger would be satisfied...much like his desire. "Do I have to crawl all the way there?" It was uncomfortable crawling around with the butt plug. It made my stomach ache.

"Stop whining and move your ass."

"Can't I at least transform?"

"That would defeat the purpose. Now hurry up, or I'll make it even worse for you."

I crawled on my hands and knees into the kitchen. The tile was even more uncomfortable than the wood. I'd have bruises for sure. At this angle, the cage tightened around my cock and pressed against my balls. I groaned and tried to take my mind off my discomfort. "I had to check on Shamar. What if he really needed my help?"

"What he didn't need was you showing up. Shouldn't it have been obvious what was happening?" Don snorted. "And to think you almost had your brains eaten...of course, based on your behavior, I'm not sure what he'd be eating."

"Are you just planning on insulting me all day?"

"Insulting? I plan on humiliating you. I don't care one way or the other if I insult you or not."

Crawling over, I waited before him. I didn't like his evil smirk. "Make sure your back is balanced and even."

"I am even…" Pouting seemed like the only option I had to defy him.

He placed the warm plate on top of my back. "Good, now follow me to the living room. And if you spill it, I'll make you eat it off the floor."

Crap. The butt plug made it difficult to crawl enough as it was, and now he wanted me to put something on my back.

It was amazing that none of the contents hadn't spilled yet. It wasn't like I was a klutz, but I wasn't a gymnast either. I had to move super slow.

"You don't think this is kinda extreme? Like really, really extreme?" I had to focus on keeping balanced as I crawled after him, trying to ignore the cage squeezing my cock. "I did what anyone else would have done in my situation."

He sat on the couch and flipped on the TV, turning up the volume to drown out my voice. "Stop here and be still." He had a bowl of cereal, some eggs, and a drink. "Now, keep quiet while I eat."

The smell of eggs had me growing hungry. "And I take it I don't get to have anything."

"Maybe later. If you're good."

"I'm pretty sure it's illegal to kill your beta through starvation." Nothing was illegal about murder in our society.

Don laughed. "One late breakfast isn't going to starve you."

He seemed to take his fucking time eating like my knees weren't aching in this position, or the plug wasn't making me feel bloated. Thankfully, the floor rug was soft.

"Stop fidgeting."

"I can't help it."

"Keep quiet."

I let out an annoyed sound, frustrated, and hungry, but

there was something else lurking in my mind. Obedience. I wanted him to punish me. I had gone against his word. As his beta, I didn't have the right to defy him. Those thoughts irked me and refused to leave. Pre-cum and beta juices seeped from my cockhead and glistened the bars as it pressed painfully against them.

The longer I knelt there, the worse those thoughts craving ownership got. I slipped up, and for a fraction of a second, I gave into them and moaned softly.

"That's a good boy." Don stroked my hair.

My pride stung. "I'm not a dog, you know?" Dogs were a beggar race that lived off other races' generosity or flat out stole it. No self-respecting wereduin wanted to be called that.

"I didn't call you a dog. Now keep quiet. I didn't ask you to speak." He reclined on the couch, sipping his drink.

I bit my tongue. But inside, I wanted him to keep me there. I deserved it. He owned me. If he wanted me on my hands and knees on the floor, then that was what I'd do. This time my moan came out in a whimper. Fucking instincts. I didn't want to obey him. I didn't want to listen to anything I was feeling right now.

"I'm hungry, you know? Geez…how long does it take you to eat?"

"You're hungry, are you now?" I didn't like the teasing hint in his voice.

My stomach growled in response.

"Well, as I can't seem to shut you up, I should probably feed you." He took the plate. "Don't move from this spot."

The moment he left the room, I sank onto my ass to give my knees a break. The butt plug pressed into my prostate, and I squirmed.

"And stay on your knees. I didn't permit you to sit."

Fucking, arrogant asshole.

"You know, I'm pretty sure there's a point when you can actually damage your knees from kneeling on a hard surface." Don didn't answer, but I heard him getting things from the kitchen. "Don?" I sighed. "I don't like this." I was whining, but the more I talked, the less I heard my beta instincts. "Are you expecting me to eat on the floor?"

He walked in, and I looked up at him, still on my hands and knees. He carried a bowl filled with three eggs. He had a glass filled with ice, and beside it, one of the bottled fruit drinks that werewolves craved. It lifted my spirits. Was he bringing me food? And the good stuff too. Also on his tray was a banana, some grapes, bacon, and strawberries. My stomach growled in anticipation.

"When can I stop kneeling?" I looked over my shoulder at him as he placed the tray on the coffee table.

"Stay as you are."

"But, Don…"

"Such a naughty little pup, aren't you?" His voice came at the level of my ear before he swirled his tongue around the shell.

"S-Stop."

"You are. I asked you to keep quiet, and yet, you can't seem to close that yappy little mouth."

I shivered. He turned my head to look at him before he devoured my mouth, kissing me hungrily. I tasted juice and the fruity flavor of his cereal, which happened to be my favorite one. He didn't even like it. Or at least that was what he'd said. Now the jerk had scarfed it down. *Asshole.*

His tongue was demanding, and I moaned into his mouth.

Breaking away, his lips hovered mere breaths away. "That's it. That's how you should sound, my little pup. I want you moaning for me." He could spot my hardening erection trapped in the cage he had put me in. "But you won't be coming. Not for a long while yet. Not until you're good and punished. And know this, the next time you defy me like that, what you're experiencing now, will be pup play."

With one hand, he removed my butt plug, and I sank onto my forearms, groaning.

He tugged my hair. "Get up."

I enjoyed the free feeling in my ass, especially since I'd been wearing that monster for what felt like forever.

He went to the coffee table and picked up one of the eggs.

It didn't smell cooked to my wereduin nose. "It-It's not hard-boiled, how do you expect me to—"

He cracked it open on top of my ass, letting it run between my cheeks. The cold yolk and whitening rolled down my skin, making me shiver. Sticky and smooth all at once, parts of it dripped down into my hole.

I moaned. "P—ervert. This isn't me eating. This is another one of your—" My breath hitched.

Don pressed fingers inside my ass, smearing the egg deep. He explored me, plunging inside, then going almost out before grinding back in. I was super sensitive from the butt plug already. Overwhelmed, I sank onto my forearms again. He yanked me up by my hair.

"I didn't tell you to get off your hands and knees." Leaning down, he nipped my ear. "You're such a naughty little pup." His arm looped around me, his fingers opening the cage. He cupped my balls before grabbing my dick. I gasped, my body trembling.

Please let me come. I didn't think I had voiced that.

"Not yet, Fern. You're still being punished." He spooned me. One hand wrapped around my cock, his other still fingering me. My orgasm sparked.

Right before I could slip over the edge, he squeezed my balls hard. I cried out in pain, my arousal rolling back down the orgasmic hill.

"F-Fuck…jerk. Asshole."

Releasing my balls, he grabbed my chin. Kissing me, he forced his tongue inside. I fisted the floor rug. He continued to finger my hole. My body approached orgasm until he squeezed my balls again.

"Godsdammit, Don…"

"See? Naughty little pup. I told you to wait for me. Keep that up, and I'll make you burn down there."

I whimpered in frustration.

"Still hungry, my little pup?" He pulled his fingers out of

me and returned to the coffee table, bringing over the banana. I knew what he planned on doing. *Pervert.* I had spent hours wearing that butt plug, and he was stuffing something else inside me?

"Fuck-ing pervert." Inch by inch, he inserted the unpeeled banana into my ass.

"There." He stood and admired his handiwork. "Much better."

The thick banana, although not as thick as him, made me ache inside. It was bigger than the butt plug. What a freakishly thick banana. Where the hell had he even gotten one like that? I felt stuffed, uncomfortably so.

"Bas-Bastard!"

When he returned, he leaned over so that his chest pressed against my back. He turned my head and pinched my cheeks. Opening my mouth, he forced a strawberry inside. I bit down instinctively, eating the berry. It was surprisingly, very sweet.

"Good, stuffing your mouth seems to do it." His eyes filled with what could only be excitement. "Let's see how much I can fit in there."

I shook my head. Letting me go, he got in front of me. "Open up, pup, or I'll shove these down your throat."

Slowly I opened my mouth. He inserted another strawberry, then another one. I started to chew. "Uh-uh, open some more. A lot more can fit in there. My little pup has a big mouth."

Two more strawberries went inside me. I wondered if he would let me choke. But I doubted it. He valued my life too much to kill me. That thought made my panic subside. I had to take his punishment, but I could rest assured that he would never permanently hurt me.

Don looked into my eyes, which had already started watering. "Much better. See how quiet you can be." He stroked my hair. He hadn't stopped me, so I chewed up the strawberries, tasting their sweetness. A strange feeling washed over me. It was grounding like I was safe and protected. *Oh no…my stupid beta instincts are back!*

I loved how much control he had over me. How he could make me take it. My well-being in his care. He could feed me more or not. Could put things into my body as he desired. I loved how firm he was with me. How he could command me, make me do it. I wasn't tied up but on my hands and knees of my own free will. I hated it too. Right there on the living room floor, he owned me.

He ran his fingers down my cheek, and I was overjoyed he hadn't used the hand that'd been in my ass.

"You're so beautiful, Fern." He leaned his forehead against mine. "So very beautiful." He moved in close until I felt him smile against my lips. I thought he would kiss me. "So untamed." I wanted it. Needed him. But he pulled away. "But I'm succeeding, aren't I? I'm breaking you in, and you know it." I shut my eyes, not wanting to see that arrogant smirk of his. "You're hungry, right? So I'll have to feed you. After all, I must care for my little pup."

He scooped me up at my waist and flipped me onto my back. The banana brushed against my prostate, and I cried out. I felt the pointed tip at the end lodged inside me, but it was round enough to not be painful, only snug. It burrowed deeper each time I moved.

Thankfully though, my knees could rest.

"Now stay put, my little pup. Otherwise, you won't get breakfast." He came back quickly carrying a red rope. I struggled to get up, but the banana weakened me, stirring around inside me, plunging deeper. He grabbed my wrists and tugged them up over my head before he tied them together. "There we go. You're so beautiful when you're docile." I gnashed my teeth, snarling. "So docile, and yet so untamed. I wonder if I can fit inside there too."

"N-No you're too big."

"Just the head then?"

I shook my head, tears already coming to my eyes as I imagine the pain of being split apart.

"All right." He spread my knees, holding them open.

"Then he's had enough time with you. It's my turn." He pulled out the banana, and I'd barely had time to relax when he stuck his cock inside me, going deep. The banana had stretched me out, so he didn't hurt, but thoroughly filled me up.

He started unpeeling the banana.

I shook my head. That would not be going anywhere near my mouth. It'd been in my ass.

He started to grind into me, making me whimper. The sensations holding me hostage. "Now open wide."

"Mmh-uh." I clamped my lips together. He thrust deeper, hungrier. I lost the battle, and my lips parted.

"Such a good boy." He stuck the banana inside my mouth, and I chewed it. "Chew a lot. I don't want you choking on me." He slowed his thrusting, so I no longer moved back and forth against the floor. He moved the banana deeper inside my mouth. I tried to chew quickly. "I love sticking this in you. Seeing it bunch up against your cheek. Imagining that as my cock."

My eyes watered as he force-fed me. Any faster and he'd be stuffing it down my throat. But at his pace, I had room to chew, however quickly.

"Good." He pulled free of me and stood up. I had a mouthful of banana, still chewing it quickly. He went into the kitchen and returned with some adhesive tape. It was a purple kind, and I had seen him put it on the card table earlier. The hell was he planning?

He grabbed my thigh, spreading my knees apart, and sank back into me. Then he leaned over me and covered my mouth with the tape. "Good, now I can fuck you in peace."

With each of his thrusts, my body moved against the floor rug. Hands bound. My mouth still full and taped shut. I was helpless, and he road me like he had every right to me.

Inside, my instincts loved that I was bound, completely at his mercy. They wanted him to hurt me. To show me how wrong I was for even thinking about disobeying him. I shut my eyes. More instincts swelled inside me, sending tingles throughout my body.

I couldn't do a lot of chewing with the tape on my mouth. But my saliva was working it through, softening it down. Sometimes I could swallow a bit of it, but for the most part, I had a mouthful and had to keep holding it, trying to chew as best I could.

"I'm still hungry." He grabbed up another egg. "I want it on Fern." He cracked it open on my stomach, the egg rolled to both sides of my waist, some of it pooled inside my belly button. He pulled out of me enough so he could lick it off my stomach.

I moaned. Feeling the tips of his fangs as he devoured the mess off my abs. Reaching up, he yanked off the tape, and I yelped.

"Fuck!" The word muffled with my mouth full. I chewed freely.

"Good, eat it down. Now, I've gotta feed you meat."

I swallowed, finishing up the banana. He continued to eat off my stomach before he reached for the bacon strips. "All right, one for you. Aren't I a nice owner?"

I shook my head. "I-I'm not a slave!"

"Eat it." He lowered the bacon to my mouth, and I took it eagerly. "Good. Here's some more." Wereduins came from wolves, so animal meat was particularly tasty. Don fed me a few strips of bacon before he rolled some down my chest and along my abs. With an intake of breath, he feasted off of me. The hungry sounds awoke more instincts. "Now it's time to feed you, really feed you. This time, my meat."

I knew where this was going, and I opened my mouth automatically, although I had yet to suck his cock. He pulled out of me, then brought me onto my knees. Moving over to sit on the couch, he grabbed my tied-up hands and placed me near his dick. "Keep your mouth on it. And if you bite, I'll remove your teeth."

I did as told and took his cock into my mouth. Grabbing the back of my head, he fucked my face. I thought I might gag, but his strong alpha prowess controlled my actions and thoughts, making me relax my throat and breathe through my nose.

I could taste my juices on his cock. My eyes watered, then he came hard inside my mouth. "Swallow it. This is all I'll be feeding you today. Just a little snack. It's high time I get more of myself inside you. You need to be tamed." He stroked my hair in a sensual, loving manner. "You want to be tamed, don't you? But don't you worry, my little beta. I'll submit you, and you'll love it. You'll love belonging to me. I'll keep you safe and hurt you at the same time."

When he had come enough, he pulled out of me. "Clean it up." I wanted to gag at its bitterness, but I licked it up anyway. The moment I finished, he tugged me to my feet and placed me onto his still hard cock. Riding him, I moved my hips in rhythm with what he was doing. I had to get off. All this pleasure was driving me insane.

"Pl-Please, let me come."

Don shook his head, and his sinister smile grew. He cupped the back of my head and kissed me fervently. Parting my lips, he entered me, his forceful tongue mapping out my mouth.

True to his word, for most of the day, he fed me his cock, making me swallow all his cum.

Then he brought me over to the bed. Tying my hands over my head, he attached my wrists to a long chain connected to the bedpost.

At this point, I was so hard—dripping with beta juices, my cock nearly blue—all I did was mewl. He had been submitting me all day. I had no will of my own at this point.

Don climbed on top of me. Moving up the length of my body, he put his cock in my face. My mouth opened automatically, and he stuffed it inside.

I whimpered. Salty tears trailed down my cheeks and into my open mouth that already held a salty taste from his cum.

He stroked my face before gripping my hair and fucked my mouth until all I felt was the glide of his cock along my throat. He was controlling me through his alpha influence, and

I didn't even cough or choke anymore—my body like an extension of his.

His cum filled my mouth, pouring down my chin.

"Good, good, Fern."

Hearing him moan heightened my arousal, and I couldn't stifle the hums and sighs that escaped me.

I ached inside. My cock painfully stiff.

"Please…" I spoke with a mouthful of cock.

"Please?" Don pulled out. He looked up at the ceiling and dragged a hand through his long hair. "Say it again, my little Fern. Again." His voice husky, lustful.

"P-Please."

He moved until he lay on top of me and cupped my face. Immediately, I ground into him, begging for release.

"Please, I need…"

"What do you need?" He held my face between his palms and moved in to kiss me.

I bucked against him and tried to close the distance between our lips. But he pulled away, hovering mere breaths from me.

"Tell me, Fern. What do you need?"

"You…Gods, Don…you!"

He licked my mouth before sucking my bottom lip. "What do you need from me?"

"You—fuck! I need you. Let me cum, please!" All my pride had long been forgotten. All I felt was my painfully hard cock, and my slick beta juices drenching the mattress beneath me.

Don smirked. "I don't know. Not sure you've earned it."

I sobbed so hard my vision blurred and my eyes hurt. "Gods…Don, I'm begging you!"

Don clashed his lips over mine, invading my mouth with his forceful tongue.

In one move, he entered me, thrusting his hips. The mattress creaked as the bed banged against the wall.

"Well then," he whispered into my ear. "Come…"

I didn't need my cock touched or his alpha essence

forcing me over the edge. He simply said those words, and my body practically exploded. I thrust my hips wildly, matching his pace. Tingles of bliss consumed me as he pumped in and out of my ass. Beta juices spurted from my cockhead. At this rate, it wouldn't have shocked me if it came out from my mouth.

A scream ripped from my throat. Then another. And another.

I moved into a state of orgasmic bliss, my mind disassociating like I'd left my body. Before I came down from my orgasm, another one bumped me back up, propelling me forward, spurred on by his movements, by my desperate need for release. I'd gone days without an orgasm.

Don's knots bulged inside me, and I swear I even felt a fourth one, but I was no longer in the waking world. It was like I'd entered Morrígan's Paradise and spent an eternity with the Goddess of Sex, feeding off her lust, rejuvenating every part of my soul, trapping me inside her realm of ecstasy.

I didn't go back to school for two more days. Instead, I served him on my knees. Him fucking me in every position imaginable—some I didn't even know were possible. All this time, he kept me high on his alpha prowess, completely stripping away my mind and will. Making my body act and do whatever he wanted. The message was clear. He didn't need to put up with my rebellion. He could force me to submit. The question really was, would I give him my loyalty of my own free will?

When I returned to school, I found Shamar at his locker. I took a deep breath and slowed my steps. I wondered how it would be between us now. I had interrupted his ceremony and had almost gotten him killed. What if Don hadn't listened to me? Would I now be at his funeral? How ironic and awful would it have been if he'd had died for real, and right after he had crossed over his First Death—something I'd heard zombies call the death they'd experienced during their Change.

Shamar must have sensed he was being watched. He turned around and our gazes met. His skin looked a darker green than normal, with a smidge of brown to it. It made his black eyes stand out. And was his nose skinnier? Were his new looks a result of his Change?

Quickly he broke away and headed off. My stomach panged. He hated me. It made sense. I had endangered his life. Still, I had to at least apologize even if he no longer wanted to be friends.

"Shamar, wait!" He quickened his steps. As a wereduin, I'd always been faster than him, now even more so. He had a shuffle in his step. One leg seemed to move slower than the other. I wondered if this, too, was permanent since he went through his Change. Most zombies shuffled when they walked, and now I knew why. "Please, Shamar, at least let me apologize, then you can hate me."

"Hate you?" He stopped so abruptly that if I had been directly behind him, we would have collided. "Me? Forgive *you*? I'm the one who nearly killed you!"

"Yeah, but that's because I stupidly came over. I mean, even Don told me not to."

"So what?" Angry and animated, his black eyes grew wide, and the saggy bags under them made him look terrifying. "It's okay if I murder my best friend!" He sighed in frustration. "I would've killed you. You…of all people! Fuck this." He stormed off. But with his shuffle, I easily caught up with him.

"Shamar, wait!"

He shook his head. "I bit you and probably came at you looking like a rotting corpse. I almost ate your brains!" Two vamps passing us in the hall turned to look at us.

"Look, you didn't, Okay?"

"Doesn't matter." Shamar sounded like he was about to cry. "I couldn't live with myself." Sure enough, he broke down sobbing.

"Hey, I'm all right." I patted his back. I wasn't good when others started crying on me. Although with Shamar, I probably should have been by now. "I can take a few bites. I'm a wereduin. That's like hugs for us."

He laughed a little bit at that.

I smiled widely. "Seriously, Don bites me a hell of a lot harder." That hadn't been the right thing to say, for his smile faltered.

"Did he hurt you for disobeying him?"

"How did you know I disobeyed him?"

"You said even he knew what to expect."

"Yeah, but that doesn't mean I disobeyed." I shook my head. "Seriously, I'm fine. I was more concerned about you, actually."

"Me?"

"Well, yeah. I mean, you weren't yourself. And then Don showed up, and he was all snarly alpha, and I thought he might kill you."

"In that case I might not hate the bastard after all."

"Did you not hear what I said?"

"Well," Shamar's smile was a mixture of shy and chastising, "I was attacking you."

"Just-Just shut up, okay? I interrupted you. If you would've killed me, it would have been my own damn fault!"

Shamar shook his head. "But you were just worried about me. Sorry I didn't explain it better to you."

"We still friends?"

Shamar looked troubled. "Is it safe, though? I'll get that way from now on. Once a month, sometimes more, I'll get the *Rage*."

"Was that what happened before? Was that your Rage? 'Cause I thought you still needed to go through your Change first?"

Shamar looked sad. "Sorry, guess I really did leave you in the dark." Anger grew in his tone, and he bunched his fists. "To think you almost died because of it."

I shook my head. "Well, it's not like I asked about it all that much, either."

"Maybe not, but…but…" Shamar looked to be trying to find the words.

"Hey, it's okay." I hoped the soothing tone I used reassured him. I was also still curious as to what I had seen.

"So, that was your Rage, huh?"

Shamar nodded. "It happens at the moment of the Change. When we come back to life, it takes a while for our consciousness to follow. And then, periodically, our minds slip again—"

"Like you die again?"

Shamar nodded. "And we revert to how we were exactly after the Change. We'll need to have another ritual to help us return."

I found all of this incredibly interesting. "Do you still remember stuff? Or is it like a complete reboot?" Obviously, they remembered things, maybe I was asking stupid questions now.

"We remember. Just like how I remember everything before, and during."

"During? You remember dying?"

Shamar nodded.

"What was it like?"

"Different. Not sure our First Death is the same as actual death, though." I pondered what he was saying. Still curious. Like I had a magnifier to look into what the actual death process felt like.

"Anyway," Shamar continued, "Those times are called the Rage. The more our minds stabilize in this world, the less it happens." Bitterness laced his tone. "It'll get worse before it gets better. But at some point, it'll peak and finally level out, but that won't happen for a while."

"Level out?"

"Yeah, like it'll happen on a regular schedule, and not so frequently. But at those times when it does happen, then it sorta becomes a ceremony, and we, uh, well, we—"

"Go and hunt humans for their brains." He wasn't telling me anything new there. But I thought that was more of a coming of age thing that happened once.

Shamar nodded. "Yeah, especially when these times become regular. We call it our Awakening. That's the one where it's like a coming of age ceremony. After that, Rage times are sacred for us. Times when we revert back to the state of our creation." He glowered. "It's disgusting. Everything about it is."

Given his pause, I think my assumption about him being embarrassed about sharing all of this info might have been accurate. But his tone, and the anger behind it, made me think that this went beyond embarrassment. Shamar hated who he was. That saddened me.

I liked everything about Shamar. I couldn't even express how happy I was that he was finally sharing more about this with me. He was my best friend, my brother—*bro from another mo*, in our case, another race's *mo*. Shamar hating his zombie-hood was the same as him hating himself as a person.

"Don't talk that way." I didn't sound angry, instead there was a plea in my voice, and he paused. "There's nothing disgusting about you."

He raised his brow.

I chuckled. "Okay, it's not *that* disgusting. But, well, I can relate. I kinda hate being a beta wereduin too. Our culture's all sorts of fucked up. Hell, I saw one of my childhood friends killed by molebats and no one will ever be held responsible for that. No one seems to even care." I couldn't hide the anger and resentment raising in my voice. "For them, it was all her fault. It's fucked up, that's what it is. So, don't, don't ever hate yourself or your culture. I mean, at least what you and the humans do is consensual on both sides, even if it is…well, deadly and gross." I really hoped he didn't participate in that. What the hell would I do if someone killed him during one of those Rage events? "I mean, I don't think you should do it. Not if you can help it, but well, you know, that's just 'cause I don't wanna see you get killed, so—"

"I'm sorry that happened to you, Fern." Shamar caught me off-guard, and I looked at him with wide, curious eyes. "About Myrtle and the molebats. I'm sorry you had to see that." His soft words made my eyes water. How had this conversation become so mushy? "I was terrified for you. And well, I still am. I don't ever want you to be put in danger like that again." His features hardened. "That's why..." He swallowed. "Like I said, this'll be my life now—the Rage. And...I don't want you a part of it."

Pain laced through my heart.

"Not when it'll put you in danger."

I couldn't help the breathy laugh that burst out. Shamar looked betrayed. "Look, I get it. You don't wanna see me get hurt. Arduinna knows how annoying you can get about that."

The corner of his mouth tugged into a smile.

"But we've been friends for like ever. Don't think I'm gonna just wanna stop. Besides, we don't gotta hang out then." I made a wry smirk. "Hey, from now on, I'm gonna go into heat once a month, and there's no way in hell I'm gonna be around. So, just make it like that."

Shamar looked away. He still seemed unsure.

"Listen, Shamar." I rested my hand on his arm and it got his attention. "You're my best friend in the whole fucking world. And I've lost so much," I didn't realize how painful it was to say these thoughts out loud, "Please don't leave me, too."

Shamar seemed to break out of his gloomy cloud. He threw his arms around me. I was happy to say that while his hugs were still chilly at best, at least the Change hadn't made them colder. Neither had it changed Shamar's mind. Not if he was being my overly emotional and clingy best friend. "All right. Okay, I won't leave. Let's still hang out."

Inside, my heart rested. I hadn't lost Shamar. Thank the Gods for that. "Okay, let me grab my things from my locker, and we can head to class."

Shamar nodded, and we walked off. I had to adjust my steps to keep to his slower pace.

Chapter Five

Perfecting You

I had never seen Don dressed up before. He stood in front of the full-length mirror near the walk-in closet, adjusting his tie. The black suit and white undershirt complemented his dark mocha skin. It also emphasized his broad shoulders and powerful chest. His long hair, tied back in a low ponytail, looked the color of twilight instead of its normal silver-brown. His eyes, although not the neon they became at night, were a striking blue. He looked, dare I say, handsome. That pissed me off. I wasn't supposed to find him anything but annoying.

"I want you to wear this." He handed me a velvety piece of fluff.

Eyeing it, I wrinkled my nose. "Not happening."

He sighed. His eyes lingered on my *Meat Skuwls* band tee and worn-out jeans. "There's no way you will be allowed in wearing that."

"Well, who says I wanna go anyway?"

"I do. It's expected of us. End of story."

"I really hate you, you know that?"

"Yeah, yeah." Don went into the bathroom, not looking back. "Put it on, or I will do it for you."

I didn't doubt it. Once again, I hated that I was born a werewolf and a Highborne at that. The celebration banquet we were attending was held by the upper echelons of our society. Werewolves of a certain caliber who had found mates and survived the Silver Offering were invited to attend. Don and I qualified. Really, ours was a good match according to all those stuffy werewolf traditions. Although, since Don had claimed me, even if I hadn't been Highborne, I would still be allowed to the event, simply because of him.

He talked from behind the door. "There will be very important wereduin there, so try not to be a brat."

"No promises." Opening the velvet nightmare, I discovered was two articles of clothing, not a single piece as it originally seemed. The shirt was skin-tight velvet with a low neckline that exposed a sliver of my shoulders. It drew attention to the two claim marks, making the red scars even more prominent on my pale skin.

Don wanted to show off the bites. It was a sign of ownership and told everyone I belonged to him. Of course, we still had one last Offering before the official claiming, so it was premature, but then Don did everything like that. He was confident and walked as if he owned the world, and if he wanted it, he would make it so. He had been remarkable that night during Silver, though. How he fought off the hordes singlehandedly, even after my blunder, which took us outside of his protection zone and on ground tipped in favor of the molebats.

The black color was that of Don's family crest. He was from an older wereduin family whose estate dated back centuries. Reluctantly undressing from my tee and jeans, I slipped it over my head and pulled it into place. The color went great with my black hair, even the parts where my natural brown had started to show. Since Don stole my flat iron, I couldn't straighten my curls. I had spent the day arguing about its location to no avail. Don was one stubborn bastard.

The fabric clung to my body. Down the front of the shirt were three claw slash marks that revealed my abdomen and bellybutton. They weren't made by Don. It was the latest fashion for Highborne betas.

I looked ridiculous and was glad none of my friends could see me. Otherwise, I'd never live it down. I stepped into the pants. The black velvet, also skintight, felt soft and smooth and shaped my body nicely. Claw marks slashed down the legs, but unlike with the shirt, underneath was blue silk.

"Looks good on you." Don stood in the hall. A comb, styling gel, and hair spray in his hands.

"Okay, so you won't let me style it myself, but now you're gonna do it?" Bitterness laced my voice.

"Well, of course, I can't have you looking like a goth street kid."

"It's not goth."

"Right."

"Just go away. Didn't you like my curls?"

Coming over, he stood behind me in front of the body length mirror in our walk-in closet.

Ours? No, his. There was no way I was thinking about this place, however nice, as my house.

He brushed my hair, straightening down the curls.

"How the hell do you know how to do this anyway? You've got straight hair."

He chuckled. "It's not hard when you know what you're looking for." He succeeded in straightening my hair and parted it in the middle, using styling gel and then spraying it in place.

"Can't I just put on a little eyeliner?"

Don raised a brow. "What do you think I'm going to say to that?"

"That you'll let me!" He smirked at my enthusiasm, then shook his head. What the heck did stupid Don know anyway? Shamar once said my eyes were one of my best features, and the liner made them stand out. He also liked the warm brown hue in the center that haloed my irises, said it made them visible in the otherwise jet-black color. Unlike Don the grumpy asshole, Shamar had great fashion. "This isn't me, you know?" He didn't know. And he didn't seem to care. "I hate alphas."

"Oh, really?" He concentrated on my hair. "Anything you do like?"

"Not you, that's for sure, rapist."

"All right, now you're presentable."

I went to grab my lip piercing from its case in the bathroom.

"Nope, not wearing that either. Geez, Fern, don't be such a pain."

"No one's forcing you to keep me. Why not return me if I'm so annoying?"

"Just come on." He went to take my hand, but I snatched it away.

"I can walk just fine."

"'Course you can. But know this, if you act like a little brat, I will punish you, and you won't like it."

Simply saying that made me want to rebel if nothing else but for that reason alone.

He locked up, leaving small lights on, so the entirety of the living room, complete with the wide oak that split through the middle, and the complimenting white couch and rug, stood out in the large glass windows. It wasn't a very private house, that was for sure. Thankfully, he lived in a wooded area, and there was a long driveway before we came across other houses.

I didn't talk to him the entire ride there. Looking out the window, I watched the dense trees, and the houses dispersed around them, with some growing through them like ours. Wereduin liked to live surrounded by forests. Open spaces unsettled most of us.

Finally, we arrived at the Grand Hotel. It was the largest hotel in the city and a symbol of Highborne influence in society. The building looked like a green screw made of glass. It spiraled around a sequoia-oak, with the bulk of it housed inside the trunk. It didn't kill the tree, thanks to wereduin architects who knew what they were doing.

I hated it and immediately wished I was in The Crone's Head, an emo-metalhead club where my friends and I hung out.

The valet out front parked the car, allowing Don and I to go inside. The velvety carpeted walkway steps gently spiraled around the base of the trunk and into the main lobby.

Don took my arm and put it through his. Grumbling, I wanted to throw him off, but stepping inside got me a bit distracted. The hotel had a wide-open lobby with crystal chandeliers and golden stairs. It was decked out for the occasion. The attendants at the lobby were quick to bow to us and directed us up the stairs to the party. My arm was still in Don's when he placed his other hand on top of mine, trapping me in place. Rolling my eyes, I let him lead me around.

Even though there were wereduins I had seen at countless holiday parties and get-togethers when I was growing up, there were still so many I didn't know.

A distinguished older wereduin called Don over. He looked like he bathed in ules. His suit alone had to cost a normal wolf's annual salary. He could have been my grandpa given his age and his gray and white facial fur. His beta, an attractive female, looked like she'd been with him for a while. She stood at his side, decked in jewels and splendor, greeting other wereduins politely.

"Ah, Donovan. It's great to see you again." The older wereduin shook Don's hand. My eyes were drawn to the salt-and-pepper color of his body fur on the back of his hand. His deep, furrowed brow made him look stern even when he smiled. A white scar ran through his eye. Although he was an older gentleman, he was seasoned in fighting with the marks to show it.

"It has been far too long, Lord Kenneally." Don then turned to me. "I'd like to introduce you to my mate, Fern."

"Ah, it is very nice to see you again, Fern." He adjusted his black top hat, revealing the peaks of his pointy ears and the ends of his thick mane, also salt-and-pepper in color. He looked as arrogant as Don. I immediately disliked him.

"We've met before?" I might have said that impolitely because Don squeezed my hand.

"Why, of course, your mother is not only legendary but quite the host. You were a pup then. I imagine you would not remember it." He stroked his goatee as his eyes traveled my body, taking me in. Beneath his mustache, his lips quirked in a lopsided smile. "I see you've grown into a fine beta." There was something off-putting about how he looked at me, like a customer examining wares in a shop.

I nodded, not knowing how to reply. Don squeezed my hand again. "Thanks," I said, taking Don's hint. It seemed weird to me how only a few months ago, I was a pup, and one birthday suddenly changed everything.

"I'd heard Pirkko's beta pup had come of age." He tipped my chin up. With a firm grip and weather-worn fingers, he made me look in either direction. I felt like a prized pig. I bunched my fist, not held by Don. "Yes, quite a fine beta, indeed. Pirkko did not undersell you. You chose well Donovan." I glanced at Don. It was strange that Don let Kenneally touch me. I thought he would tear him up for sure.

When Lord Kenneally released me, I took a half step back. I hadn't realized I'd stepped behind Don until he put his arm around me. Kenneally gave me a thin, belittling smile. I bristled. I didn't want to appear weak around that asshole. Don's scent soothed me. I couldn't believe Kenneally unsettled me enough that I sought out Don's comfort. Worse yet, how natural it felt to rely on him. What the hell was wrong with me?

"He looks quite fond of you." Fucking asshole talking about me as if I wasn't even there.

"Thank you, I am quite fond of him." I expected Don to sound threatening, but he was still the gentleman he'd been since we arrived. Perhaps I was overthinking this, but Don acted more arrogant than normal. Sounding like the pompous Highborne he was, standing around talking about me as if I wasn't present. *Asshole.*

"He's okay." Both looked surprised when I responded. The disapproval on Don's face was obvious. Fuck him. That was what he got for disregarding me like that.

Kenneally's furrowed brows managed to narrow even farther. Not taking his eyes off me, he addressed Don. When he spoke, his voice remained the posh tone of a gentleman. "He's quite untamed, Donovan. I hope you can handle him."

"Never been one to want it easy." Smirking, Don stuck out his chest, tilting his chin up.

Lord Kenneally's eyes found the shiny bite marks between my shoulders and neck. Immediately, I wanted to cover up. He made me feel even more vulnerable. "It's nice to see your family's emblem strong and proud." Bitemarks had a similar look across families, hence why the bus driver allowed me to pay the fare when I went to Shamar's that time. Don marking me wasn't just an indication that I belonged to him, but to his family, as well.

For a moment, Lord Kenneally looked so pleased I feared

he might try to touch my bitemarks, but he didn't. Perhaps that would be crossing the line. What would Don have done if he had? I was curious, but I didn't like the idea of some stranger touching me. Inwardly, I growled. Since when did Don stop being a stranger?

Don didn't seem on edge at all, nor did he cover me. Instead, he showed off my bare shoulders—his marks red and ugly against my pale skin. I wondered if Kenneally knew Don was flaunting. And if he did, was he bothered?

They talked about boring things and paid little attention to me. At least they no longer talked about me like I wasn't right beside them.

"Come, I want to introduce you." Kenneally directed Don toward other stuffy looking Wereduins, all looking pompous, rich, and annoying.

Don was the perfect gentlemen throughout the night, politely shaking hands, choosing the right dinner conversations. It made me sick, but also made me curious. Don was nothing but a bully in my eyes. He didn't dress poorly by any means, but seeing him in such a fancy suit, speaking with important wereduins, and not looking out of place, was new to me. He treated me like an adult, not his child or his burden. I was his mate.

Don had been right about his clothing choice for me. All the other betas were dressed in their best. I didn't look out of place at all. In fact, wereduins kept complimenting me, or rather complimenting Don on my behalf. And that jerk was looking even smugger.

There were many pairings. That trio was there, the two alpha males and their female beta. She had another shiny mark on the other side of her neck, in the valley between her shoulders—the same place Don had bitten me. Her bite marks were doubled, one over the other. Both alphas had bitten her. She followed behind one of them, hugging onto his arm, her face wistful. Her other alpha's hand rested on the small of her back. Both alphas were engaged in conversation, laughing about something I couldn't hear. Now in the light, they looked strikingly similar enough to be twins. That would explain why they shared a beta. Twins in our culture were special and always kept together.

Then I saw a muzzled beta. His alpha had also collared him. His bite mark, especially the one on the opposite shoulder, was shiny and off and a bit glossy as well. *Wait a minute?* He wasn't one of those reclaimed betas, was he? Upon closer look, that appeared to be the case.

The alpha who had claimed him in the Hunt must have lost him to another. I wondered what had happened to him. I had seen the molebats get one alpha. How many others had they gotten? Had the beta's alpha shared that same fate? Or maybe he had let him go? There was the third option, and that was the new alpha challenged the last one and won.

Don's hand rested on my ass for a moment and brought my attention back to him. Then he took my hand, intertwining our fingers. For a moment, my senses thought of nothing but him. It made me lightheaded. I mentally kicked myself. I didn't want to get *wobbly-legged* for an asshole like Don.

The celebration was the opposite of the rest of the Offering events. Here, wereduins wore suits and dresses and ate off of refined porcelain plates and drank expensive tea. There was no sign that nights before, some of them had thrown children to monsters to be devoured. My thoughts returned to poor Myrtle. Was her asshole alpha here? Papa had told me he was a Highborne, too. I wanted to track down that bastard and kill him myself, alpha or not.

Instead, I let Don lead me around. He opened doors for me and even pulled out my chair. I sat at the table and ate the fancy foods I grew up with on special occasions. But this time, I wasn't as hungry. I should have felt comfortable because I had been around parties like this my whole life, but I didn't.

Afterward, Don introduced me to yet more wereduins. An older female alpha introduced Don to three ancient-looking Highborne werewolves, and they all ogled over me like I was choice meat. I forgot all their names the moment I heard them. Through all this, however, Don kept me close. Sometimes he would lead me by a hand on the small of my back. Other times his hand found mine, but he never left my side the entire night. Of all the wereduins I met there, Lord Kenneally was the most unsettling.

When we finally got home, I was exhausted after all the pomp and wanted to laze on the couch and binge on a series or maybe stream some movies. Shamar said *Fadeaway Tomb 2* was an even better movie than the first one. Since the producers had gotten Maggot Lore to return, odds were good that Shamar was right. All of Maggot Lore's movies were awesome. He was one of my favorite zombie actors—he kicked ass in horror films.

I changed into some sweats and my *Fangorre* tee before I collapsed onto the couch. Don came out of the bedroom. He no longer wore a suit, but a gray tank top and jeans. His broad shoulders and muscular chest looked sturdy and a little sexy.

Stop thinking that way about stupid Don! There's no way I'm accepting that arrogant jerk as my alpha.

"We're going out."

I had just flipped on the TV. "What?"

"I gotta take care of a few things."

"Uh, okay, have fun."

"You're coming too."

"What? Why?"

"Because it's dark out, and I don't want you to get hurt stupidly trying to run away again."

"Who said I'll run away?"

"I do." Don put on his shoes. "I'll barely be down the street before you'll be out the door. Besides…" He looked over to me and smiled, catching me off guard. "I wanna take you somewhere."

"Somewhere?"

"Yeah."

"I'm tired, though." I was also curious.

"Yeah, me too."

"Then why go out?"

Don rolled his shoulders before popping his neck from side to side. "Let's just say everyone has their own way of letting off steam." His smile was in his voice.

That made me more curious, so I got up and went to put on my shoes.

Instead of taking his car, we used public transportation into the city. The subway was quieter at this hour. I was about to ask Don where the heck we were going, but his cell rang.

"All right, we're almost there," he said into the phone, quirking his lips in a half-smile. "So, you can bitch to me in person." When we came to our destination, he tugged my elbow to get me to follow. We walked a few blocks to a rundown, dark alley that slowly descended into the city's underbelly.

"The Underbelly?"

Don smirked at the fear behind my tone. "You're not scared, are you?"

I puffed out my chest. "Yeah, right."

The Underbelly lay below the city. It was made up of drainage tunnels, sewers, and other underground rivers and caverns. We walked through a large drainage sewer, avoiding the stream of water winding through the center. I stayed on the stone ledge, hugging close to the stone walls. The air was damp, and the smell was just as bad as one would expect. Finally, the tunnel opened into a medium-sized cavern. A dock spread across the two banks separated by a subterranean river—sludge and grime from the sewer streams ran into it. The river itself ran in either direction.

Longboats were docked. They resembled those the God Arawn's servants used to ferry the damned souls into the Shadows. Toward the end of the dock on the other side of the river was a dilapidated inn. Tunnels surrounded it, venturing farther into the Underbelly. This was definitely a black-market port. All sorts of illegal wares were sold there. Not to mention events that went below the radar of our society. Street peddlers occupied different corners. It probably had illegal fighting, gambling, and even drug trafficking as well. Representatives of various races were all around us.

Several wereduins and trolls loaded things on and off boats while two goblins had digital rosters in hand. One argued with a boat captain. The tall human towered over the goblin, who didn't seem intimidated in the least. They were too far away to hear what they said. Three zombies passed me. Two rolled a large cage containing several barely dressed humans. A large werewolf stalked beside them, seemingly serving as the zombies' bodyguard.

My stomach sickened. I wondered if this was how the zombies procured human flesh. Normally, human flesh wasn't sold but won over by zombies from battles with humans—not this. It served as a grim reminder that I was with society's lowlifes.

What the heck did Don even want with a place like this? He was a Highborne, correct? What business did he have in the Underbelly?

We entered the inn. It wasn't large, but standard size and very rundown.

A few hags were at the tables trying to sell their wares. One called out to Don.

"Lo there, handsome. Fer dat ponytail a urs, I'll give yeh good fortune."

He flashed her cold eyes and didn't stop. He guided us down into the cellar. Inside was a boxing ring, and bets were being taken. At the center of the ring, a troll with a crooked nose and large tusks fought against a wereduin in full werewolf form. Its massive size dwarfed the troll. Blood spattered all over the mat.

"W-What are we doing here?"

"Ah, the rat lives!" A gnarly old werewolf slapped Don's back in a friendly gesture. "Thought yah might be dead."

"Mites," Don greeted him like they were old friends. "Promise is a promise. Besides," Don smiled, "last I recall, someone owed me a drink."

"And you owe me a win!" Mites's grin revealed two

chipped fangs. He didn't even bother to leave werewolf form, nor did he cover himself with clothing. Thankfully, his thick, matted fur hid his crotch.

"Well, then lucky for you, I lived through the night, and you can get your money back."

"Money back? Win?" I tugged Don's arm. "What are you talking about?"

Don didn't get a chance to answer me before two more wereduins greeted him in the same manner. These two looked around his age, maybe a bit older. One was a large beast of a wolf. The other was smaller than Don. That was when I noticed the smaller of the two carried a chain. Behind him was a beta, her eyes covered with a blindfold. Bruises covered her cheeks and arms. She wore next to nothing, so it was easy to see where she was hurt. Was she a slave beta? Anger ran through my veins. Who the hell were these assholes?

"Brawny," Don nodded to him. Brawny tugged the beta against his leg, using the chain to yank her. "Looks like Mites smelled a rat after all." They broke into conversation. It didn't seem like Don was bothered in the least that Brawny dragged around a battered beta.

Don was different here. More untamed. Nothing like the gentlemen he had been inside the celebration ball. So far, I had seen three different sides to Don. The pervert, the gentleman, and the ruffian. Brawny turned his eyes on me.

"Oh? Snagged yourself a cutie?" Brawny's hungry leer revealed his jagged fangs. His yellow eyes matched the color of his spiky hair that went past his pointed ears.

I didn't like that I was suddenly the center of attention, especially from these guys. They had an aloofness as if they were talking about the latest toy Don had purchased.

Don's arm went around my shoulders. I wanted to throw him off, but this didn't seem like the best place to show my rebellion, not with stray alphas straggling about. I didn't want to be left alone with his friends, either. I hated how uncomfortable I felt, but Don had taken me out of my element. I wanted to go home.

"He's mine, so don't get any ideas." Heat radiated from Don's side. His arm around me felt secure. I despised it, but I didn't want him to stop holding me.

"So, we haven't had that win, Donny boy?" Don's other friend, that large beast of a wereduin, looked over to the ring. The troll had won. Perhaps size wasn't everything.

Wait a second? *Win?*

Surely Don wasn't planning on fighting? Inwardly I shook my head at the thought. *Nah.* I knew Don liked fighting and all, but street fights? Surely, even he hadn't sunk that low. They must have been talking about Don placing a bet.

"You know, Jut," Don addressed the gigantic wereduin, "I've yet to see your fat ass enter." He arched an eyebrow, giving a superior little smirk. "'Course, Mites wants to win back his money tonight."

Jut scratched his ear with a large claw, his deep tone nonchalant. "All this talk, Donny boy, and how did last time turn out?"

"Just wanted to see Mites shit himself when he lost those bets." Don was cocky as always. And it seemed like, yes, he did plan on fighting.

What the hell? Did this guy ever *not* want to fight? He already trained a lot with his sects and served as a trainer, too. Plus, *spawn* was a pretty vicious sport when it came to fighting, and Don was auditioning for the pros. I'd have thought he'd had his fill of it. Apparently not. It looked like fighting was to Don what music was to me.

Jut made even Don look small. Unlike most wereduins, he didn't have pointy ears. They looked like giant human ones. The tip of his huge nose was round like a ball. *Wait a min*—was he a half breed?

They were rare among wereduins because of the shame, but Don's friend Jut definitely looked the part. He kind of reminded me of a giant. Of course, the only giants I'd seen were on TV, mostly because they were a mountain race. The ones that did mingle tended to be superstars and guaranteed parts in movies that needed giants, kind of like how oboe players were coveted whereas flute players were plentiful, as I had learned when I took band my first year of high school.

Still, wereduins, like vampires, were all about racial purity. Maybe that was why Jut was in a place such as this.

"You better not be sayin' you lost on purpose, asshole!" Mites grumbled, but I cut him off, grabbing Don's arm.

"What are you doing? You're not gonna fight, are you?"

"Why?" The amusement in Don's tone made me want to punch him. "You worried about me?"

"You wish! I just don't wanna end up dragging your bloody ass home."

Don grabbed me so quick I had no time to react, and he tugged me close. "I'd like to see you dragging me home." His warm breath tickled my ear before he nipped the piercing in my cartilage. "But you've started to call our place home, and you're worried about me. Should I call this a win?"

I tried to shake him off, but no such luck. He tugged my back against his chest and nibbled my neck before his hand invaded my sweatpants, and he played with me for a bit. I screwed my eyes shut, not wanting to see his friends' leers or the other scruffy patrons. I continued to struggle, but it only excited him more.

"After this," he said low into my ear, "I'm gonna be so worked up. Think you can handle it, little pup?"

"G-Get off."

"Not happening." His husky whisper made me shiver.

Brawny's voice interrupted us. "Well, are yah fightin'? Or are yah just gonna eat that tasty beta of yours?"

Don's chuckle tickled the light fuzz on my lobe. I felt his reluctance when he let me go. They all headed to the ring, leaving me behind, talking about things I didn't know the context of. When they made it to the ring, Don pulled off his shirt to reveal his well-defined chest, solid like a rock, with smooth dark skin over firm muscles. I swallowed. He was unbelievably hot!

That pissed me off. *Don, hot? Yeah, fucking right!* Why the fuck had he made me come? I didn't even like him. If anything,

I hoped he'd get so beaten up that I could escape.

Don climbed into the ring; Mites went up with him. It reminded me of some of the boxing movies I'd watched.

"You shouldn't stay too close, pup. Unless you wanna get a blood bath." Brawny's voice stole my attention. He and his beta were a few paces behind me. I didn't want to be covered in blood, so I joined them.

Don and the troll got face to face. Both breathing harshly, focusing. The moment the ref's hand went up to tell them to begin, Don transformed into a werewolf. In an instant, the two of them were fighting. Like the other werewolf, Don was taller than the troll. But the troll, closer to the ground, was more compact and could move quicker.

Don slashed across his chest, but he got out of the way. Quickly he turned and gored his horns into Don's shoulder. He drew blood. Don's eyes lit up, a smile ghosted on his lips. Was he enjoying this? As the fight continued, the idea of wanting him to get hurt diminished.

Don backed the troll into a corner. Instantly, he crouched and attacked into the troll's stomach, his claws slashed through flesh, sending blood onto the floor. The troll howled in pain and rammed his tusks into Don, leaving bloody protrusion marks on his chest. Don seemed to get more excited, both in the way his upper lip curled and the quickness of his movements.

With a series of kicks, the troll used his horned toenails to do damage. He was very quick, but Don was quicker. He was more like the Don I had seen during the Silver Offering—a different werewolf than the one who'd started out. He had the troll on the defensive. His teeth tore into the toes of the troll's kick that was too slow. Don had him on the floor, rolling around. They scratched each other, creating long deep gashes. The Troll's tusk split Don's shoulder, and he hissed in pain.

The Troll got a good kick in and jumped to his feet, only to be attacked from below. He fell, head smashing into the side of the ring. Blood from his mouth and nose sprayed all over the floor. And all over me. When the hell had I moved closer?

Damn it! I loved my *Fangorre* shirt. It was one of the most comfortable tees I owned. And given that *Fangorre* had stopped touring, I doubted I'd be able to replace it. They were an older band, although they still rocked. Thankfully, I had turned, and the spray ended up covering my shoulder and not the *Fangorre's* classic logo—werewolf fangs dripping with blood. The green might be hard to get out, though. *Fucking troll.*

Don wiped the floor with the poor guy. It looked like he had even broken the troll's arm. Even though the troll tore Don up wherever he could, he was getting his ass kicked. I wondered how long the fight would go on. The other werewolf had needed to be carried out of the ring. Would Don end up doing that to the troll? Don sank his teeth into the Troll's back, and he collapsed to the floor. Cheers broke out all around me.

"Finish him!"

"Break him open!"

What? What the hell? "No, don't!" He probably couldn't hear me, but I yelled anyway. "Please! Don't!"

Don's jaws opened, his fangs dripping with the troll's green blood. Scratches on his shoulders and his chest, he was bruised all over. He met my eyes. I watched him, unable to say anything, but my fear had to be apparent.

The ref tugged Don's arm up in the air. "And the winner!"

The announcer took over from there. "What's this? Floor's too clean? No entrails tonight? Has the Black Beast gone soft?" Then he looked at the troll. "Looks like Splinter is *Puker* now!" The troll leaned over the side and vomited green chunks into the crowd. I thanked every Goddess and God I knew that we were not on that side.

Don jumped down from the ring, reverting back into a Wereduin. His pseudo-clothes reappeared. Now that I thought about it, a lot of his clothes were pseudo. Not like that should have been surprising given that he was an alpha, and they changed forms constantly, unlike betas. Mites and Jut surrounded him. He was covered in sweat. The red blood on his shoulder was stark against his dark skin.

"So, what did you think, little man?" Brawny came over and was about to put his arm around me but thought better of it. "All wet and ready for him now?"

"Fuck you." I shoved away from him. "Dammit, Don! What the hell were you thinking?" I wasn't sure why I was acting like the worried mother hen, but the words just rushed out.

Don went to put his arm around me, but I pushed him away. He stank of sweat and blood.

"Get off! I fucking love this shirt! There's no way you're touching me before you shower."

His friends laughed. It pissed me off more.

Brawny guffawed. "Already got a little *pup maker*, don't cha?" I wanted to punch him even more than I wanted to rip off Don's haughty smirk.

The crowd swamped in on us, coming to retrieve or give up their money, depending on their bets. I would have been pushed to the outside, but Don shielded me from most of it.

I took out some gauze, cloth, and rubbing alcohol from above the sink, as Don took a seat on the closed toilet. The master bathroom was covered in mirrors, so I saw him moving his long hair to the side and looking over his shoulder at the wound.

He must have felt me watching, for his gaze found mine. Quickly, I returned to my task of pouring the alcohol on the cloth.

"Are you doctoring me, my little Fern?" Don said with a half-smile when I came over to his side.

I grumbled and took the cloth dipped into alcohol to his shoulder. "I got your *little* right here!" He hissed in a breath as I dabbed his skin. "See, this is why I told you not to fight. Now you're getting all sorts of wrong ideas from me doing this." I wiped the blood from his wound and listened as his dark mocha skin sang beneath the cloth. I hadn't noticed that he had three little brown birthmarks on his shoulder before. When he looked at me, I paused. "I told you not to get any ideas." I touched more alcohol to his wound, and he sucked in a breath.

He watched me from one of the many mirrors, and a slow smile grew. "Then stop putting ideas into my head." He grabbed my hand.

"Let go."

He shook his head.

"I'm not done cleaning up your injuries yet."

"Think I care about that?"

Anger welled up, although I didn't know quite why. But the more I looked at the deep gashes on his body, the angrier I got. "So, you let yourself get beaten up, and now you won't even let me doctor you!"

His eyes widened, and he released my hand. Quickly I went to wash out the blood from the cloth, so I could use it again. I didn't want to see his face, but I caught it anyway through the mirror.

"Do you care about me, my little Fern?"

"'Course not. I just don't want you to get an infection and get us killed in the Third Offering."

He laughed. "So, you're accepting that I've won you over?"

"I didn't say that." I moved to his other shoulder, also injured. "Take off your shirt."

His smile showed his teeth more as he looked at me and tugged his tank over his head, first revealing his rock-hard abdomen, then his well-built chest. His shoulders looked even broader without his shirt on. Don was surprisingly handsome if I allowed myself to think that about another guy. He held eye contact, and I swallowed hard. My hand trembled as I dragged the rag along his collarbone and down his pec. Looking away, I focused on the task at hand.

Cleaning more blood off his skin, I treated it with alcohol. His body heat seeped through the cloth and warmed my fingers. When I went to clean his back, I could no longer avoid looking at him with all the surrounding mirrors. His pensive blue eyes grabbed hold of me, and I couldn't look away. I rubbed the wet cloth over his broad shoulders before I trailed down his defined back, tracing the contours of his large back tattoo.

I had a chance to really study Don's tattoo. The Twins of War looked even more menacing. Their vivid colors made them appear ready to jump off his skin and attack their unseen foe. I trailed the rag up and down his back, removing blood from Babd Cath's torso and from Camalus's fist weapon.

"Like what you see, my pet?"

I glanced away, but with those damn mirrors, the only safe place to look was at his skin.

Shaking my head, I couldn't reply. I was already trembling, a low ache filling my groin. I wanted him to take me in his strong arms. I wanted to drag my claws down his back. I wanted…to hate myself for these thoughts, but my brain was growing numb. If I focused on the task at hand, I could keep control. But as I continued to touch his firm body, the feel of his skin along with his masculine scent, all began to awaken my desire.

I cleaned the cut on his side with alcohol after wiping it down. His hand snatched mine, and I dropped the gauze, alcohol spilling onto the floor. He pulled me into his lap, and I straddled him.

"St-Stop." I could barely breathe, my heart in my throat.

Forcing my head back, he attacked my neck. I cried out as his teeth tore into the second claim mark, reinforcing it. My eyes found the mirrors on the ceiling, where I saw him devouring me from an entirely new angle. With my mouth still open, the moans wouldn't stop. His dark physique dominated my pale, smaller frame as he held me in his muscular arms. I looked so helpless, but it didn't upset me like I wanted it to.

"I told you, you better be ready to handle me." I wanted him to remind me again—to make me realize who I belonged to. To fuck me, again and again, until those words drilled into my brain. "You're thinking about it right now, my little Fern? Aren't you? Thinking about all the ways I'm going to submit you." My bottom lip trembled as he licked up my neck to my cheek. Cupping my face, he kissed me with deep, open-mouthed kisses.

Clutching my ass, he stood and took me over to the wall. He pressed me against it and yanked off my clothing. I wanted to grab his pants, unbuckle his jeans, but my pride stopped me.

"Go ahead. You can do it. Touch me." Holding me up with one hand and the wall supporting me, he took my hand and placed it on the buttons of his jeans. "Go on," he whispered into my ear, giving me goosebumps. "Give in to your desire. Free my cock, so I can stick it inside you."

A moan ripped from my throat as he dragged his tongue down my neck and littered kisses on my skin, all the while continuing to whisper naughty, little bits of poison into my ear. "Like you did that first night when you ran into that dead end. You saw it, didn't you?"

I shook my head.

"Don't lie, Fern." His hand took mine and slid it into his pants, popping open the two buttons. "You saw the exit, that if you took the right, you'd escape." He kept moving my hand down. "But if you took the left, you'd be trapped. You'd be mine. And you chose the left."

"N-Not true."

He attacked my mouth with a harsh kiss, forcing his tongue inside, playing with mine—my body surrendering, even if my mind still felt it had a chance at resisting. As he continued to fuck my mouth with his tongue, he brought my hand into his boxers.

"You did, and you know it. That night I saw it in your eyes. What your body painfully craved." He closed my hand around his cock, holding his hand over mine so I couldn't pull away. "And do you know what?" I ached so badly it hurt. My beta juices ran down my thighs, and my dick grew painfully hard. I couldn't believe how much he worked me up, and he hadn't even touched me. "You wanted me inside you. You ached to be mine."

He was right. I did remember seeing what looked like an exit behind a shrub, only my body didn't take that path.

Subconsciously I had taken a left. Somewhere in my heart, I knew I was running to my doom. I just hadn't wanted to think about it. All I focused on at that time was to be free. Not to be claimed, or fucked, or turned into someone's beta, but even if my mind had not wanted it, my body had.

He brought my hand out from his pants until he pressed it against the mirror. "Look, Fern." I hadn't realized I'd shut my eyes. "Look at yourself. Look at how you're responding to a few, simple words."

I cracked my eyes open, and I saw myself in the mirror. That wasn't me. I couldn't be that person flushed and panting in his arms—cheeks red, mouth open, hot breaths against the closest mirror. My body trembled. The blush went down my neck and onto my chest. A few words had reduced me to putty in his hands. His sensual smile turned devilish. "Now free me, Fern." My hand trembled. "Free my cock."

Slowly, I reached between us. I brought the jeans' zipper down as far as it would go.

"Go inside, all the way in."

My hand descended into his boxers, and I wrapped my fingers around the thick, pulsing flesh of his cock. He moved enough to allow me to take it out. He cupped my chin and made me look at him. Trails of liquid escaped my eyes. My body so turned on, trembling, gasping, unable to stop the sound of lust. It was embarrassing how he was able to bring me to this state. Embarrassing. Degrading. How he could own my body simply with his voice.

"Good. Now sit on my cock."

I lifted my hips, and he grabbed me. Aligning his erect cock to my hole, he thrust inside me. My mouth fell open. He rocked into me, holding me tightly, his hips nailing me to the wall, my ass cheeks making smudges on the glass.

"Gods, look how much you want me." He thrust me down on his cock as he plowed up into me. From the new angle, it penetrated a different section of my inner walls. Pleasure burst behind my eyelids. My moans were loud in the room, filling it up with sounds I didn't recognize.

"You wanted me then too, didn't you, Fern?" All I could do was cry out. My face contorted in pleasure-pain at the intensity.

"Answer me."

I nodded, tears trailing my cheeks from want, from need, from pushing my body to the limits of arousal. All I wanted was release.

"You wanted me inside you. To be the first to open your ass. To make you know your place beneath your alpha. Didn't you?" His tone turned harsh. "Didn't you!" His demanding voice pulled the answer straight from my soul.

"Yes!" I tried to brace against the wall with my sweaty hands, tried to reach for some control, but it didn't matter what I did. At that moment, I was completely without power while he held it all. He could move my body how he liked. He could enter me as deep or as shallow as he desired. He could plug me up all night, and I wouldn't be able to stop him. And maybe I didn't want to. I had a tough time knowing what was going through my head during the Hunt. Maybe it was as he said? Maybe even in my darkest thoughts, I wanted him.

"Again, Fern. Admit to that depravity inside your heart that begged for me. That wanted me to force myself inside you. That wanted me to make you take it, no matter how much you didn't like it. That bestial force inside you that would stop at nothing to see you fucked and mated. To have my cock inside you, claiming you hard."

His teeth sunk into the first claim mark, blood trailed down my neck and shoulder as he tore open the wound. My mind was overcome by him. He was breaking down all my defenses.

Was he right? Did I want to be caught? To be trapped? To be raped in that dead-end, where no one could save me. If I hadn't, why hadn't I chosen the other path? I told myself it was because I'd been too distraught to see clearly. Maybe that wasn't the case.

As his fangs bore into me and his cock invaded my body, those words poisoned my mind, warring with my memories of that night. Coloring them with what he told me had happened. Brainwashing—mind-fucking me. I wasn't sure what he was doing to me. Morphing my thoughts, owning not only my body but my mind as well.

Giving in to him, I cried out in ecstasy as my cum burst out over our abdomens pressed together. My mind was too lost to get out from under his words. I replayed that night over and over in my mind, seeing myself willingly running down that path, hoping he would catch me, even if I didn't want him to. I didn't want him to stop until he took my virginity, fucked me hard, raped my unwilling body because I belonged to him. I belonged to him from the first moment I saw him, looking majestic with his shining black fur.

He held me tightly, and I sagged against his chest. Spent. His loud breaths against my ear condensed on the mirror behind us. Now that I was coming down, the reality of what I'd said hit me hard, and I trembled in his arms.

"Shh." He pressed a kiss to my temple. I couldn't stop shivering. Had I really wanted to be raped? What was wrong with me? Fear jolted inside me.

I don't wanna lose myself.

"You won't," Don whispered softly in my ear. Had I said those things out loud—revealed a bit of my heart to him? I felt so vulnerable. Like someone could break me open and shatter me all over the floor. "I won't let that happen. You're safe with me, Fern." He secured me in his arms, pressing another kiss to my temple. "Submit to me. Submit to your alpha. I won't break your trust, nor will I abuse my power." His warmth slowed my shivering. Surprisingly, his gentle words were exactly the reassurance I needed to hear. "Don't worry, I've got you."

He leaned back, and I screwed my eyes shut, too embarrassed to look at him. Tenderly he kissed my forehead and cheeks and along my nose. I still couldn't look at him but was relieved when his warm lips covered mine. He cupped my face between his palms.

"Fern? Look at me?" Rapidly, I shook my head. His exhale sounded like a laugh. "Suit yourself." He kissed me again, his mouth gentle. Even though my thoughts were still jumbled, I savored his taste and the warmth of his kisses.

The next morning, I awoke to an empty bed. For a moment, I studied his side of the mattress and the indent in the shape of his body. Honestly, I was kind of shocked to find him gone. I thought for sure he'd attack me first thing in the morning, especially after what he did to me at my school that one time I left without us having sex. Don was so confusing.

Rolling over to his side, I nuzzled his pillow and inhaled deeply. It smelled strongly of him. For a moment, I wanted to roll around in his rich scent.

My mind strayed to memories of the night before. He had said that I wanted him, even that first night when he claimed me at the Hunt. But was he right? Had I wanted him to catch me that night? I had no idea. I couldn't remember. There may have been some of those thoughts in my head. Had I chosen the wrong path on purpose? For him to make me his? That thought sent a thrill up and down my spine. Shaking my head, I tried to compose myself. More than likely, this was another one of Don's ploys to get me to say super embarrassing things. *Godsdamned pompous jerk.*

My mind returned to last night when he'd held me.

I won't let that happen. You're safe with me, Fern. What had he meant by that? Did he really plan on letting me still be me after the mating? Should I even trust him? Alphas didn't have to give their betas much freedom; our instincts pretty much blinded us to them regardless. Losing myself like that was what scared me most. I didn't want to become someone else without a will of my own.

You won't. I won't let that happen. I recalled the strength of his body and how secure it had felt being held by him.

Now thoroughly confused, I got up and got ready. When I made it into the living room, Don was on the tail-end of a phone call. I wouldn't have cared except for that last part he said at the end of the conversation.

"Morning," he said when I came into the kitchen. He sat

at the kitchen table, sipping his coffee. He'd finished his plate and was reading the Daily Fang.

"Morning," I said under my breath, but he smiled at me as if he'd heard it. Quickly, I searched the pantry for cereal.

"There's breakfast still on the stove if you wanna heat it up? I left it for you."

I shook my head and retrieved a bowl. "Did you really make a formal request to my mom?" I poured myself some cereal.

Don didn't look up at me. "Of course, I told you I'd wanted you for a while. And like I said, I know your mother. She'd place her pup into the Offering as soon as you came of age."

"What does that even mean anyway?" I dug into my cereal, talking with my mouthful. "Not like you'd have a claim on me before the Hunt."

"No, but most Highbornes take bids for their betas, especially if they're highly priced in lineage." Of course, Mom talked nonstop about Papa's lineage and how that was a reason why she claimed him. Then she would say something gross and lovey-dovey, and I'd get out of there fast before they started going at it. As a wereduin, seeing sex was something I was used to, but that didn't mean I wanted to see my parents doing it. And Mom had a habit of taking my papa on the kitchen table. *Gross.*

"That's what she kept going on and on about when my birthday was right around the corner."

"A year before, actually."

"And did you really memorize my scent?" That was the tail-end of Don and Mom's conversation that I must have heard incorrectly.

"Of course." I hadn't expected him to admit it right off the bat. Because, come on, the whole notion was ridiculous. Laughable, even. Especially when I pictured him sniffing my shirt. Still, Don had never lied to me before, so I wasn't sure why I thought he would evade the question.

"When did you even do that anyway? You never came to

our house."

"It goes along with making a request."

"And what? My mom let you sniff my underwear?"

Don laughed. "Something like that. It was why I was able to find you so quickly in the Hunt." Given the several hundred participants, maybe I should have wondered why Don was able to locate me as fast as he had. After all, he had stopped the first alpha who tried to rape me.

"So, you've been sniffing me all this time. Kinda creepy." I sniggered. "Like a stalker."

Don just shrugged as if it were the most normal thing in the world. "It's commonplace when you make a bid." All this time I thought Don hadn't even noticed me, and here he was memorizing my scent. "You had a fair amount of suitors. What did you think your mother was doing when she was talking with them?"

"Well, I certainly didn't think she was giving them my items so they could creep on me. Besides, I got chased a lot, but not by *that* many people. So, I couldn't have had *that* many suitors."

Don laughed. "You really are just a pup, aren't you?" Leave it to Don to never miss an opportunity to humiliate me. *Asshole.* "What did you think I was doing in the times you were able to get away from me?"

"So…you were fighting them all off?" My eyes widened. "Don't tell me you actually killed them."

Don spoke nonchalantly, like I was asking about him skipping practice, not ending people's lives. "Maybe? I didn't stick around to know. I've seen a few of them since then, so some lucked out." He looked up from his newspaper and his eyes fixed on me. "I would have, though. I'd kill them all for you, Fern. Every last one."

His piercing blue eyes were so intense. Quickly, I glanced away, my face feeling uncomfortably hot. I needed a distraction, especially since Don hadn't stopped looking at me.

I thought back to the two attractive alphas who had almost caught me at the end of the Hunt. They looked to belong to our caste. Don must have known them. "So, um, those alphas that almost got me before you claimed me?" Thinking of Don claiming me had been a mistake. I remembered it in vivid detail, and it made my lower body ache. *Shit!*

Thankfully, Don said, "What about them?"

"They're not dead, right? I mean, you probably know them, right?"

"Why?" Don narrowed his brow. "If you're thinking of seeking either of them out, you can forget it."

"So, then, you didn't kill them?"

Don shook his head. "Nah, they made it. But know this, Fern. You're mine." He cupped my chin, forcing me to maintain eye contact. "I'll never let you leave me."

I tried to pull away, but only succeeded when he let me go. "Jeez, someone's possessive."

"You better believe it."

"I didn't ask because I was interested in them. Sheesh…they're guys."

"Your point being?"

I glared at him. "Point being is that I'm straight!"

Mischief lit up Don's eyes and brightened his smile. "Not to me you aren't."

Bastard.

I was still curious about those two alphas. It would also piss him off if I asked. "So, were they some of those suitors you were talking about?"

Don growled. "Stop mentioning them."

"Fuck, I can't be curious?" Now he was being ridiculous. "I said, I didn't want them."

"Does that mean you want me?"

I shook my head. "Hardly." The look on his face told me he hadn't taken me seriously. *Bastard.*

"Then, yes, they were suitors." Don straighten up and his chest puffed out. "And they lost." He caught one of my curls, twirling it on his finger. "Like I said, you got quite the number of offers. You're very desirable, my little Fern."

I shivered at the words, feeling the urge to surrender to him and beg him to fuck me. Growing angry at myself, I slapped his hand away. Don's smirk turned challenging, like a predator that had spotted its prey. I knew what he planned to do.

Pushing out of my chair so that it screeched against the wood, I raced for the bathroom. I'd been able to lock myself in once, but I'd had to come out. And the moment I had, Don assailed me, took me to his room, and submitted me. It had been humiliating how he had gotten me to whimper and beg.

I heard the thrill in his growl, but I didn't stop to look back. Dashing into the living room, I used the couch to steady myself to turn the corner when a weight crashed into my back. He grabbed me and tackled me right over the couch, and I landed face down into the cushions.

Don purred into my ear, licking his lips. A moan slipped from my uncovered mouth. He sank his teeth into the second claim mark on my left shoulder. I cried out.

"Mine," he growled through his fangs. Slowly he peeled off my clothing, his teeth never leaving my skin. My body tingled at his touch. I ached inside, wanting him. Once naked underneath him, he entered me with one thrust. I moaned into the pillows. "You know this, my little Fern. Your body craves mine. You crave to be beneath me, taking my cock up your ass. Marking you as my own." He released my neck and licked my ear, nibbling on the shell. "Give it up. I already have you. There's no way you can escape me now." My grip on the cushion slacked the more he thrust into me, and I lost the battle not to beg him for release.

Afterward, I brimmed with anger. Damn that full-of-himself jerk. He was right, though. My body did want him. Maybe I even wanted him to catch me that night. But fuck no, I was not going to submit to that arrogant jerk. Be damned if my body wanted to or not, he didn't own me, and that was that.

Chapter Six

Obedience Training

The stadium we entered was noisy and bustled with alphas and their betas, along with some other races trying to make a buck selling beta bondage gear.

Before we entered, Don had to register us. The whole thing was premature since we weren't official in the Goddess's eyes, but it was the time in the mating month where bonds were already being formed. That made it the perfect time for alphas to start schooling their betas for submission.

I scoffed. *Schooling betas? What the fucking fuck?*

We weren't property. This was beyond degrading.

The line we stood in was relatively short because Don was always ungodly early for everything in life.

They had me shift to werewolf form and take my handprint. I thought they'd need a canine paw print too, as werewolf hands were humanoid, but it wasn't necessary, so I didn't have to revert into a worg.

Don immediately had me transform into a wereduin again, and I cursed how naturally it felt to obey him that my body did it almost on call.

It wasn't hard to shift between forms because Don hadn't allowed me to put on any clothes this morning. I had fought him and tried to get out of it but to no avail.

They took a blood sample, sticking me in-between my shoulder blades with a large needle.

Dagda's Balls, that hurt!

Next, they sat me on a chair and poured warm gel into Don's initial bitemark on my neck.

Ten minutes later, it was finally dry. I kept wanting to scratch it, but every time I did, Don swatted my hand.

Bastard! Let's see him wear this crap.

When it was finally ready to come off, I expected it to hurt, but the gel, which felt a lot like rubber, simply popped right off.

Once we had been registered, we were allowed to enter the stadium.

I licked at the ink on my hand, trying to remove the stain. "Geez…why can't they give us something that doesn't stain the skin…now I have a black hand."

"Thought you liked black."

"Yeah, when it looks cool. This is lame."

He stopped and smirked at me. "Want me to clean it for you?"

I bunched my brows. "Yeah, right!" Like I wanted him to do something so embarrassing.

He laughed and took the lead again. A chilly wind nipped my skin.

"I'm freezing my ass off. Can't I be a werewolf?"

"Nope."

While I still had fur as a wereduin—as all of us do—it was so sparse it might as well have not been there. As a werewolf however, my lush fur would have kept me warm, although beta fur wasn't nearly as thick compared to alphas.

We stopped at one of the vendors in the open area before the bleachers, where concessions were normally sold during games.

I crinkled my nose. "Please tell me you're not interested in that."

The goblin at the booth was selling three different kinds of body-length girdles—collars that looped the neck before they circled the chest, leaving holes for the nipples. Then they went down the abdomen, shaping around the navel before they fanned out around the butt and crotch. Of course, the ass cheeks were left exposed, and by *crotch*, it was a mere ring around the dick and netting for the balls.

"Ah, come come, see yer checkin' out *Black Beauty*?" the goblin said in a rickety voice. I raised a brow at the ridiculous sounding name. "This here beauty's fer more unruly betas. Each section can be restricted individually, or the entire thing restricts as a whole."

"There's no fucking way I'm wearing that stupid thing."

The goblin chuckled. "Perfect fer this kinda one here."

"Fuck you."

"Fern, keep quiet." Don took the girdle from the goblin and examined it.

"See here, there's a button on the leash that chooses specific sections to restrict." The goblin trailed a talon-shaped thumb over the button, drawing Don's attention there. "'Course, it works as a standard choker too. Including the ol' step-on-the-leash submission route."

This was ridiculous.

"I'll take one."

"Fuck, no! I'm not putting that on! Not happening, not ever."

We came out of the dressing room with me wearing that hideous, demeaning thing. He had fondled me the entire time while he'd put it on, and once again, I was powerless to stop him.

"Think of it this way, Fern. At least now you're not so chilly." Don's teasing smile made me wish I could punch him, but there was no way I'd be able to get a hit in given how much of a fighting-freak he was.

"Not like my ass isn't still freezing off, and my nipples…geez, just about every spot that could freeze off, is conveniently missing."

"Of course, what do you expect? This is Obedience Training. You're not supposed to be comfortable." Don swallowed down his laughter and pulled me against his chest. The collar squeezed my nipples and cock, earning a yelp from me. "And I like your sensitive bits showing. Or should I say *my* bits?"

"Fu-Fucker, per-vert." His warm breath against my ear had me trembling, and my body heated up despite the cold. "S-Stop."

Don nuzzled my neck, and the collar restricted my throat. It wasn't tight enough to affect my breathing, but enough to make me feel trapped, to reaffirm that there was no way out of this.

He fondled my balls from outside the netting before he squeezed my cock, and I moaned. "Definitely worth the purchase."

Shame made my cheeks burn. "I-I hate you."

"Hmm." He licked my ear.

"We-We gonna stay here? Thought we're gonna do that stupid *Obedience* thing."

Obedience Training. Papa and Mom had told me about that. An all-encompassing *How to Submit Your Beta* was what it really should have been called. It also opened the gate for championships. As a Highborne beta, I was expected to win championships to make my future offspring more desirable.

Papa had won two championships, something flaunted by Mom during the year before I came of age, and longer according to Don. I had absolutely no desire to compete in that beauty contest. I didn't want to be *the Most Obedient* or *Most Beautiful* or whatever other bullshit title alpha judges gave. And while Obedience Training on its own didn't require championships, it was a gateway for the upper-class to make the right connections and steer their betas in that direction.

Knowing that arrogant jerk, showing me off like a trophy was exactly what he wanted to do—one more thing to bloat his gigantic ego.

He inserted his tongue into my ear before he pulled out and nibbled my lobe. My lower body began to ache. Smirking, he let me go. My face flushed as I looked down at my hard cock.

"Fucking jerk."

Still looking too pleased with himself, Don stopped restricting my bits with the collar and led me toward the main stadium. I glowered as he kept me on a tight leash. I squeezed a finger in between my collar and my neck, trying to loosen the damn thing. If only it could come off with a simple buckle. But no, the asshole had to get one that required a key, which Don kept on his person. Once more, I was powerless against him.

Since I ran track in school, I was very familiar with the

stadium. Seeing it made me want to run again. It felt like ages since I last jogged, let alone ran. It also made me wonder what my friends were doing at school, since Don had taken me out of class today so he could *school me in other ways*. His words.

A large podium stood at the center of the field. All across the field were different *activities* as they were called, which were nothing more than ways in which alphas could humiliate us.

Papa had told me some of his and Mom's experiences with a few of these *activities*. I always found it strange that he remembered them with fondness.

Alpha and beta pairs were selecting spots on the grass around the track. Don and I stopped at a comfortable distance from others.

"Sit."

"What the fuck? I'm not your goddamn dog."

"I didn't call you a dog, but you will take your seat at my feet."

"Fuck you."

Don's eyes narrowed. The next moment, I was on my belly, and the spikey grass made me want to itch. He stepped on the leash, close to my collar. Thankfully, we weren't directly on the track, or this would have been even more painful. "That's better."

Moving caused me to choke, but I did anyway. "Fuck-er."

He pressed my head into the grass with his shoe, the tuffs muffling my sounds. "Much better."

"Mmmm." I struggled against him, but it was no use. He was too strong, and he stood on the leash.

"Welcome, mating pairs." The voice of a priestess of Elaine, Goddess of Obedience, came from the field's center— probably at that podium, I'd seen earlier. "Today starts the first of your Obedience Training. I see some of the unrulier ones are already being subjugated. Let that be a lesson for any beta who chooses to disobey. Alphas take as long as you need to get your beta in line."

Even as she said that I kept struggling. The collar restricted my body, shortening even more of my breath as it tightened around my chest and neck. When it squeezed my ass and groin, a tingle rushed up my spine. I twitched at the sensations. Feeling utterly trapped, confined. The grass still tickled my skin, but I had no way of scratching. A sound too much like a whimper escaped my lips. Don was teaching me my place, and I didn't like it.

Don's foot pressed me farther into the grass. "If you want to suffocate, by all means, keep it up."

The priestess hadn't stopped speaking. "Betas that aren't misbehaving take a knee behind your alpha. Alphas rest a palm on your beta's head. This is called the Praying position. This will be your starting position. Each class will begin and end with this position. Now, let us begin the prayer to the gracious Goddess Elaine."

Don whispered into my ear, "Shall I fuck you, my little Fern? Right here, while you're helpless and exposed."

"Uhm uhmm," I tried to shake my head. He grabbed my ass, his fingers trailing along my crack, itching to enter me. I didn't wanna be fucked. I wanted to be free, but that wasn't going to happen. Either I stopped struggling, or he'd fucked me right here on the grass.

I fought anyway. I didn't want him to fuck me, but I'd be damned before I rolled over onto my belly for him.

The leash squeezed my cock, and I moaned, thankful for once that the grass muffled the sound. But Don still heard it.

"Too late." His belt buckle clanked, then he was on my back, pressing me into the ground even more. His cock nudged into my pucker. In one brutal movement, he thrust into me, tearing my skin a bit, and I cried out. The pain bordered on pleasure, the pleasure bordering on pain. Don's alpha prowess already began healing the hurt.

Now that he was no longer shoving my face in the grass, I could see around me. Other betas were being fucked on the grass. One beta was being taken up the ass, her large alpha pounding her into submission. She kept trying to get away, to no avail.

My groin ached. Something about the scene was hot.

Maybe it was the submission. Maybe it was Don pumping into my ass, riding me hard, biting my shoulder. The suit stiffened around my body everywhere Don had tightened it. I lay, mouth opened, panting on the grass. My body rocked against the ground in line with his thrusts. I wanted to keep struggling, but I was tiring. Soon I couldn't move a muscle; the girdle was so tight.

Don was heavy on top of me, whispering words into my ear.

"How about it, Fern?" He nipped my cartilage, tugging it between his teeth. "Gonna stop fighting me? Or do you wanna spend the entire class with my cock up your ass." He closed a hand over my mouth, so I couldn't answer him.

I could no longer think. My eyes rolled back into my head as I surrendered to the pleasure.

Then he came hard in my ass, and all I could do was moan. When he came, I fell over the edge with him. But it was different this time like my orgasm was dictated by him. I'd heard of this—when an alpha makes his beta force-cum. It was unlike any orgasm I had experienced. It rushed through my body, drawing all of me into the feelings of pleasure, of pain, of my owner. That's what it felt like—like he was the one in control over my body. Not me. He took the energy from me and left me lethargic. I felt his influence settling in more places inside me.

He forced me into another orgasm. It was more than simple pleasure. This was entrapment. The more I came, the more it sucked the fight out of me. Making me docile until I lay motionless beneath him.

"Good boy." He stroked my sweaty hair. The moment he let up on the leash, I dragged in a deep breath. My body still tingled from the sex.

Don tugged the leash until he had me on my knees. "Praying position, come on. Get up onto one knee."

Exhausted, I bared my teeth. The girdle tightened around my cock. I whimpered, still sensitive from having come so furiously. The pain forced me to comply. "I hate you."

"Keep quiet. Bow your head to the Goddess."

At the mention of Elaine, my head bowed on its own. Don rested a flat palm on top of me, making me look down even farther. I grumbled at his touch. His semen pooled from my hole, leaking down my cheeks until it collected in the net holding my balls.

I couldn't have felt more owned. I had bent the knee for him. His cum still dripped from my ass. His hand on my head prevented me from looking up. I briefly wondered how long we would be in Obedience Training. In my mind, I saw me with a full belly carrying his pup still returning here until he got every bit of rebellion out of me. I trembled, my instincts overwhelmed me completely, and I shut my eyes, feeling Elaine's blessing upon me, schooling me. She, too, wanted me to submit to my alpha.

Don must have felt my shift, for he growled approvingly. That only rekindled my will to rebel. I was still too weak to do much fighting, but I began to regain my energy. There was no way, absolutely none, that I would give in to him so willingly. I wasn't his mate yet, nor did I want to be. I tried to shut off the thoughts inside me that spoke otherwise. We still had one more Offering to get through—along with Betas Night right around the corner. I had to stay strong.

"Alphas begin warming up your betas. Betas, as you trek in a circle, know you follow in the footsteps of the great Goddess Elaine, who calls you to obey your alpha. Walk your place with pride, pride in yourself, and in your alpha."

A sharp tug on the leash brought me to my feet. The force almost choked me. When Don began walking, I had to move fast, or he would drag me by the leash.

"Fuck, this *is* like a dog…" I was still exhausted, only my will to fight kept me going, but I felt peeved. Pride in myself? *Yeah right!* I had no idea how a beta could feel proud of being walked on a leash. We were not slaves, and certainly not dogs.

"Alphas keep your beta close. If you need to punish them, please step off the track to do so as we must keep the procession moving."

As we walked, a heady rush came over me, making me lightheaded, awakening innate feelings of submission, making me feel connected to him on an entirely new level. Papa had told me walking the track with Mom holding his leash had put him in the proper headspace for obedience. I hated how I now understood him in a way I never even imagined. My alpha's will awakened my body, opened my soul. I could still feel his thick cock moving inside me and hearing the sounds made as my beta juices slicked my hole as he pumped in and out of me. My knees weakened, and my foot slipped.

Instead of falling, I was caught in his strong arms. Despite walking behind him, he had kept me from falling and pulled me against his chest. Hearing his strong heartbeat thudding against my ear soothed some of my anger.

"Shh, I've got you."

His seductive voice made my heart feel like it was about to leap out of my chest.

"Let-Let go." Inside, I begged him to submit me, to own me. Those feelings were so strong, I was trembling.

"And let you eat the dirt?"

"B-Better th-an this…"

"You really are stubborn, aren't you?" Don steered us out of the circle, and I knew what was coming next. My groin ached. It didn't matter that his cum was still warm inside me. I wanted him back to fucking me. I wanted his cock all day, all night. I wanted him to make a baby inside me.

He thrust me onto my belly. This time, Don got on hands and knees on top of me, pinning me to the earth. Tightening his grip on my leash, he forced me to stay down, my head rested to the side. I panted, billowing the turfs of grass. I felt his breath against my neck. Felt his weight—not enough that I couldn't breathe—only enough to leave me feeling confined.

It was the strangest sensation—feelings so out of control of my body—so many emotions. I clenched my fists to get out some of my anger. My erection, painfully stiff, pressed into the ground, leaking with beta juices.

"Are you enjoying this?" Don whispered into my ear.

"St-Stop."

"Not gonna happen." Don's sharp, somehow still seductive tone sent a shiver running down my spine. "For the next hour, you're going to be obedient to me."

I wanted him to fuck me again and again, and it pissed me off almost to the point of killing my erection. Almost, because the longer he stayed on top of me, the more my beta instincts consumed me. Trailing his hand down my back along the leather girdle, he cupped my ass. His fingers cool against my sweaty skin.

"I think you need more of a reminder of who's in charge here."

I swallowed. "N-Not yo-u." Speaking grew difficult. "Tha-t's fer s-sure. I w-on't—"

Two fingers pressed against my pucker before they pushed into my hole. My face burned with embarrassment at the sloshing sounds his fingers made in my beta juices.

"You really want this, don't you, Fern? Your tight, little hole craves to be filled with cock." My helpless whimper had me gritting my teeth. "My cock." As he continued to fuck me with his fingers, colors and dots flashed across my vision. "Such a perfect little hole," he whispered into my ear, "I should really call it *my* cum hole." Then he nibbled the lobe. "It looks even sexier stretched around my cock, taking me all the way in." Heat coiled in my stomach as his warm breath caressed my skin. "But I'm not going to fuck you again. If you behave for the remainder of the class, then I'll give you what you want. I won't even wait until we get home. I'll fuck you long and good right here on the grass."

I still wanted to rebel and push him away, but fighting my instincts was nearly impossible.

"If you don't behave, you won't be getting any cock. I'll keep you aching for me for as long as it takes. I don't mind. I love seeing you helpless beneath me. But you…you'll feel it. I'll make you feel it." The collar squeezed around my cock, and I yelped at the pain, tremors of need making constriction all the more painful. "So, are you going to behave?"

My tears muddied the dirt, my body trembling all over, but I nodded as if beyond my control.

He got off me and pulled me up to my feet. My prominent erection bulged around the girdle, so there was no way for me to hide my arousal. I screwed my eyes shut, so I didn't have to see his satisfied grin.

He pulled me against his chest and licked from my neck to my ear before he ghosted a claim mark, and I trembled. "You may not like it, but you're mine now, Fern. And I will submit you, and then you'll be seeking me out, begging me to fuck you. I won't even have to ask. That's how trained you'll be."

I sagged against him.

"Come on." Taking my leash again, he led us back onto the track.

Several betas glanced at me. Alphas too. It was easy to spot the alphas who weren't quite satisfied with their betas given the hungry look they gave me. I didn't want to see it, so I shut my eyes. Quickly, I opened them. I didn't want to fall on my face.

Don was by my side. "It's okay to let go and close your eyes. I won't let you fall. And I won't let them hurt you."

I trembled as his arm went around me. He still held my leash firmly in his other hand, but his arm around me helped steer me and even provided me with speed, so I was no longer trotting to keep up.

We passed another alpha whose eyes raked over me. This one was a golden bronze, muscular beast. Not as beautiful as Don when he was a werewolf, though, although it was obvious that he was also Highborne. *Stupid self! Stop finding stupid Don beautiful!*

Giving in, I closed my eyes.

By the second lap, Don had let me go and had instead walked me on the leash. I still felt the alphas watching me, and it was unnerving. I had no way to stop them from seeing my painfully hard cock. My juices flowed from the tip, dripping to the ground. They also leaked out of my hole and down the backs of my thighs. Still, I didn't bother opening my eyes or fighting him. Instead, I let go and felt the leash moving me along. Leading me, and I knew I was safe.

"It is now time to begin the activities for those pairs that wish to participate. Otherwise, alphas, keep submitting your betas. We've got twenty minutes before class is over."

The priestess's voice jarred me to reality. I had no clue how long I had zoned out. I couldn't believe we had twenty minutes left. That meant he'd been walking me for thirty minutes straight. It had felt like I'd followed him for hours.

Don stopped walking, and I almost banged right into him. He turned to me with a look of love on his face, and it stole my breath away. "I think we can leave the activities until next time. You've submitted so beautifully today, Fern."

I swallowed, unable to look away as he tucked a curl behind my ear and brushed a kiss on my forehead. I wasn't sure why the words slipped my lips, but they did, much to my dismay. "R-Really? That's it?" The note of disappointment in my tone was unmistakable. Where the hell had that come from?

"Oh." His lips quirked into a sly smile. "Want some more?"

Frantically, I shook my head.

"My dear little Fern." He petted my hair again. "Such a contradiction you are." Without another word, he swept me off my feet. "All right, if you insist. How about we try an easy one to start off with. Next time, I promise we'll do harder ones."

"Wait!" I squirmed, trying to get away. "I didn't mean that I wanted to do more! I didn't. That's your perverted mind thinking—"

His firm kiss took the words straight from my open mouth, his tongue brutally exploring inside, ripping a moan from me.

"Oh, you meant it."

"Shouldn't I be the one deciding that? Given, I'm the one who knows what I feel?" I was tired, but not enough to miss the opportunity to be sassy.

"Nope."

"Bastard."

The activity he brought me to was close to the track, some meters away.

The stocks were open, and Don fitted my head and wrists to the device before closing it up. Immediately fear butterflied in my stomach. I couldn't move, and Don could do whatever the hell he wanted to me…

"Shh." Don stroked my ass. "This is no different than how I've submitted you before. Relax into it. I won't hurt you, nor will I leave you."

"I-I don't want this."

"Yes, you do."

I tried to shake my head, but I couldn't move.

"Fern, you asked me to do this."

Closing my eyes, I inwardly cursed myself. What the hell was with these stupid beta instincts? It was like they wanted me to be properly fucked until I willingly submitted. I had asked for this. I hadn't wanted to, but I had. If I complained too much, it would only excite Don. But giving in altogether wasn't something I could do. At least not yet.

"Fine…not like your perverted ass would have not found a way to humiliate me more before we left this circus."

Don pressed his lips against my ear, and it made me shiver. "Now you're getting me, Fern."

I nibbled my bottom lip.

"You ready for me?"

"Do I have a fucking choice?"

Don's breath was warm against my butt cheek. "Nope. Now give me everything, Fern. Don't hold anything back."

My beta instincts went crazy at his words, his tone demanding my surrender.

Shit. Shit. Shit.

I was losing the battle. *Fucking instincts.* Once again, I hated that I was born a beta wereduin.

A wet sensation licked across my asshole, and I jumped.

Don licked me again.

"Fuck…stop." It was more than embarrassing. I was too exposed. "Fuck…" I bunched my fists as his tongue breached my pucker. He pressed his mouth to my ass—the stubble on his face tickling my ass cheeks.

"Mmm, Fern, you taste so good."

"I-I seriously d-doubt that—" I had to stop talking when his tongue turned forceful, and he fucked me as strongly as if it was his hard shaft thrusting into me. "D-Don!"

He squeezed my cheeks. "You want more?"

I couldn't nod, so I let the words fall from my open mouth. "Fuck…Don. Yes…yes!"

Don's fingers joined in and struck a spot inside me, and I saw stars. I didn't think I could come without his hands around my dick or his cock inside me. The orgasm hit me so hard, and I twitched and shook, tugging against the stocks that bound me.

"Fuck, I need to be inside you." Don didn't wait until my orgasm finished. His cock entered me as if it were another push of his tongue, but thicker, and it dragged me right back up the orgasmic cliff and over the edge. I cried out, far too loudly than I wanted to.

Unable to control my body, I was so under his influence that my fists gave way, my body going limp, and he moved me like one of my little sister's rag dolls. His thick fingers dug into my hips as he fucked my ass. At this rate, there was no way I would be walking home. In fact, I briefly wondered if I'd be able to walk tomorrow, either. But my mind couldn't stay on that thought long before another orgasm consumed me.

His fingers shoved into my mouth, successfully gagging me. Instinctively, I sucked them, taking them deeper into my throat.

He was doing it again—hollowing out that place inside me, breaking down even more of my inner walls, making a space in my body to incubate his young—our young, our pups.

I panted as he worked his magic. It both hurt and felt amazing. Each motion stole my breath away, sending ripples of pleasure throughout my body, only to be followed by an equal amount of pain. I groaned at the sensations, but I didn't even try to fight him. My body was so ready to carry his pups.

The intensity must have knocked me out. When I awoke, he held me in his strong arms. I vaguely remembered the wooden stocks being released from my wrists and my neck able to move again, but it was hazy.

Inhaling his alluring scent, I sighed against his chest, feeling satisfied. Whole. Needed. Like I found the place where I belonged.

Something nagged at the back of my mind, like mosquitos trapped in a jar. But I was too fatigued to open my eyes, let alone chase down the irritation deep inside me.

"All right. That's all we have time for today. Alphas, submit your beta."

Don put me down, and I was directed to take a knee. His large hand was warm on top of my head, keeping me steady.

"Let the blessings of Elaine purify your hearts, let it bond the two of you. Betas, please the Goddess, submit, and be obedient to your alpha. Alphas, have zero tolerance for disobedience so that Elaine may bless your mating. Go in peace."

At her words, those nagging mosquitoes escaped the jar.

What the fuck?

I'd shown almost complete submission to Don while trapped in the stocks. I wondered how many wereduin saw me that way. They were all around me, some mated alphas disciplining their betas or doing other activities, and some loners simply watching me being tortured.

I felt violated, so I took it all out on Don.

Immediately, I growled. Without a second thought, I sprang up at him, intending to attack. I saw him smirk—like he wasn't surprised at all by my actions—before he knocked me to the ground. His bodyweight was crushing. He didn't even try to keep from crushing me.

"Are you angry, my little Fern?"

"Fuck you. Fuck you! Fuck you." I broke down sobbing. I couldn't take the humiliation any longer. All of those eyes on me…and the way I acted? I was mortified, and it washed me with rage.

Don kissed my head gently. "Yeah, let it all out, Fern. Let that stubborn will of yours be broken."

I kept shaking my head and shoving uselessly into him. Despite the gentleness of his kisses, he still hadn't let up on me.

"You will, Fern. You will let me in. I promise you; it's already happening." He nipped my ear. "Don't fight it, Fern. It'll be less painful if you don't resist."

I sobbed in frustration.

"I don't want to hurt you, Fern, but I want your obedience, your utmost obedience." He nuzzled my head. "And I will get it. I always get what I want." His arms encircled my body in a hug, and this time he did let up some of his weight, holding me tight, but still with unusual gentleness. "And you want it, Fern. You didn't want to go home, not without experiencing a sample of what lies ahead. You know this, Fern. You know, deep down, you have already surrendered to me." He nuzzled my hair and pulled me closer. "Accept me, my mate. Accept me, and I'll keep you by my side forever."

When he entered me again, I was so wet inside that I almost didn't notice. His cock felt so normal, like there was never a time when I didn't know his body.

He rocked into me with each gentle thrust. Kissing my hair, loving me in ways I hadn't experienced before. Was this the mating bond forming?

Leftover tears trailed my cheeks. I couldn't escape him. He had made that clear. And I wondered how many times we would have to return to this awful place, but he was right on some level. I hadn't wanted to leave until he properly submitted me until I had experienced these activities that Papa remembered so fondly.

As we reached climax, his voice grew gruff in my ear, with

none of the gentleness he'd used only moments ago. "From now on, I want you to keep your body ready for me, as I will be taking you whenever I want, any way I want. Do you understand me?"

Nodding uncontrollably, I relinquished control, but those mosquitoes were back, and I clung to them. They were my lifeline preventing me from giving myself completely over to my new alpha. Like mosquitoes, I knew that they would not live forever, but at least for now, they provided the inner peace I needed to grow accustomed to my new life with Don. That, or they would help me bide my time until I could escape him and all of his perverted ways.

Apparently, Obedience Training came with homework. *What the hell? Assholes.*

For the next few days, he had to have his cock up my ass any time we spent together. Rather than this being about fucking, it was about getting me accustomed to being underneath him. This was known as Coupling. A practice where the alpha stayed inside the beta while pretending to go about everyday life. I say *pretending* because, at some point, Don inevitably gave in to his instincts and fucked me sideways.

That evening Don trapped me beneath his strong body and the living room rug. Propped up on his elbows, he read a book he placed beside my head. His cock rested inside me.

I had to lay there and take it.

I couldn't stop fidgeting. Don wore his silver-brown hair tied in a ponytail. Every time he leaned closer to flip the page, it peeked out from behind his shoulder. The next time he changed the page, I made a grab for it and started playing with his hair.

"You're heavy."

"And you're small."

"Am not!"

"To me, you are."

"That's 'cause you're a giant."

"I'm your alpha."

"Do we have to do this? My ass is sore."

"Really? How are you going to make it through the next few days like this if you're already sore?"

"My fucking point exactly," I growled.

Still pretending to read his book, he started to thrust his hips, slow and taunting. *Fucker.*

As he was way too heavy for me to move, I could do nothing to stop him. He wasn't going to get off me, and however much my ass hurt, it belonged to him. That was what this exercise was supposed to demonstrate. His dominion over me. Me, his newly captured mate, assuming he could hold onto me through the rest of the Offering.

The next day when I came home from school, he was waiting in the living room. "Come here, Fern."

"Fuck, no!" I knew what he planned to do. Dropping my book bag, I raced for the bathroom. I barely made it two steps before he trapped me. Then he was carrying me into the living room. It looked like it would be another Coupling session. I was thankful for the soft rug around the couch. Otherwise, we would be lying on the bare wooden floor.

"I've got homework!" I hated doing it, especially the tedious stuff my Culture Studies teacher gave. But ever since I'd moved in with Don, it was non-negotiable, and he would punish me if I tried to skip it. Of course, I'd take having to study the boring customs of other races over *this* any day. Now I would have to do both at once?

He shoved me down onto my knees and pulled down my skinny jeans, taking my underwear along with them. I heard him unzip his fly before his weight crushed me into the floor. He hadn't even fully removed his clothes—simply freed his cock—and then he was inside me. I muffled a moan into the thick carpet of the floor rug.

"I need to grab my homework first."

"Already did." He dropped my bookbag in front of me. Sitting up, he let me get onto my forearms, then placed my textbook beside me, and I opened it up. "That's a good boy."

I growled. I didn't want him on top of me, nor did I want him fucking me. But our *homework* would last for the next few days while we honored the Goddess Elaine. I'm surprised he let me go out and didn't Couple me at school. Surprised but thankful.

I had no intention of reminding the jerk, else he might actually do it. The idea of the whole class seeing him stick it in me burned my face with embarrassment and made my stomach ache. At the same time, those instincts inside me stirred.

"Thinking a lot, aren't you, Fern?"

"Well, what else would I be doing? It's homework, jerk."

"I think it's time I punished you for that little mouth of yours."

Oh shit.

He stopped fucking me and stood up—stuffing himself back into his jeans and zipping them up. "On your knees."

"What?"

"You heard me, beta."

I swallowed. He was pure alpha in front of me, his werewolf rising.

"I-gotta finish my—"

"Later. Right now, I need to put your mouth to good use. It's about time you learned how to pleasure me."

Shaking my head, I scooted up onto my knees and tried to crawl away.

"Do I need to go and get the girdle?"

So embarrassing. "Fuck you…" I hung my head and crawled over until I was right in front of him.

He smirked with his usual arrogance. "That's it. I'll make a fine beta out of you yet." He brought his hand to his fly. "Come here. I want you to unzip this with your teeth."

Come again? "Is that even possible?"

He nodded. "Do it." His commanding tone held no room for debate.

I sought out his zipper until I held it between my teeth. Then I glanced up at him.

He gave me a nod.

I tried to tug it down, but it didn't budge. "I told you that's not possible. Jerk."

"I can make you do it if that's more helpful." Amusement hid behind his smile.

I swatted his hands away.

"I can do it, jeez." I hated how he belittled me. I could do this. After all, it was just a zipper. My resolution made, I tugged the zipper with my teeth, pulling it all the way down, tasting the coppery metallic flavor.

"Take it out." Werewolf features prominent, his cold eyes promised pain if I refused him. Slowly, I obeyed. "All the way. Expose my cock down to the sack."

I followed suit.

"Now, put your mouth on it. Wet it with your saliva." His thick, rusty-red cock was coated in a layer of my beta juices. It had been inside me. *Gross.* "Am I going to have to make you?"

I bared my teeth. "It's been inside my ass."

"Like I care. And right now, you don't either."

"Fuck! This is gross."

"Do it, Fern. Now." He clasped my head, taking me down to his cock until my juices smeared on my nose, and I grimaced. "Lick it. Lick all over."

My tongue hesitated at the pungent taste of my beta juices on his cock. Licking it off made my stomach ache from the bitterness, but he didn't let me stop.

"You're such an asshole, do you know that?"

He tugged my hair. "Stop talking and put your mouth to good use for once."

When he was satisfied with the slickness of his cock, he had me take him into my mouth. It was enormous. My lips had to stretch around it.

"Good, slow. Nice and easy. Take it deeper. I want to feel your throat constricting around me."

I tried to do what he wanted, but I gagged and pulled away, coughing.

"I didn't say you could stop."

"B-But I can't breathe."

"Use your nose, not your mouth, and keep going. I'm already agitated. I want to fill your mouth. But you're no good as you are now. You need to be trained."

"Fuck you, I'm already being trained." Grumbling, I put my lips around his cock again.

"Take it in."

"I'm trying!" I didn't remember it being this hard during my punishment after the whole Shamar episode. But then he had completely taken away my mind, and controlled my body with his alpha prowess.

Cupping my face, he tipped my head, exposing my throat, then he stuck his cock inside my mouth. It dragged along my throat, and I gagged.

He didn't let me pull away. "Breathe through your nose, or you're going to suffocate."

Tears clouded my eyes, both from his cruelness and practically choking to death.

He stopped forcing me and stroked my hair. "You can do this, Fern. Trust me and let go. This won't hurt you. I won't let it. I'll take care of you. But you must trust me. Let go, let my cock go down your throat. If you fight it, it'll get worse. Let your body relax."

I didn't want to listen to him, but I was afraid he genuinely might choke me. The gentle way he stroked my hair helped to soothe some of my fear. Slowly, I relaxed my throat and took a deep breath through my nose.

"Grab the remainder that can't fit into your mouth and glide your hand up and down it, following my movements."

It was getting easier the more I did what he told me. Inside, though, I still was panicking. It felt like we were overcoming an obstacle together.

I pumped the part of his cock that couldn't fit in my mouth. His shaft moved in and out before it slid down my throat. When he struck the end, I gagged again.

"Relax, you're okay. I won't hurt you, Fern." He stroked my hair. This time, his hand simply guided my head instead of forcing it. "You can do this. Your body longs to obey me, give into me, and I promise to keep you safe. Know this, Fern. I would never do anything to physically put you in danger. Ever. If I am asking this of you, know that it's safe."

His words lulled me into a sense of security, and I let myself go.

His breath hitched. That made me open my eyes. When had I closed them? But hearing his arousal got me wet inside, and my cock stiffened. Curious to hear more of those sounds, I stroked his shaft inside my mouth with my tongue.

His head lolled back. "Like that, Fern," he moaned, "like that."

I trailed my tongue all around him, aiming for his cockhead when that got more of a reaction. He cupped the back of my head, and it allowed me to relax until he supported my weight. He wasn't holding my head to simply make it easier on me. He used his grip to have me pick up speed. Again, I gagged, but this time I didn't pull away and let him fuck my mouth, feeling owned by him. My instincts made me lightheaded, and my body responded on its own. Releasing his cock with one hand, I started fondling my dick in rhythm.

"Good, Fern. Pleasure yourself. You're such a good beta."

I bristled at that deep inside, but my instincts were overwhelming, and I was lost on the climb towards release. He forced me to take it deep and fast, and soon he came in my mouth.

If I wasn't gagging before, I was now.

"Drink it. Let it go down. Drink all my juices. One day I will grow our pup with this. I'll grow our pup inside you."

With a moan, I chased my orgasm over the edge. His cock slipped from my lips, and any leftover cum spilled down my chin.

When I came down, I sagged against his legs.

He petted my hair.

"Beautiful, Fern. You did beautifully. My little Fern. My mate."

His last words made me shiver. My instincts flared up,

and I nuzzled his legs.

He released a sigh. "Now, someone needs to go do his homework."

"Are-Are you serious?" I grumbled up at him, still too tired to get up.

"Uh-huh." He scooped me up and carried me to the dining room table, sitting me down.

Don went into the living room and returned with my notebook and textbook. "I'll be back in later," he flashed a lecherous grin, "for round two."

Chapter Seven

Freeing You

"So yeah, um...I sorta got this thing at Crone's Head tonight."

Don looked up from the book he was reading on the couch. I was already decked out in my usual garb, complete with a lip piercing, industrial bar, curls flattened, and bangs hiding my left eye. I even put some eyeliner on and glistened my lips. I had dug out my baggy jeans too, dangling chains from the pockets, and slipped on a *Zombie Blood* tee. I was pretty proud of it since it contained the band's new logo—a voodoo doll pinned to a wall with its brains and intestines dripping from its ripped stitches. I wore a black scarf to cover up the claim marks around my neck—it fit perfectly with my outfit.

Don gave me the once-over. Something in his eyes made me feel embarrassed. He didn't say anything at first, but a smile crept over his face. I looked away, blushing, and I hated it. Dammit, what was so embarrassing about Don seeing me like this? Fuck him, this was me. If he didn't like it, best he realized it now.

"So yeah, it's tonight, so um, I'm gonna go..." *If you let me.* I didn't say it. Instead, I left it hanging in the air. I didn't have to. I knew that he could stop me, lock me in the house. After the punishment I'd received for disobeying him and going to Shamar's, I had no plans of ripping up the tree net this time if he locked me in the bedroom. My knees and ass ached at the memory.

A pang of dread knotted my stomach. What if he didn't let me go? Worse yet, what if he didn't even let me be me?

"You play?"

I had forgotten I was holding my electronic guitar case. "Oh, uh, yeah." Why was I so fucking nervous? It was just stupid Don.

His smile grew. Was he laughing at me? "All right, let's

go."

"Us?"

"Well, yeah. No way I'm gonna let you go by yourself."

"Uh…" I was shocked. I really thought he would stop me altogether. Of course, I'd been preparing for a fight because there was no way in hell I'd miss my band's first gig. We'd booked it over a month ago. "You don't have to come."

"'Course I do."

I rolled my eyes. "It's not like I'll try to run off again."

"I didn't think that."

"But you still wanna come?"

"'Course. With the way you are now, there's no way you won't be attacked." Oh. I hadn't even thought of that. I was of breeding age, going through the Offering. There was a very real possibility that some asshole alpha would try to claim me. From what I could remember, Crone's Head wasn't a non-fight zone.

Normally stores and other shops had non-fighting zones. Otherwise, wereduins would have a hard time living with the other races. It was etiquette to refrain from fighting in those areas and take it outside. One time that happened to Mom and Papa in *Playland*. We had barely started the line for the roller-coaster, *Roaring Banshee* when Mom had to go to a fighting zone and face a challenger. I was never afraid of my mother losing. It never crossed my mind, even though the challenger would've killed my sister and me if he won, and Papa became his mate.

I sighed. "Fine."

"Besides…" He tried to mess up my hair, but I dodged his hand. "I wanna hear you play."

"Why? I'm not that great."

"I'll be the judge of that."

"Whatever, let's go."

We were locking up the front door when he turned to me and spoke in a serious tone. "If we do get a challenger, don't engage them. You wait for me. I'll most likely smell them coming, but don't ever run."

"I know that."

"Do you?"

"Yeah."

Don quirked his brow. "No repeat of the molebats."

Low blow. "Jerk. You know why I did that."

"Just come on."

"That's my line."

We drove in silence. I stared out the window. The familiar buildings of downtown stirred up nostalgia. The last time I came here, I'd been unmated. I wondered how it would be now. How my friends would take this. *Oh yeah…*

"Lucian is going to be there, so please don't mess with him." *Please? What the fuck?* Why was I saying please to Don? The asshole was going to get even more stupid ideas.

Don's lips curled into a snarl. "Is this a mixed club?"

"It's a bar. But yeah, it's mixed. Gotta problem with that?"

"Actually, yeah."

I swallowed but still mouthed off. "Well, too bad—"

"Listen here." His tone stopped me. "I'll go along with this game, but only because Lucian is a brat. Stay the hell away from adult vampires, or I will attack them."

Shit really? "Isn't that a bit extreme?"

Don huffed. "What planet have you been living on? Extreme? It's far too tame for their lot."

"But—"

"Don't push it, Fern."

"Fine." It wasn't like I hung around many vamps, anyway. Lucian was the only one. Well, there was another. He was also goth, more goth-metalhead, so sometimes he came with us to gigs and hung around us at school. "You know, I know you're an old man, but you're young enough to have gone to a mixed school."

All the races going to the same school was a relatively new thing. My parents had been at the tail end of wereduins-only schools before the mixed schools happened, so tension was always higher among the older persons. Don had gone to my school. He confirmed it when he told me he'd rescued me from Brig that one time in the gym lockers.

"You really have been sheltered, you know that?" Maybe what he said was true. I never once felt afraid of anything living with my mom—not vampires or alphas.

"I don't think I'm sheltered."

"'Course you don't."

Finally, we arrived in front of Crone's Head. It was a little dive outside of downtown, right on the edge of the bogs. Given its close proximity to the bayous, lots of zombies came there. That made even more sense when most metalhead and emocore groups were made up of more zombies than the other races.

Dirt lots surrounded the building, and that's where we parked Don's car. Overall, it wasn't too crowded, but we still ended up parking close to the water. Here the gnats were thick enough to catch them between your fingers when brushing them away. The pungent smell of detritus from the nearby swamp stung my nose.

"I'll carry that for you." Don reached out for my guitar case.

I shook my head. "Please don't."

"You really don't know how to accept a good thing, do you?"

"Good thing? Well, aren't you full of yourself?"

Don smiled, and this time he succeeded in messing up my hair.

"Dammit, Don!" The moment I put down my case and went to correct my hair, he stole it and carried it the rest of the way. *Ass.*

The bar was more of a hut with wooden steps up to the porch. There wasn't a cover, so we could enter for free. When I pushed the door open, a thick cloud of Nightshade cigarette smoke invaded my nose and momentarily made my eyes water. I wondered if Shamar had brought along his pack. It felt like years since I last had one. What would Don think about me smoking? Some of his friends smoked, but I had yet to see him with a cigarette. I briefly wondered if he would stop me if I tried.

Crone's Head also didn't card at the door, which was great. Hopefully, Kina would be there, so I could at least grab a drink. The zombie bartender was awesome because she didn't ask for ID.

"Okay, can I have it back now?" Don's gaze roamed around the room like he was making sure it was safe for his mate. Overprotective much? His distraction allowed me to snatch it back.

The smell of crispy human fingers and fried frog wrinkled my nose. Since most clientele were zombies, a lot of menu items involved human flesh, but not all. My mouth watered as I watched two zombie cooks at the fryer—the pan sizzling, adding to the small pub's cozy atmosphere. "Maybe we could split an order of fried sparrows later?" I said over my shoulder. "They're my favorite! Their wings got just the right amount of crunch." I'd never splintered a fang on them yet. "Oh wait...lemme see if Shamar's here."

A side door let out to an awning overlooking the bogs. Shamar liked to come early and sit at a table. He said the humidity helped maintain his body. That was a bit weird— wouldn't the humidity make zombies rot quicker? But apparently, that wasn't the case. Not like I knew anything about Voodoo replenishing spells.

I peeked my head out, but surprisingly he wasn't there.

Shrugging, I went back inside. "Come on, the stage is downstairs."

Don hung back. "Thought you wanted to get sparrow wings?"

Yeah, I had asked him, but I'd said that without thinking—momentarily believing I came here with my friends. I never expected him to listen to me.

"Oh, well, we normally play first."

Don studied me with those pensive blue eyes, and I fidgeted under his stare. "All right." His face took on a gentle expression, and for a moment, I couldn't look away.

Stop it! Stop fawning over stupid, jerky Don!

Spinning on my heel, I stormed off. Not sure who I was angrier at—me or Don.

The wooden floor creaked between my feet, and my shoe skidded on the grease.

Before I could fall, Don caught me. "Careful."

I shoved out of his strong arms. "I-I'm fine."

A stairway led into a speakeasy. Halfway down the steps, I saw a makeshift stage. A hybrid of metalhead and emo décor filled the space with lots of blacks and grays. None of the usual metalhead, metalcore, and emocore music played tonight because my band was scheduled to perform.

Alphonse was setting up on the stage. I still didn't see Shamar. Lucian wasn't there either. I was kind of dreading having Lucian around Don. I wasn't sure if Don would be an asshole or, at the very least, be rude to him.

It was weird to see Alphonse without Lucian. Almost immediately, he noticed I had company.

"Oh, uh, h-hi." He ran his hand through his long, shaggy auburn hair streaked with black. "D-Didn't know you were-were bringing some-someone." Alphonse held out his hand to Don. "Think we g-got off to a bad start. I, um, I'm Alphonse, ni-nice to meet you." I was shocked at Alphonse's assertiveness. Even though he still stuttered, he was definitely more courageous tonight. Of course, I really shouldn't have been surprised given how different Alphonse acted on stage. Maybe he was pumped for the gig.

"Riiight." Don returned the handshake sounding more patronizing than friendly. "Don."

Alphonse either didn't notice his behavior or else didn't care. "I hear you're-you're a *spawn* player? Are you really gonna play for the Furies?"

Don popped his forehead up, looking down his nose. "Didn't know you goth brats like *spawn*."

Alphonse turned bright red. "Uh-um, well, yeah."

"We're not goth, and fuck you." I went to the back of the stage and started setting up my *Ailill Mac* guitar. Its sleek black color and silver skulls caught the stage lights whenever we played. *Ailill Mac* guitars were arguably one of the best electronic guitar brands ever. They took their name from one of my idols, Ailill Mac—a badass wereduin and one of the few, most guitarists were zombies, with some humans in the mix.

"Fern, I'm getting a drink." Don didn't even ask me if I wanted anything. I got the feeling he'd prevent me from drinking tonight.

"So, Fern. Te-Tell me you brought a-another pick? Lucian seems to, um, have lo-lost his. Think he might've gone home for-for it."

"He did?" I sighed. Even though Lucian rocked on the bass, he went through picks like blood-drinks. Sometimes they broke, but mostly he dropped them and wouldn't bother looking for them. Said it would be his signature if we made it big.

"Uh, yeah, he was talking to Fa-Father on the phone, and it see-seemed like if Lucian d-didn't make the trip, Father will c-c-come here."

Shit! Lucian was the favorite godchild of his coven's leader, who they all called Father, and he always went out on a limb for Lucian. I'd heard some vamps our age complaining, saying that he probably outranked Father's own son. Something they thought would complicate things when Father chose an heir.

I searched my case, praying I had a few extra spares. "Please tell me Father's not coming here." I didn't even want to think of what Don would do when he saw the leader of Lucian's coven walk down those steps.

Just then, Lucian came gliding down the stairs. His platinum-blond long hair shimmered and offset the parts he'd dyed black. The black and the blond alternated down the length. It looked like a chessboard. His goth makeup was enhanced with red lipstick. He had a few picks in hand, and most importantly, he was alone. *Thank Arduinna!*

"Found them, huh?" I beat Alphonse to the question.

"Nah." When he didn't come off arrogant, Lucian

sounded bored. "Loretta brought them to me."

"Loretta? Father's daughter?"

Oh shit!

I should've figured that Father wouldn't run errands for a teenager, no matter how special.

"Yes, I couldn't get her to leave, either," Lucian grumbled. "She even brought Elliot. Figures she can't leave her stupid, half-blood lover behind—" Elliot was also her seedling. Perhaps that was why Lucian disliked him as strongly as he did.

"Whatcha g-got against half b-bloods?" Alphonse asked. "They're kinda cool. I m-mean, they unite our f-families, Lue."

Lucian blinked at Alphonse, and his expression softened. "Uh, yeah, I guess."

Alphonse brushed against Lucian's shoulder—having to bend down to rest his head. "S-Sure, you guys are your own r-race. Y-You were born a v-vamp, but since hu-humans can become vamps—"

"Half-vamps," Lucian cut in.

"O-Okay, but that still s-supports my theory of everyone c-c-coming from us."

I stopped listening, too busy fretting. "Shit."

"What?" Lucian raised his brow at me.

"Don's not gonna like that."

"Don? Your alpha?" Lucian's bored tone tinged with irritation. "Wait, he's here?"

"Yup!" Alphonse said happily and stopped leaning on Lucian's shoulder. "And I-I introduced myself pro-properly this time." He tied up his long hair into a ponytail, leaving the black strands around his face free.

Lucian's eyes narrowed at me before he glared at Alphonse then scanned the crowd. "Why the fuck is he even here?"

"Who's here?" Shamar came down carrying his drum cases.

"Fern's asshole alpha."

Shamar's nose wrinkled in disgust, and he blew out a sigh. "Don't tell me he wouldn't let you come here without him?"

"Bingo." I attached my extension to the plug socket and started tuning the guitar.

"What the fuck? Is he going to try to dominate every aspect of your life until you aren't even your own person!"

"Wasn't planning on it, brat. But it's not a bad idea now that you've said it." Don stood behind him, holding his drink. A faint pink entered Shamar's green skin. The dark tone made it more noticeable.

He went to put his stuff down, putting space between him and Don. "Well, I think that's horrible. And degrading. Fern isn't a piece of property."

"Yeah, yeah, yeah." Don cleaned his ear with his pinky finger. "I'm taking a seat over there." I was kind of shocked he didn't tell Shamar off, but then Don didn't seem to give a shit about my friends' thoughts and opinions.

"Fern," he leveled me with narrowed eyes, "remember what I told you."

I nodded. "Yeah."

Shamar knitted his brow, and his pupils darkened. With the blacklight causing his glossy stare to glow, he looked terrifying. "Did he just ignore me?" He sounded like he wanted to chase after Don and punch him in the face.

"Forget it. He's an asshole." He always treated me like that. It was apparent he would win against me in a fight easily. But I wasn't lesser because of that. The least he could do was not belittle me. It seemed like he did that to everyone he considered *not worth his time*—arrogant jerk.

I could tell where Don was because Shamar kept glaring at him. I wondered if Don would really start doing that—trying to dominate every aspect of my life. It wasn't far from the truth. Otherwise, why was he here, anyway?

Other alphas.

He was here to protect me against other alphas. I hadn't been to Crone's Head since hitting breeding age. Would I really be attacked? That scared me. Not the alphas, but the idea I might no longer have my freedom to go places on my own. That pissed me off. Shamar must have read that to mean anger at Don.

"I'm working on a curse for you." He kept glaring at Don.

For some reason, only the Gods knew what, I didn't want Shamar to do that. There was no way I was going to voice it, though. I had a reputation to keep. "Won't hear me complaining." Holding my *Allie Mac*, I looked at Lucian. "Ready?"

At his nod, we played a few notes to get in tune and warmed up. Don's eyes watching me from the crowd.

My fingers trembled, and I missed a note.

Fuck!

What the fuck did I care that Don was looking at me? It wasn't like I was trying to impress him. I decided to focus all my attention on my music.

Alphonse's loud—"Hey, hey guys, thanks for coming out!"—came a lot quicker than I thought, but I was warmed up and ready to play. "We're *Unalive!*" Hearing him say our band's name made it feel final like up until now we'd been trying it on for size. "Thanks for having us tonight. We're gonna play a few-few classics for you guys tonight. But I wanted to start-start us off with something I wrote." Alphonse had a habit of hogging the spotlight. It was weird, given how much he stuttered. But put him on stage in front of an audience and he shined. It even helped his stutter get better, if not eliminated entirely.

From the corner of my eye, Shamar bristled. Personally, I didn't care if Alphonse mentioned me or not. I wanted to finally play this song to a live audience. Alphonse had written the lyrics while Shamar and I hammered out the composition. Lucian hadn't helped at all. Typical pureblooded vampire. Just sat on his prissy ass while everyone else worked.

The song started out with Lucian's bass solo. He always had good rhythm skills. Finally, it was time for my part.

Closing my eyes, I let the music flow through my fingers until my *Ailill Mac* felt like an extension of my body. My soul rested for the first time since the Offering had started. I felt like myself again. Felt *normal.* I wasn't a beta forced to mate with some jerk. Or a newcomer into wereduin society that needed to be trained. I was simply Fern. How I used to be, and I stopped focusing on the fact that Don watched me from the audience and got lost in my music.

The four of us played great together. Shamar and I composed most of our music. All three of us took turns writing lyrics. Sometimes, Shamar and Alphonse hit heads, especially since Alphonse wanted to scream once per song. Shamar, being overly sensitive, preferred ballads. As we played emo with a metalhead punk, we were able to incorporate both of their styles.

When we stopped, the small crowd clapped, even those at the bar. I surveyed the room, watching all the people on couches—mostly wereduins and zombies, but there were several humans as well—some had been nodding to the music. Others had been out on the small dance floor, headbanging or jumping around. My gaze found Don's. He smiled at me—not teasing or mocking, but a genuine smile. My heart jumped. Was he proud of me?

That last thought pissed me off again. *Proud of me?* What was he, my papa? But the thought of impressing him got lodged into my mind, and I couldn't shake it.

Alphonse grabbed everyone's attention again. This time he jumped into the song. He and Lucian started off, then Shamar joined in and then me. This song had a unique arrangement. We played around with music to make the vocals simply another instrument. This time I led, the other guys, including Alphonse, played backup. It was like Alphonse and I communicated to each other through song. Our parts bounced back and forth like a dialog. Shamar had written these lyrics while I wrote the musical arrangement.

My eyes strayed into the crowd. Don watched me, his face neutral and relaxed. Immediately I felt on display. Beneath my black scarf, the bites on the valley of both my shoulders ached. I sucked in my bottom lip.

Alphonse stole my attention. He leaned against my shoulder, and I focused on our music—the four of us creating something together. I leaned back into him.

Lucian's bass solo came at the end. Alphonse migrated over to him with a bounce to his step, unlike how he normally walked with slumped shoulders and nose to the floor. Lucian and Alphonse leaned back-to-back. Lucian playing, while Alphonse kept harmonics.

When the last notes rang out, more people in the audience clapped. That was exciting and more than encouraging because this music was something we created together, not a cover of our favorite bands.

I looked over to Don again, only it wasn't his hungry eyes staring back at me. This alpha looked around my age. His eyes blood-red, and lines of drool trailed down his chin. Gradually, he shifted into a werewolf. Fear punched me in the gut. In milliseconds, I was terrified. His face told me he enjoyed causing me fear.

Fuck him. He was my age. Maybe I had to submit to Don, but not this junior. Swallowing down my fear, I extended my fangs. Slowly, my werewolf rose, and my wereduin features changed. My ears lengthened, heightening my hearing. As a werewolf, they should have been much pointier and furrier than a wereduin. However, much like they did in wereduin form, some of my worg features still lingered. Like my damned ear—the tip still drooped.

The more I transformed, the more my vision sharpened. My eyes grew larger, and distant objects became clearer. The sparse fur on my arms grew noticeable, heavier. In full werewolf, it wasn't shaggy but sheen, luxurious and warm. My tail grew—a trait that wasn't present in wereduin form. It also was lush, and would have been more uncomfortable if I hadn't been wearing my baggy jeans. My shirt too was starting to stretch as I grew taller, my body becoming stronger. I cursed not having pseudo-clothes.

A hand on the alpha's shoulder drew my attention to Don. At his deep growl, the smaller alpha turned around. The confrontation wasn't very loud, but it captured the interest of those nearby.

The alpha lowered his tail between his legs. Dropping eye contact, he quickly went back to the couches hidden behind the steps.

Don reverted to a wereduin.

I returned to wereduin form as well—my clothes probably thanking me. My front fang still hung outside my mouth before it softened too. The world around me also returned to normal.

A scoff came from the other side of me, toward Lucian.

"Leave it to the *dogs* to show their fangs in public." Loretta narrowed her violet eyes that glowed in the darkness. "I supposed it's too much to ask for dogs to not be dogs."

Like all Vampirean aristocracy, she was tall with a long face. She had pale skin and wore her platinum-blonde hair straight down her back. Her perfectly straight nose and beauty mark gave her a regal look. Her resemblance to Lucian was uncanny. The major difference between them was their height. Loretta, unlike her cousin, was very tall, and I had to look up at her.

Don snarled at her. He was much taller than Loretta and her companion.

"W-Woah, woah, woah!" Alphonse didn't look like he was afraid of Loretta. Maybe because she was like a big sister to Lucian, perhaps he thought she wouldn't attack him. He stepped between her and Don. I wondered if he considered Don like that, too. Safe, family. For a moment, I liked that he thought of Don that way. Then reality hit, and I dashed it down. "Co-Come on, guys, we're about to-to start an-another song—"

Loretta's long nails moved along Alphonse's cheek, the tips leaving faint marks on his skin. The signet ring she wore, which also matched Lucian's, sparkled. Her silver necklace drew my attention to her full breasts, barely contained in her black evening gown. I'd heard that vampiresses never went out in public in anything but splendid, lengthy dresses. Apparently, that was true.

She shared a mocking smile with the male vampire at her

side, Elliot. "How is it that weak human pets think they can speak in our presence?"

Alphonse flinched.

Lucian lowered his bass. "Don't you dare talk to him like that?"

"Lu-Lue?" Alphonse's eyes widened, his mouth trembling.

"You do not touch him, Loretta." He stepped off the stage, close enough to see that his hair had the same tiny, intricate braids around the sides of his face and down his back. I had missed that detail because the dark sections hid parts of it.

Lucian grabbed Alphonse's arm and jerked him out of the middle of what was becoming ground zero. He stepped in front of Alphonse before he drew his fangs. "Put another hand on him, and I'll remove it." Alphonse was taller, so he could still see Loretta over Lucian's head.

Loretta spoke to Lucian, still not looking at Alphonse. "You keep poor company, cousin. Human, zombie," –she sneered at Don— "and a *dog*."

"Want me to tear your throat out, bloodsucker? Keep talking." Don's handsome features were replaced with a full werewolf, about to make good on his threat. At that moment, nothing blocked Don from the vampires.

"Don!" I went to him, not even sure why, and I placed a hand on his chest. His thick fur both coarse and soft beneath my fingers. "Please don't."

An evil glint flashed in Loretta's pretty eyes. "Aw, is this your little mate?" Her forked tongue licked along her ruby-red lips. I should have known she'd keep poking the fire. If only I could wish her away. I had been counting on Lucian's family being too pompous to visit a dinky joint like Crone's Head.

"Fuck off, Loretta," Lucian interrupted her. "If you get me kicked out, Father will surely hear about this."

Elliot joined her side. He looked at Alphonse and me like he wanted to skewer us with his fangs.

Fuck him. I wasn't afraid.

Alphonse tugged on Lucian's shoulder, then grabbed mine. "C-Come on, g-g-guys. We need to get ba-back to p-p-playing."

Don took my hand off, directing me toward the stage and out of the way. "By all means, don't let us stop you." He narrowed his glowing neon blue eyes at Loretta. "Right this way, bloodsucker, if you wanna fight."

"Don, don't." I grabbed the back of his pseudo-shirt.

"Stay out of this, Fern." He wasn't cruel, but he wasn't friendly, either. Then he turned to me. "Go back and play. I'll meet you back here."

I shook my head. I didn't want him to go out and fight. I heard Lucian's family was strong, but it wasn't that I thought Don would lose. I didn't want them to spill blood. Lucian and I were friends.

"Look, whatever you have against us isn't worth it, so just fuck off." I spoke to Loretta like I had the power to make her listen. "If that alpha B.S. bothers you, how about not watching?"

"Lucian?" She looked right at me as she addressed her cousin. Her fangs extended. "I think your little friend would look cuter in red."

It happened too fast. One minute Don faced me, and the next, all I felt was a rush of air before he was gone. The first thing I heard was the clashing of his claws against her blades.

She had produced twin daggers made of steel, engraved with pearls on the hilts. His claws were enough to meet them and provide resistance. He was an alpha. They were made for fighting, and everything about their physiology said as much. Those blades didn't even come close to cracking his lethal weapons.

Don used his claws like daggers, but unlike with other alphas, he didn't rely so much on his size. Instead, he used the more elegant speed-fighting similar to what he'd done in the Second Offering.

The tops of his claws fended off her attacks before his lethal tips slashed at her. When she blocked, he supported her weapon's weight evenly among his claws. He moved like a dance with twists and flips. Despite the elaborate moves, he still fought within his space. Immediately, I remembered the Underbelly when he'd fought in the confines of the ring.

Loretta fought with agility and grace, also using intricate moves. Her sparkling daggers formed elaborate patterns, all the while, she kept up with his pace.

Don's claws slashed right through her chest with intent to skewer clean through. Only for her to burst into smoke, black clouds like mist in the club lighting. Her high-pitched laughter filled the air. She reappeared right behind Don, thrusting her small silver blade at the back of his shoulder.

My heart leaped into my throat. "Don!"

Turning in mere seconds, he blocked her weapon with his claws. Loretta scowled. "What a pestering dog." Elliot joined in, but he didn't fight quite so elegantly and took down a nearby *Zombie Blood* picture. Don easily warded off Elliot's attacks. Loretta was more challenging. Still, he parried their blades, blocking and attacking them in turns. Perhaps it was too early to tell, but Don appeared to be winning.

That was as far as they got before they were asked to leave. Don left without question. This was a challenge, and as a wereduin, once a challenge was entered, it was final. Loretta and Elliot didn't follow and instead left in the other direction. I got a better look at why wereduins and vampires butted heads. For a challenger to initiate a fight and not finish was shameful in our culture. Trickery, games, and having someone else join the fight—things we considered weak and cowardly—seemed commonplace among vampires. Attacking in the shadows after walking away seemed like something they would do.

I didn't like the idea of him alone out there with those two. They didn't fight fair. There was no telling how low they would stoop. I had a flashback to when Don had come to pick me up that time when my friends and I walked home, how he had called Lucian an untrustworthy bloodsucker. Maybe this was where Don was coming from. If those assholes came back with a group of them, and if they managed to hurt Don, I would kill them.

Inwardly, I shook my head. It was ludicrous to think anyone would be able to hurt Don. He took on a whole colony of molebats! Vampires seemed scarier, cleverer. Wait a second...why the hell was I so upset over something happening to an asshole like Don? Stopping my thoughts, I let out a curse.

"You still with us, Fern?" Lucian said by my side.

"Yeah." I tried to shrug it off. "Why wouldn't I be?"

"Oh, I don't know, 'cause your boyfriend went out to fight my cousins." Lucian shook his long hair out of his face. His headbanging had caused some strands to slip free of his braids and hide his eyes.

"He's not my boyfriend...gross." In my mind, I felt him kissing me, saw his eyes closing as his kisses turned tender.

"Right..." Lucian humphed. "Just don't fuck us up."

"Fuck you." I shook off my thoughts. For the next two songs, I focused on the music.

Another alpha in the audience stalked closer to the stage. *Fuck.* This guy was nothing like the junior alpha who had threatened me earlier. He was older, and based on the size of his bulging physique, definitely in Don's league.

But Don wasn't here. I was alone.

Fear knotted my stomach, and I gripped the neck of my guitar until my knuckles whitened. Don had told me not to run, but as this older stranger approached, my instincts screamed *get out of there!*

Shamar stopped playing and stood up. It stole my attention. "You need to back off, man." He advanced on the alpha. Was Shamar standing up to an alpha with bloodlust growing in his narrowing red eyes?

Without a thought, he slashed Shamar, who put up his arm in time.

"Fuck!" I went to help him. "Shamar!"

"Okay, someone escort the alpha out of here," said one of the barkeeps.

Shamar grimaced. "Shit..."

"Back off." I stepped in front of Shamar.

The alpha leered. His eyes roamed over my body before he whispered, "Run." He revealed sharp-looking canines. "I want you to run."

I swallowed. *Shit.* I wasn't an idiot. Running from an alpha was a fantastic way to get killed, not just claimed.

I shook my head. "Back off. We're trying to play. If you've got an issue, take it up with my alpha outside."

"Mi maji saa uwe. Mi maji toki ten *uwe."* Shamar's voice grew with intensity, *"Ooneka! ooneka! Kuuwae tuka mi!"* He took out a voodoo bag from his baggy jeans pocket and threw it at the wereduin's feet.

"See that, asshole?" A gleam appeared in Shamar's black, bulging eyes. The underlying emotion was unknown to me. Menacing, terrifying. If he wasn't my best friend, I might have been scared. "I just took ten years off your life. Keep away from Fern unless you wanna lose ten more."

Two barkeeps, both large trolls, took the alpha out.

"You're mine, boy." The alpha looked at me the entire way up the stairs.

Don! My heart hammered in my chest; adrenaline pumped through my veins. Where was he? I never thought I'd actually want to have him by my side, but that alpha had scared me more than I realized.

Shamar's arm was slashed open. As a zombie, he didn't bleed, but he still needed to prevent infection. Perhaps he needed to more because he was a zombie. *Shit.*

That pretty much ruined the night. We had one song left, but Shamar needed to tend to his injury. We left Alphonse and Lucian to finish the gig, and the bartender got some alcohol for Shamar.

Don had been right. I could no longer move about as I pleased. That struck me hard.

I went into the bathroom with Shamar and held the cloth bandage we received from the bar's first aid kit. Shamar washed his bloodless wound underneath the water. My eyes drew to the whiteness beneath the cut, white and purple, not living blood or flesh.

Shamar looked away. "Is it gross to you?"

"Huh?"

"My skin. Is it gross to you?"

"Nah, why the heck would I find it gross? Geez, sometimes you make no sense." I nudged him in the shoulder before my voice turned serious. "You didn't have to do that. He could've seriously hurt you."

Shamar shrugged. "I couldn't think of anything else to do. The asshole looked like he was going to hurt you."

I scoffed. "So…what? You get hurt instead?"

Shamar shrugged again. "Better than him hurting you."

"Don't see why. Come on, you have to patch this quickly, or you'll get infected." I didn't like how long Shamar was taking. Zombies had to be careful about infection. There was a very real chance they could start rotting inside if exposed to something harmful. Their skin protected them from most ailments, something they used voodoo to enhance, but it could mean death—real death—if injured.

"Just don't do that again, okay?" I suddenly felt angry. I didn't want Shamar to get hurt for this stupid werewolf mating shit. "There's probably gonna be a lot of them from now on. Leave it to Don, please."

"He's not the only one."

"What? 'Course he's not. That's why I said there will be more of them."

"I mean, who can protect you. Don's not the only one."

"Against them? He sure as hell is. You and me? We don't stand a chance." Whatever I said must have hurt him since Shamar grew quiet. The silence felt awkward, so I focused on helping him apply the alcohol and not whatever the heck was going on in his head. "Look, thanks for helping me. I just don't wanna see you get hurt over this dumbass mating bullshit."

Shamar looked at me. "I stopped him, at least."

"Yeah." Tension drained from my body, and I gave him a faint smile. "Guess you did. But, dumbass, don't do something like that again." I didn't want to lose my best friend. Not to this. I had already lost my independence—my life. I didn't want to lose Shamar. I nudged him again. "You stopped him, but next time, I think I'll run."

"You fucking won't," Shamar said with intensity. "He'll kill you."

"Yeah...that's what Don said, too."

"Well, in that one aspect, that asshole and I agree. Don't ever, ever run, Fern."

"You know, I don't like seeing you get hurt, either."

Shamar smiled forlornly. "Sorry about that."

"You-You both better be!" Alphonse stood in the bathroom doorway. His hands on his hips. "You-You guys left Lucian and I to carry the weight."

"Well, seeing how Loretta started it and drove Don away, it serves him right."

"What the-the fuck, Fern?" I didn't expect Alphonse to get angry. "Is this a-a-a vampire versus wereduin thing no-now?"

"What? No."

"Since-Since when can you control Don? Why blame Lucian and think-think he can do the same?"

"Sorry, sorry." It probably did sound like I was taking sides. "I, well...I kinda would've liked Don to be there. Then that asshole wouldn't have been able to take a go at Shamar."

"Is-Is it bad?" Alphonse's anger faded.

"Nah," Shamar brushed it off.

"Well, in all fairness, Lucian t-told them to leave. Loretta just-just likes to cause trouble." Alphonse looked from Shamar to me. "B-But you didn't do much to-to-to drive them away. Honestly, y-you just provoked them more."

"What did you want me to do, beg them to leave?" I growled. "Yeah, fucking right."

"Be-Because they're vampires?"

"No, because I don't beg to anyone. Fuck, no."

"Okay, all right, guys. Let's not fight. I'm good." It was weird that Shamar had stopped a conflict when normally I had to stop conflicts between him and Alphonse.

We left the restroom, and Don was waiting outside.

"You? You're back!" I smiled without thinking, but it faded as I took in his appearance. "You've been fighting?"

"Had a couple of rounds."

"With the vampires?"

"Those bloodsuckers? Nah, they ran. Typical. Fucking cowards. It was just some alpha that got thrown out. He was eying you, so he came to the right spot."

"Good." Anger seethed through my words. "Hope you ripped him up."

"Wow." Don looked surprised. "First you don't want me to fight, now you want me to tear him up."

"That asshole clawed Shamar."

"Oh? Your friend all right?" Was Don caring about Shamar?

"Uh, yeah. He was able to get patched up from the first aid kit."

Don nodded before he swore under his breath. "Fucking bloodsuckers. I should have been there."

"Lucian's not like that."

Don snorted. "Yeah, for now."

"For *ever*. Lucian has been my friend since I first started high school. Maybe his family can be assholes, but he's not. So don't hold it against him."

"Just be careful, Fern." I expected him to fight me more. Maybe he realized Lucian wasn't much of a threat? "You okay?" Don rested his hand on my head before trailing his fingers down my face.

"Hey!" I didn't have time to push him off before he let go.

"You're pretty good," Don smiled. "So how long have you been playing?" Was Don curious about one of my interests?

I tried to fix my hair as I led the way down the stairs to the speakeasy where my guitar and amps waited. "Since Mom gave me one when I was in middle school."

"Was that around the time I protected you?"

I thought about it. "A little before, actually."

"You protected Fern in school? When?" Shamar was putting away his drum set. Alphonse and Lucian were still closing their gear.

"Not really any of your business, is it?"

"Geez, Don!" I glared at him. "He's just asking a question." I turned to Shamar. "Yeah, it was from Brig and his group." Shamar and I had become friends in the second year of middle school, so he was familiar with the group of senior alphas who used to bother me.

Shamar eyed Don skeptically.

"I'm gonna grab another drink." Don didn't seem bothered when Shamar's skepticism turned into a glare.

"Wait," I called him back, "get me one."

"I'm not buying you alcohol."

"The fuck, Don? Since when are you my parent? Come on, if you're my mate and all, then you have to share—"

Don looked at me with wide eyes. Stepping into my personal space, he cupped my chin and kissed me hard.

I pushed him away. "Wa-Wait!"

"You called me your mate."

I shook my head. "Slip of the tongue."

"Well, your drink that I had changed my mind about getting you just slipped *my* mind."

I growled. "Jerk. Can't you be nice to me for once?"

"Who's not nice to you?" The corner of his lip rose in a smirk. "Say it again, say that I'm your mate, and I'll get you something to drink."

"F-Forget it." Kina, the bartender, liked me. She would give me *Jars Lite*. She was cool like that. I didn't need to stoop so low for alcohol. "Never mind. I'm tight with the bartender. She'll give me something."

"With what money?"

Oh. With Don present, there was no way he'd allow me access to his family's Vault like I had on the bus to Shamar's.

"Fuck it, I don't need anything, anyway." I turned and

continued putting my guitar away, trying not to take my anger out on the instrument. I was pissed. The chasm between Don and I widened even more. He was the one with the money and the power in this relationship. He had age, and soon the law, on his side too. What did I have? I couldn't even go to a bar with my friends without being attacked.

I turned around and glared at Don at the bar. *Jerk.* He lived to humiliate me. That was why he had to point out that he had money while I had none. I had nothing without him.

I sat my guitar case next to the coffee table where we normally liked to hang out after a show and have a drink. Alphonse had already claimed some couches. He kept looking at Don with large, dreamy eyes—probably wondering how he should ask for an autograph. Alphonse and his stupid *spawn*.

Shamar already had a drink. "Got you one. If you're up for it?" He passed me a *Jars Lite*.

"See? I knew Kina was working tonight!" I took a swig before my smile weakened. "Oh, wait. I don't have any ules this time."

"Pay me back later."

"With what money?" Don held a drink in each hand. "Here." He placed one down in front of me.

It was one of the warm liquor-based drinks. Fancy, but not overly high in alcohol. About the same as a *Jars Lite* and probably tasted much better.

"He already has a drink." Shamar snarled at Don, narrowing his brow—it made it look like he didn't have eyebrows, and that made his eyes stand out. He looked like the menacing zombie that he was. "He doesn't need to be in any more debt to you."

"You really are an annoying, little brat. Aren't you?" Don picked up the *Jars Lite* Shamar had given me and took a sip.

"What the hell, jerk?" I couldn't believe he drank from my bottle.

"Fine. Have it your way." He placed the *Jars Lite* back in front of me. "Drink this crap. Or...you can have the good stuff. Your choice?"

I sniffed the warm drink. It smelled heavenly. But Don was the one offering. Should I take it? Shamar looked pissed like he wanted to hit Don but thankfully thought better of that. Of course, Don ignored him like an unruly child, which, I imagined pissed Shamar off even more. Don was such a belittling jerk.

Sipping the warm drink before I could stop myself, I tasted it.

Wow.

"See? Told ya." Don's smile widened, and I realized I spoke out loud.

Shamar's look of betrayal made me feel guilty for drinking it.

Despite coming of age in wereduin society, somehow, I still wasn't old enough to drink. Funny how I was now allowed (required?) to join the Offering and potentially get killed in the stupid mating game. Not to mention forced to mate with some asshole alpha, but Arduinna help it, if I actually wanted to get drunk. Our society had its priorities up its ass.

"Well, it is kinda good." I snubbed Don. "Not like I'm gonna thank you."

Don looked irritatingly smug. "And yet you did."

"I'm going home." Shamar collected his things.

"Shamar!" I went after him when Don grabbed my hand.

"He has to accept you're mated now. Otherwise, I have no intention of letting him come around." If Don could have picked the worst possible words to say to me then, he did.

"What the fuck?" I tried to yank away from him, but he was too strong. No surprise there. "Maybe you expect the whole world to think what you're doing to me is not wrong, but Shamar isn't like that!"

"Wrong? You're my mate. I'm not doing anything wrong to you." With his free hand, he chugged his drink. "We're going."

"W-What?"

"We have to get up early for tomorrow, anyway."

"But I haven't even finished my drink yet?"

"Then it's a good thing you didn't want it. Let's go."

"No."

"Fern." His tone was low, challenging. "Are you trying to test my patience? If you don't want to get thrown out of your own bar, pick up your stuff and let's go. I won't say it again. We're leaving."

I wondered if I should challenge him. But…I really liked this bar. As it was, they were giving Don unwelcoming looks. If the two of us started fighting in here, I might not be allowed back.

"I fucking hate you. You know that?"

"Come on." He downed the remainder of his drink and headed up the steps. "You've got five minutes to get your stuff, or else I'm dragging you out of here, got that?"

"Fern?" Alphonse had been silent the entire time. Lucian had gone home to prevent Loretta's story from being the only one given to Father. Oddly, even though he was alone, Alphonse didn't look afraid. *Weird.* "You really ought to be nice-nicer to-to him, you know?"

"What?" I exhaled sharply like he'd socked me in the gut. "Me, be nice to him? You were right there. You saw how he treated me!"

"Well, I saw you f-fight-fighting him. He even got you that-that drink you wanted. Honestly, he's a-a nice guy. Maybe in-in-instead of fighting him, y-you should try and get t-to know him."

"Fuck you."

Alphonse held up his hands. "S-Sorry, I don't wanna butt my nose in."

"Then don't. Fuck…just 'cause he's a *spawn* player, that's all you're thinking about."

"No. I mean, yeah, but besides all that. He's like th-the nicest alpha I've met. Really. I don't think he'd be mean to you, if-if you didn't act the way y-you do."

"The way I do?"

"Ye-Yeah…"

"He threatened to drag me outta here. And he would too!

He pushes me around. And *he's* the nice one? Fuck this." I grabbed up my guitar case and stacked my amps on top of it, carrying it up. Alphonse's words lingered.

Don had gotten me a drink. He hadn't prevented me from going tonight. He'd even showed interest in my playing. Though I wasn't sure how I felt about him coming with me, it was nice to know that he was there to keep me safe. Still, Don, nice? He was a jerk, right? He was a rapist. He kidnapped me. He ordered me around. He threatened to not let me be around Shamar. I scoffed. Like I would ever stop hanging out with my best friend.

Still, I couldn't get Alphonse's words out of my head though, regardless of how hard I tried.

...to be continued in book 2!

About the Author

Rosary is an author of erotica ranging from sweet and fluffy, to dark and taboo. She aims to foster a sex-positive experience for readers to indulge their fantasies in a fun and safe space. Sometimes she uses her writing to journey into the often hidden and taboo depths of human sexuality, and hopes readers will take away from her stories, not an acceptance of violence and sexual abuse, but rather a way to embrace their inner desires often shamed by society.

Follow Me on Social Media

Website:
rosarydeville.com

Facebook:
facebook.com/rosary.deville

Rosary's Devilish Delights FB Readers Group:
facebook.com/groups/RosarysDevilishDelights

Twitter:
twitter.com/DevilleRosary

Instagram:
instagram.com/rosary_deville_69

Newsletter:
rosarydeville.com/newsletter

Amazon Author:
amazon.com/author/rosarydeville

Goodreads:
goodreads.com/author/show/20782176.Rosary_Deville

For a complete list of all my social media, see my linktr.ee:

linktr.ee/rosarydeville

Also by Rosary Deville

HENRÍ, À LA CARTE
À la carte, book #1

It's another year, another birthday for Casey until his lover gets other plans.

Henrí never expected to be asked to join a threesome, but when he's asked by his crush's boyfriend, how can he resist becoming a side dish to the couple's sexual appetites.

THE OFFERING SURRENDER
Wolves of Wereduin, Book 2

Fern's fate was never his to decide, and now Wereduin Society challenges him in the most brutal way possible.

The Offering is nearing the end, and Fern will become a mated beta. So far, he's been unsuccessful at escaping his alpha, Donovan Blackfang. But in their world, where it's dog eats dog, Don might be the key to Fern's survival.

Don't miss the riveting conclusion of the Wolves of Wereduin series.

Glossary

Alpha Wereduin

- Developed to be strong, dominant, and vicious
- Most have Irish-sounding names – although they do not know the origin
- Tallest of the races, they can reach heights over eight feet in werewolf form
- Have the ability to influence their betas with their alpha prowess—mental arousal or physical essence that can be consumed by betas
- Follow strict rules of societal behavior, which is based on class
- When they come of age, they devote themselves to a sect of one of the gods. Most, if not all, involve some kind of fighting

Alphonse

- Fern's human friend
- Like all humans in this society, he is a descendant of the legendary Van Helsing and a family of Vampire Hunters. But it's been centuries since they have hunted vampires. Now the two races live side by side
- Fern thinks he's a scaredy-cat with the courage of a mouse
- He has a nervous stutter and, although tall, slouches when he walks to not draw attention
- He will return in a spin-off

Arduinna, Goddess of Hunt

- Alpha goddess known as the mother goddess, because she created the wereduin race from her two hunting worgs
- Her beta mate is Cerowain, God of Fertility

Arawn, the God of Death

- Beta mate to the Twin Gods of War

- Souls go before him and are judged accordingly, with those found worthy sent to the Moon Vale and those who are not are sent to the Shadows, where they will be forgotten
- Legend has it that the Twin Gods of War protected their beta, Arawn the God of Death, from the old gods who wanted to rid *Death* from the heavens. From that, alphas from the Twin's sect swear an oath to do likewise for their betas

Ayida-Weddo

- In the Voodoo religion practiced by zombies, she is the creator of the zombie race, and they revere her as their Mother Goddess
- She is the most powerful of all Voodoo loa, and the closest to the Supreme god, who later turned her into a goddess

Bayous

- Swampland where Zombies live in medium-sized communities
- The Voodoo spell that helps maintain and animate their bodies requires a lot of water, so the humid air is perfect

Beta Wereduin

- Smaller wereduin born to be subservient, as is their natural state, *before society made it something to strip away one's personhood,* as Fern said
- Birth young, regardless of gender
- Typically are named after flowers or plants, i.e., Fern, and Rose, etc.
- Can be influenced by alphas' prowess that calls forth their instincts to submit to their alpha
- Werewolf form developed for beauty, not strength or fierceness

- Prized in society for lineage and often treated as a commodity. When born, they belong to their parents, and then ownership is transferred to an alpha upon mating. Legally, they are the property of the alpha
- When their alpha dies, they are buried with them, often put to sleep to ease the process
- Are accepted into alpha's den if they have one

Blackfang Den

- Don's family den
- Highborne den with family crests and estate

Bloodwhispers

- Creatures that hunt after molebats have finished their attacks
- They secrete mists to make their victims comatose, then attack from the shadows
- These are silent blood drawers, crave live blood
- Evolved to be deathly silent since too weak to attack in the open.
- They are long and skinny and inch along the ground like a caterpillar. Their centipede-like bodies are covered in soft hairs
- They're roughly two feet long
- To draw blood, they use their long feelers that resembled antennae on both sides of their head
- They can draw blood without inflicting pain and can drain their prey dry without being noticed until it's too late
- Most live close to molebats to take advantage of their leftovers
- Molebats sometimes eat them, but mostly, bloodwhispers wait until the colony has left the arena before looking for food weakened by the molebats

Bog Homes

- Zombie homes. These circular homes have wooden porches and steps leading up to the door. The poles on either side stick into the mud and prevent the home from sinking

Brawny

- One of Don's lowlife friends whose crude humor and abusive nature toward his beta make him particularly distasteful
- He likes to taunt Fern, which borders on harassment and later puts him at odds with Don
- Alpha werewolf who's smaller than Don and roughly around his age

Brigacos or Brig

- An alpha who used to bully Fern in school
- Fern had been in middle school, and Brigacos had been a senior in high school
- The bullying stopped once Don intervened, even though Fern didn't know it was him who had done so

Cerowain, the God of Fertility

- Beta god, with stag horns on his head
- Mate of Arduinna
- Formerly was a stag that gave Arduinna such a hunt that she turned fell in love with him and turned him into a werewolf

Change, the

- The zombie rite of passage into adulthood. A zombie is subjected to a curse that kills them before reanimating their body, and awake as a full-fledged zombie

Coupling

- A practice where the alpha stays inside the beta while doing other tasks unrelated to sex. The idea is for betas to get used to being under their alphas

Crones

- Also known as hags, these are usually older witches that had sold their souls to Cursed Phantoms, or Sprites
- They lived off body parts to survive
- Begs for body parts to eat or use in spells
- These witches were banished from the witch community, who feels like the crones have earned the entirety of their race a bad name

Dagda the All Father
- Father of the Gods
- Alpha and mate to Luna the Moon Goddess
- Despite being the creator of the gods, neither he nor Luna created the Werewolves, so Arduinna is their mother goddess
- There are sects devoted to him, as there are to other gods

Days of the Week
- *Dagasday* (da-GAST-day) = Sunday. Named from the God Dagda, the All Father
- *Belsday* (BELLS-day) = Monday. Named for the Sun God Bel
- **Dweensday** (du-WEENS-day) = Tuesday. Named for Arduinna, Goddess of the Hunt
- **Twinsday** (TWINS-day) = Wednesday. Named for the Twin Gods of War
- **Morriansday** (MORE-ends-day) = Thursday. Named for the Morrigan Goddess of Sex
- **Surensday** (sur-RENS-day) = Friday. Named for the God Cerowain, God of Fertility
- **Alunsday** (a-LOONS-day) = Saturday. Named for Moon Goddess Luna, the Life-giver and Mother of the Gods

Druids

- Wereduin dedicated their lives to serving the gods. Most are betas, but a few alphas occasionally take vows. Seldom do they leave werewolf form

Elaine, Goddess of Obedience

- Alpha goddess in whose honor Obedience Training is done

Family Vaults

- Sometimes called Den Vaults, these act as a communal bank for the entire Den
- They are expensive to own, so only Highborne families have them
- They are maintained by gollums, which is why they cost so much. See gollums

Fangorre

- A metal band of werewolves. Their logo is a set of fangs dripping with red blood

First Death

- The death experienced by zombies during their Change. Unlike regular death, while it kills their body, their mind is restored afterward because of the Voodoo spells and concoctions that are used in the ritual

First Offering, the

- See the Hunt

Hands of the Moon

- Cult of priestess and priests devoted to the Goddess Luna, the Life-giver
- Betas that are impotent and thus not desired by alphas
- They dedicated themselves to serving the community

Highbornes

- Wealthy wereduin in the top echelons of werewolf society

- Each belongs to a Den, having started out being a child of the Den leader and lives in the mansion. Those who were not direct heirs later move out into their own homes but are still considered members of the den
- A Highborn den, such as the Blackfang den, has a family estate as well as a vault
- Fern's mother is the daughter of the Brightwood Den leader, while Don is the son of the Blackfang Den leader
- A beta will become a member of his alpha's den and will need to be initiated after he is officially mated

Hummock Prairie

- A vast prairie littered by dunes, or hummocks, in the countryside
- It is the home of molebats, and the Second Offering is held there to test if werewolf pairs can survive the night

Hunt, the

- The first of three Offerings where alphas hunt their future beta
- Done in honor of the Alpha Goddess Arduinna, Goddess of Hunt who legend has it hunted her mate Cerowain and turned him into a werewolf
- Alpha can only take one beta unless the others are slave betas
- After the Hunt, the beta can move into the alpha's home and must be subservient to them

Iron Furies, the

- A professional *spawn* team that Don has been a fan of since puphood

Jabir Zelaji

- A zombie guitarist from Zombie Blood who owns a brand of acoustic guitars

Jut

- One of Don's lowlife friends who's part giant and part wereduin. He's one of Don's friends that Fern likes, and who in turn is kind to Fern
- Likes to taunt Don using the nickname *Donny boy*
- He's so huge, he makes Don look small. Since he's a half breed, his ears aren't pointy like wereduins, rather they look like giant human ears, and the tip of his huge nose is round like a ball

Loa

- Spirits that serve as intermediaries between the zombies and the supreme Voodoo god
- Zombies perform rituals and acts of service to them to performing spells and hexes

Lord Kenneally

- A distinguished Highborne wereduin who rules the Kenneally den
- He has salt-and-pepper hair and a deeply furrowed brow that makes him look stern even when smiling. He also has a white scar across his eye, a mustache and wears top hats
- The first time Fern meets him, he makes Fern uncomfortable

Lucian

- Fern's vampire friend
- Aristocratic vampire who lives in a coven, as most do, and is the favorite of the coven leader, known as Father
- He's the true goth of Fern's group, dressing in an antiquated style
- His closest friend is Alphonse, and he's quite protective of him – including standing up for him against his cousin, Loretta, Father's daughter

- He and Shamar can hit heads mostly because of the zombie-human conflicts that effect Alphonse, and so Lucian gets upset
- Will return in spin-off

Luna, Beta Goddess of the Moon

- Known as Luna the Life-giver, she is the mother of the gods
- The beta to Dagda the All Father
- Despite being the creator of the gods, Luna did not create Werewolves. Arduinna is their mother goddess

Mating Song

- Equivalent to the official wedding vows alphas and betas say to each other after the Final Offering to bind them together forever

Mating Quilt

- Made to honor the God of the Offering,
- Used to consummate the mating vows during the Offering
- Made by beta parents to their beta children
- Alphas cannot enter the Mating Quilt of a beta claimed by another alpha

Mating Week

- First week wereduin couples are officially mated. Most pairs spend the entirety of it in bed. To conceive during Mating Week is good luck

Meatheads

- Another metalcore band Fern's into and wears their band tees

Meat Skuwls

- Zombie metalhead band of zombie players

- Logo is a Voodoo doll with pins stuck to it. Dripping blood. The expression on the face is showing teeth. Part of the brain is exposed
- One of Fern's favorite bands and he often wears their tee shirts

Mites

- A flea-bitten old werewolf that's one of Don's lowlife friends. Unlike a lot of his other friends, Mites shares a connection to Don that sets him apart from the others

Molebats

- They are a mixture of bat and rodent with faces resembling bats with their beady eyes, pig-like snout, and large bat ears. Inside their mouths, two fangs protrude on either side with rows of tiny, jagged teeth. Their skinny arms stretch like a bat, but they don't have wings. They have knife-like, retractable talons on their three fingers. They walk upright on two legs or crawl on all four. They have rat legs, toes, and tail, and they scurry when they move, much like rodents. While their arms are naked like bats, their faces, bodies, and legs are covered in fur

- They live underground in burrows, which are a complex network of tunnels. Molebat drones gather prey and bring the carcasses back to the colony

- Although much smaller than werewolves, they attack in vast numbers. Often entire colonies attack at once and can overcome a lone wolf, or a small group

Moon Vale

- Wereduin equivalent of heaven in the afterlife

- A place where the gods live and only those mortals who are found worthy may enter after death

Myrtle

- Fern's acquaintance that was turned into a slave beta that he sees in the Second Offering

Nightshade cigarettes

- Cigarettes made specifically for Zombies, created from the deadly nightshade plant
- Only werewolves and zombies can smoke this. It's strong enough to kill humans

Non-fighting zones

- To keep civilization flowing, as well as to appease the other races, there are places called non-fighting zones where werewolf fights are illegal

Nomans Forest

- A vast woodland that said to be named by prehistoric humans, those that existed long before the Van Helsing line. Today various races used it in their Rites of Passage ceremonies

Offering, the

- Ritual that exists to produce couples
- All werewolves, alpha or beta, must participate in this Ritual to be allowed to mate. The exception is for slave betas that are born into slavery
- The ritual is a month and consists of three Offering ceremonies spread out evenly, with the days in-between for other ceremonies, banquets, and bonding time between couples. The very last week is the week of the full moon and mating week.

Obedience Training

- An all-encompassing *How to Submit Your Beta* is what it really should have been called. It also opens the gate for championships

- Takes place in a large arena where alphas dominate their beta, walking them on leashes and taking them to other activities—those designed with sex in mind

Pirkko Brightwood
- Fern's mother
- Her father is the alpha head of the Brightwood Den, and her older brother inherited the Den when her father stepped down
- Highborne wereduin that cares greatly about appearances and forces Fern into the Offering
- Is kind and loving to Fern's papa and contributed to Fern being sheltered from his harsh society
- Also, one of Don's trainers/teachers, and he refers to her as Teacher Brightwood. He also addresses her with high respect
- Don had informed her of his intentions to pursue Fern before the Offering

Pseudo-clothes
- Clothing made from a special fabric that doesn't rip while shifting between forms
- The fabrics shrink down to mere threads that fit between the fur follicles and are thus not visible when in either wolf or werewolf form. In wereduin form, the clothes fill out and act as regular clothes
- Most pseudo-clothes are made for alphas, with a few for betas. Fern has a few pairs
- All kinds of clothing exist as pseudo-clothes. Shorts, pants, shirts, dresses, robes, shoes, etc....
- Created by witch technology

Pup maker

- Derogatory name for a mated beta

Rage, the

- A period when zombies become mindless eating machines and will kill friends and lovers alike. These states begin after the zombie has gone through the Change. What's happening here is their mind is temporarily dying—reverting to the state they were in upon their First Death, but Voodoo spells and concoctions are used to restore their minds. The Rage never goes away, and in fact, gets more frequent before finally peaking and leveling out with maturity and age. At first, the Rage can occur several times a month, but eventually can dwindled for months in-between, even longer. Zombies will feel the Rage coming on like the start of a migraine—most detect it a day before it happens, and so are able to prepare. Despite the results, the Rage period is important and even sacred to most zombies, and has great significance in their Voodoo religion

Second Offering
- The second of the three Offering used to weed out weak alphas an unprotected betas
- Done in honor of the Twin Gods of War
- The alpha must keep their beta alive through the night while fending off molebats and bloodwhispers
- Also known as the Silver Offering

Sequoia-oak
- An ancient tree large enough to house buildings inside it.
- Some of these monstrous trees can even hold up entire palaces, like the City Hall Tower

Shamar
- Fern's zombie best friend
- Has green-colored skin, mangy black hair that always looks uncombed, like he has recently gotten out of bed. He sprinkles a bit of dirt on it

- Walks with a shuffle
- Overly emotion, loyal, and strongly dislikes Don

Silver Offering

- See Second Offering

Spawn

- A professional sport where the goal is to capture the opponent's trident and bring it back to home base while keeping theirs protected.
- Gets its name from the origin of the Twins of War. When war broke out in the heavens, the Dagda and Luna *spawn*ed the Twins of War to fight and so protect the heavens from the old gods
- Its origins might be wereduin, but *spawn* is a mainstream game in society that multiple races enjoy
- A particularly vicious sport that requires teamwork, strategy, and a lot of fighting
- Playing fields, or tracks, can be huge. Sometimes half the city gets roped off. Often, they're made up of obstacles. Beasts are sometimes added to provide additional challenges. Fields frequently change, depending on the stages of difficulty
- Two teams start out on opposite sides of the playing field at their home temple. Inside the temple is the trident of the gods. The goal is to protect their trident while also stealing the opponents. The first to achieve this goal wins

Twin Gods of War

- Also known simply as the Twins of War
- These are the War Goddess, Cath Bodva, and her twin, the God Camalus
- Their symbol is a pair of silver, crisscrossing blades

Ules

- Pronounced yew-els, (like *jewels* with a y) are the currency of this society. When not represented digitally, ules are pieces of gold

Unalive

- Fern and his friends' emo-metal band

Underbelly

- A series of drainage tunnels, sewers, underground rivers, and caverns that lay below the city. It is a shady place full of criminal activity, such as the black market, gambling, and drug trafficking

Vampires

- They did not start out as humans, although that is disputed by humans. They are a living race, but not alive in the same way as Fern and Alphonse.

- Have platinum blond long hair, pointed ears that stick out past their heads, pale skin, long faces, and high cheekbones

- All vampires have purplish eye color

- Speak *Vampirean*

- Live in covens headed by *Father*, a name they give their leader

- Have forked tongues

- Their fangs extended longer when about to feed

Vampirean

- Language spoken by Vampires

Wereduin

- The humanoid form. Most werewolves stay in this form because it requires less energy than werewolf form

- Form between wolf and werewolf forms

- This is the normal state most wereduin live in

- Wereduin require more energy to stay in this form, which is why it takes pups time to transform from wolf and stay as wereduin

- Beta wereduin can transform into wereduins by around age six or seven
- Alpha wereduin can transform earlier, some as early as the first year of life

Wereduin Housing

- Live in tune with nature. Their houses often have trees growing through them, as opposed to cutting them down. Sometimes they are built inside of a giant tree

Wereduin Reproduction

- Beta wereduin are always fertile except when already pregnant
- Betas go into *heat* once every so many months. During this period, the beta is highly fertile and more likely to produce alpha offspring. This period cannot be brought about by an alpha
- During the gestation period, male betas need to have their pup fed by their alpha's essence during intercourse to keep growing and developing. This is not the case with female betas. Although additional nourishment can be provided by the alpha, it's not required as it is with male betas
- A gestation period for wereduin is roughly six months, anywhere between 26 to 28 weeks
- To give birth, all betas must go into wolf form

Wereduin Society

- Another name for Werewolves society in this fictional world

Wolfsbane

- Drug that prohibits the wereduin from shifting into werewolf form

Worg

- A wereduin's wolf form. Prehistoric wereduin started out as large wolf-like beasts, but over time they ended up looking like regular wolves. Alphas still have features present from their prehistoric forms, such as their size

- It is a wereduin's natural state, so it doesn't require additional energy to maintain, which is why it takes pups a little time to learn how to shift into wereduin and stay there. Often the result is to have some features still present from wolf state even while in other forms
- Fern still has remaining worg features—his ear droops at the top, and he has discoloration on his nose that looks like freckles

Zandien

- A language spoken by Zombies

Zombies

- The living dead, Zombies are a race that lives in the bayous in bog homes. They practice the Voodoo religion
- They have a first death when their living flesh dies, and they truly become the living dead. This is known as the Change
- After they go through their Change, they periodically will experience a bloodlust state. When this happens, they normally go in large hordes and attack humans. This is why humans and Zombies are at odds, and Shamar and Alphonse's friendship is so strange

Zombie Blood

- A metal-emocore band Fern likes and owns an acoustic guitar that's named after the band's guitarist *Jabir Zelaji*